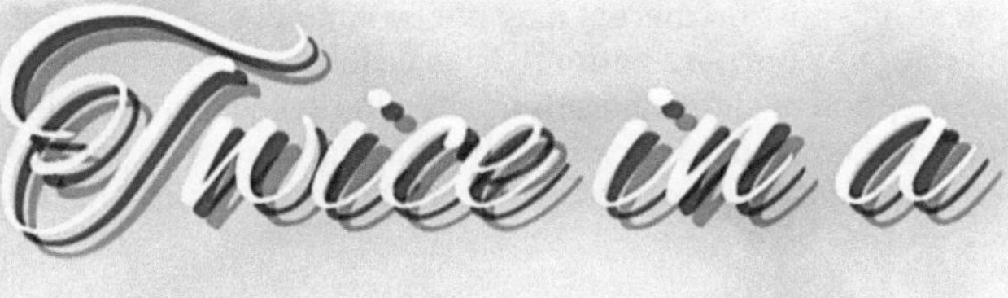

Twice in a Lifetime

A Contemporary Romance Novel by

Breyanna I.L. Evans

Twice in a Lifetime

breyannaevansauthor@gmail.com
breyannaevansauthor.com
@breyannailevans

For Bay.

CONTENT WARNING

Readers, please be advised:

This book contains heavy topics such as loss, death, depression, alcohol use, and covers sensitive topics such as losing a loved one, grief and therapy, complicated family relationships, and healing or "moving on" from loss. Although this book does not contain any graphic sexual content, it does contain sexual and offensive language, as well as talk of divorce and miscarriage.

Twice in a Lifetime

A Contemporary Romance Novel by

Breyanna I.L. Evans

A Note From The Author

Dear Reader,

I wrote the majority of the first draft for this book back in 2019. Partway through the initial drafting period, I lost a dear friend with whom I had not spoken in four years. Writing this book helped me find my way through my first real experience with this kind of loss, and I was able to finish the first draft by February of 2020.

It has been years since I finished the story, and I've kept coming back to it, but I honestly wasn't sure how (or if) I ever wanted to publish it. Although I do enjoy writing and publishing in various genres, I wasn't sure if this book really fit. Over the last year, however, I have found myself returning to this book often, and it's amazing how working on its contents has helped me heal from other new kinds of losses I have experienced over the last few years.

I hope that you enjoy the story within these pages, and that it gives you something special you can take with you... just as it has done for me.

Wishing you the very best life has to offer,

Author Breyanna J.L. Evans

Chapter 1: *The Beginning*

ADAM AND I WERE IN LOVE. I'M NOT TALKING PUPPY LOVE OR THE college sweethearts kind of love; I'm talking the real deal. Love of cosmic design. Love that comes along only once in a lifetime—and that's if you're lucky. Adam and I were supremely lucky to have found each other in this crazy world of billions of possible matches. We were soul mates.

As it did often, this idea played through my mind as I rode the bus home from UpAndComing Advertising, my place of work. Our quaint little apartment was on the side of town opposite my work, and the bus ride typically took about an hour. I always had time to think while I came up with ideas for new art projects on that bus ride, and today I doodled the different kinds of flowers I might want at my wedding.

I was in a particularly good mood. The early autumn sun shone brightly outside, the bus's radio was playing one of my absolute favorite songs, and I was on my way to meet the love of my life for a picnic he orchestrated on his own. All in all, it had been a good day, and it was looking to be another good night, as well. I danced through the bus's crowded aisle as I made my way to the front, down the steps, and out the open door.

The bus sighed and groaned as it took off behind me, and I could smell the thick exhaust fumes as the breeze changed directions. As soon as the scent cleared the air, I drew in a deep breath, just happy to be alive. I pulled out my cell phone, desperate to play the song that had been playing on the bus.

I spoke into my phone's receiver and asked it to continue the song that had been playing when I stepped off the bus.

I laughed as the cheery yet robotic voice repeated my request back to me. The automated female voice always cracked me up for some reason. I guess I always just imagined an actual person on the other end, face clear of any emotion, voice almost completely monotonous, no matter how much personality its programmers intended for it to have. Something about that image always made me smile.

I danced the entire three blocks from the bus stop to our apartment building, which had once been two small offices before the entire upper level of the building had been converted into two living spaces. I entered through the lobby, where the glass doors were always open. Once inside, I climbed the stairs that led to the second floor and faced the door to the right: Apartment 2. Our building still had two businesses beneath us, but they were both closed before seven in the evening., so we never had to worry about bothering downstairs neighbors after quiet hours began.

There were so many little things I absolutely adored about this apartment, like how hard we had to try to get the door open. Adam had always been irritated by the fact that it sometimes took and upwards of five minutes to get the key into and out of the lock, but I thought it was something that gave our apartment character. I jiggled the key into the lock and fiddled with it until I could finally twist it and turn the knob.

I loved our apartment, and I always joked with Adam that even if we hadn't moved in together, this apartment would have been mine: I was destined to live there.

Our entire apartment consisted of a kitchen, a living room with a balcony that wrapped all the way around to our bedroom, a tiny bathroom, a laundry room, and a spare room that doubled as my art studio and Adam's weight room. Every room in our small apartment was painted a different color, with our bedroom containing some of each color throughout.

When I got inside, I swung my oversized burlap purse on the island in the kitchen, dropped the keys beside it and made my way to the bedroom to get changed.

As always, our apartment was spotless. While I did my part, doing the dishes, cleaning up the bathroom and picking up after myself, it was always freakishly clean because Adam made a point to deep clean twice a week, always before I got home from work. The couch had been tidied, rugs vacuumed, floors swept and mopped, all pictures dusted, all the walls had been wiped down.

As always, the entire apartment smelled like lemons, and the scent spread a feeling of warmth through my body as I undressed and scoured the closet for something cute to wear before tossing my work clothes into our empty laundry hamper.

I settled with a light green tank top, a pair of white skinny jeans, and a fringed leather jacket that had long sleeves but only covered my torso to about the bottom of my ribs before the fringe took over.

I fixed my makeup and released my long blonde hair from its twisted up-do before straightening it. Smiling at my reflection, I turned, making my way down the hall and back to the kitchen. I put on my black high-top sneakers, tying them tightly around my feet and wrapping the excessively long laces around my ankles.

"All right, Kalli," I said to myself. "Let's go get that soon to be husband of yours."

The park where he'd asked me to meet him was only a few city blocks from our apartment, so I was happy to walk. It was a large park with rolling green hills, two playgrounds, and several tennis courts. The spot which we always picnicked, and the spot that I found my fiancé predictably waiting for me, was much more private, at the edge of the park and surrounded by tall trees on three of four sides.

"My, my, my," I said as I approached Adam, who sat on our large patchwork quilt with a straw basket, a bottle of red Moscato, and a Boston-cream cheesecake all laid out next to him. "What is this handsome devil doing in my picnicking spot?"

Adam smiled up at me, simply beaming. His white teeth sparkled in the shining late-afternoon sun.

His eyes, as they always did when they caught the light just right, looked more golden than brown. I bent, pulled him in by his purple tie, and gave him a sweet, soft kiss.

"How was your day?" I asked as I sat cross-legged on the blanket across from him.

I opened the basket and picked a few grapes off their vine before popping them one at a time into my mouth.

"It was good!" he said, still smiling. "I got three more events on the calendar today, and the Bronson wedding is just about good to go."

"Cool! Do you have any more pictures? I want to see what decorations they ended up going with."

Adam pulled his phone from his jacket's inner chest pocket and swiped the screen a few times before finding the pictures I asked for. He held his phone out to me, and I took it excitedly.

"Wow, babe. These are beautiful," I said.

I swiped through picture after picture of elegant yet rustic looking decorations of deep reds and soft blues. Apparently, the Bronson family had also chosen a venue this week, too. Its brick walls reminded me so much of our apartment, but across them were strung large bulbous lights that intertwined with the red and blue silk tulle that was strung delicately around the ballroom.

Just looking at the things my soon-to-be husband could do made me shiver with excitement at the thought of what he would do for our wedding. Although he would never admit it, Adam had an artistic eye of his own.

"Incredible," I whispered, finding it hard to take my eyes off the decorations and the flower arrangements he had prepared with the vendors he often worked with.

"The venue allowed me to set up for the photo shoot to give them some samples. The decorations will look better on their big day," Adam said, as if they didn't already look amazing.

When I did finally pull my eyes from the strapping décor, I noticed the strange look on Adam's face. It was almost as though he was lost in some bittersweet thought. He shook off whatever it was for a moment and met my gaze.

"They're so happy with the job I've done that they invited me to their wedding. Would you like to be my plus one?"

He held his hand out, and I took it and squeezed it tightly.

"Absolutely."

One of the many things that I loved about the work Adam did was that his customers were rarely anything but thrilled with the job he did. As a result, he was often invited to the events he planned for, and because he ran his own business and didn't have to clear the time off with any boss, we were always going to events like this.

I grinned, excited for yet another business success for him, and another elegant party for me to attend.

"Well, then, I propose a toast," Adam said. He grabbed the bottle of wine, popped the cork, and poured each of us a glass. "To the Bronson's. May they have a long and happy life together."

I raised my glass. "And may they always remember the fantastic job you did for their future party planning needs."

"Hey, I'll toast to that!"

We both laughed and clinked our glasses together.

Adam had packed the most delicious ham and cheese sandwiches I had ever tasted, and I was finished with my sandwich long before he had eaten half of his. As he usually did when I ate faster than he did, he grinned at me as though I'd achieved greatness, but he said absolutely nothing.

Still thinking of those incredible decorations he showed me, I asked, "So you're going to decorate like that for our wedding, right?"

"But of course," he replied. "Whatever you want, my love."

He held my hand up and pressed it against his lips, and the gesture made my stomach flip.

We were just getting into the cheesecake when that strange look reappeared on his face.

This time, however, he said something about it.

"Kalli," he started, and I couldn't disregard the sad tone of his voice that he hid behind that gorgeous smile.

"Yeah?" I swallowed a large bite of cheesecake and smiled back at him. He hesitated for just a moment.

"Now that we're officially planning our wedding, I think that there are some things we need to discuss."

"Okay, shoot. I've got your answers right here. Yes, I would totally be down with getting a Great Dane, but no, we are not getting a male. They don't listen worth a damn," I joked, jabbing at our many previous arguments about how I thought dogs were an excellent substitute for children.

"Noted." Adam nodded. "Actually, this is a little more serious. I know you don't really like to plan ahead for or talk about stuff like this, but I think it's important. So, I'll try to keep the conversation as brief as possible, okay?"

"Uh... okay, sure." Suddenly feeling uncomfortable, I shifted my weight and tried to keep my attention from wandering.

"All right," he said. He straightened his back and looked me in the eye. "I think it's important that we're fully prepared and say everything we need to say. That way, should anything happen in the future, we will know what to do. I've made a list."

He reached into the same jacket pocket that had held his phone and pulled out a small notebook with a black cover. He flipped a few pages in.

Although I was dreading whatever it was he wanted to talk about, I couldn't help noting how I adored that he insisted on keeping a notebook nearby and planning his events out on paper first, even though his cell phone was more than capable of keeping things organized for him. I loved that this full-grown man had a list for everything.

"First thing's first: I've decided to change my driver's license status to show that I'm a donor. I've been thinking about that conversation we had when we first started getting serious, and how you told me you thought it was pointless for our bodies to rot while others were out there in need of organs. I've changed my mind. You're right, and I want to be a donor. I'm going to change it tomorrow morning."

I beamed at him. I loved it when he admitted I was right, but even more than that, I was thrilled that he had decided to donate his organs when he died. I'd always believed that was the right thing to do, and the fight we had that had resulted from him telling me he didn't want to donate after our first year together had almost broken us up.

"Great!" I said. Now I just had to convince him to be cremated like I wanted to be so we could be spread across the wild together, not being buried in a rotting wooden box for the rest of eternity. I found myself laughing out loud.

Confused, Adam frowned at me.

"What are you laughing for?" he asked.

"Well, I've just realized that we've never had such a morbid conversation on a romantic date before. It's kind of kinky."

I smiled at him, and after a moment of complete shock at my strange use of the word kinky, he smiled back.

"You're weird," he said, scrunching his nose at me.

I gave his shoulder a gentle push.

"You know you love me," I tell him.

"I guess you're right," he said. "Now, onto the next order of business. In the case that I die before you do, I want you to have everything: My business, the apartment, the furniture, my bike, the guitar collection at my parents' house, everything. I've already met with my lawyer, and we're good to go. He'll take care of everything."

"I knew I was marrying you for something." I winked at him, and he chuckled. "And if I die before you do," I continued, "you can have my art and the waterbed at my parents' house. Sound good?"

"Sounds like a fair enough trade." His full attention went to his little pocket notebook as he crossed out the first two items on his list. When he was finished, he set the notebook down on our picnic blanket. He took both of my hands in his and squeezed them lightly, making me turn to face him directly.

"Now for the hard stuff. I love you, Kalli Morgan. I honestly believe that I was made to be with you. You're the most amazing person I've ever met, and you've touched my life in ways that no one else ever has."

Like the romantic I was, I couldn't help tearing up at his sweet words.

"Because of this," he said. "I want to spend the rest of my life making sure you're happy. I always want you to be happy. That's why, if I did die before you, I would want you to find someone else to love. I believe I'll find you again in the afterlife, and we can duke it out for your favor there. But I don't want you to be lonely. I want you to find someone that will keep that smile on your face."

I leaned back as though the extra few inches of space would allow me to see him differently. My stomach began to ache, and it had nothing to do with the fact that I was now on my second helping of dessert.

"Woah, woah. Are you joking right now? Hell no, I'm not moving on without you when you die!"

"If. Only *if* I die," he said.

"You're serious."

I dropped his hands and stood up, running my fingers through my hair, turning away from him. I couldn't make myself believe what he was trying to say. He stood up also and almost tripped because his leg had fallen asleep. He stumbled a little, and then he caught himself.

Adam reached out to me.

"You've got to know by now how much your happiness means to me. Please, Kalli. It's not like I'm going to die tomorrow. Just promise me you'll think about it, okay?"

I wasn't going to agree to this. It was stupid.

"No way. I'm not going to think about it. I'm marrying you for a reason: Because I want to be with you. Why the hell would I just move on to somebody else if you weren't around anymore?"

I was angry with him for even suggesting such an idea. We hadn't even started the rest of our lives yet, and he was already trying to get me to agree to being with somebody else. I was irritated with myself, also, for getting so worked up about it, but the thought was just so infuriating.

A couple tears trickled down my cheek, and I faced him, fuming.

"It's important that we plan..." he started, but I held my hand up to stop him from saying anything else.

"No, I think you should just drop it."

"Kalli..."

"Drop. It."

I turned and stormed down the hill toward one of the playgrounds.

Plopping down on the jungle-gym's bottom step, I played with the little holes in the stairs with my fingers, kicking up wood chippings with my feet.

A few moments later, I caught sight of Adam walking down the hill toward me. When he reached the playground, I whipped my head around to hide my splotchy red face from him. "I don't want to talk about it," I mumbled with my face still turned away.

He sat down beside me and put his steady hand between my shoulder blades, brushing my hair to one side so he could rub my back.

"All right, I won't say anything else about it, but I want you to remember what I said. It's important."

"Fine. Whatever." I let out a huff of air through my nose, and we sat in silence for the next few minutes before I finally turned to look at him. I studied his face. "What if I die first? Are you going to move on? Just like that? Like we were never together in the first place?"

He pondered my question for a moment. Clearly, I'd caught him off guard, though it was unlike him to only consider one outcome of any given scenario. He leaned in close, put his forehead against mine, and said, "Not a chance."

The setting sun cast vibrant pinks and oranges across the clouds that dotted the sky. It was just like a painting, and I snapped a picture of it with my cell phone and moved it to my "Paint Later" folder.

The view was breathtaking. With every moment that passed, the warm colors grew richer, blending together and standing in stark contrast to the ever-deepening blue above them.

I rested my head in the crook of Adam's neck and breathed in the scent of him, listening to the familiar sound of his heartbeat. I wouldn't want to share a moment, a sunset, like this with anyone else. I couldn't.

We waited until the warm colors had completely faded, then I stood up and brushed loose wood chippings from my back pockets.

"I guess we get headed, huh?" I asked.

Adam stretched and let out a long yawn.

"Yeah, I guess we should."

I sighed. Shooting a wry smile through the ever-darkening space between us, I said, "Race you to the basket?"

"Oh, I don't know. I'm in a suit, and I don't really want to... Go!" he shouted, and the two of us were off, racing through the cool night to the sounds of chirping crickets.

By the time we reached the top of the hill where he'd set up our picnic, both of us were out of breath and sprawled out on the limited free blanket space. I reached over, pulling him toward me.

We kissed, and then I rolled away from him, cleaned up our meal, and stood with our basket and blanket in hand.

"Let's go home, lover," I said, wanting nothing more than to put the unsettling discussion of the evening completely behind us. He stood, taking the blanket from me. We walked home with our free hands clasped tightly together.

We spent the rest of the night in each other's embrace in our full-size bed. I lay in his arms, trying to get myself to go to sleep. I was beat, and my eyes hurt from crying earlier, but despite my exhaustion, I couldn't get myself to fall asleep.

Finally, as he did every night, Adam looked over and kissed me on the forehead, whispering, "Goodnight, kid."

With my sweet Adam at my side, and his calming goodnight, I was able to put my nagging thoughts to rest.

Chapter 2: *A Night with the Girls*

BY MORNING, I'D ALMOST FORGOTTEN THE EMOTIONAL CONVERSATION Adam and I had had. Still groggy, I dragged myself out of bed and into the kitchen, where Adam had left breakfast and a quick note with his neat handwriting that made my heart squeeze in my chest.

> Good morning, kid. I had to go to the DLD.
> I love you more than life itself. Have an
> amazing day at work, and I'll see you tonight.

After breakfast, I got dressed and threw on a silky, salmon-colored scarf. We were technically still enjoying the summer heat, but the scarf was pretty much cute with anything, and it covered me just in case it got cold.

I walked to the bus stop, rode the bus to work, and stopped in the lobby to grab a caramel macchiato from the small coffee shop we recently added to the building. There was a guy in line in front of me with a bunch of folders and notebooks tucked up underneath one arm.

He wore a brown leather jacket that said he definitely felt like he was the biggest badass in town and a comic strip backpack, which was brightly colored and—I'll admit—pretty badass. From the look on the barista's face, this guy had been there for a while, and it didn't look like he was going to order any time soon.

I waited a minute or so longer, pulling my phone out of my purse to check the time. I still had a few minutes, but I liked to get to work early so that I could settle in before starting my projects for the day.

After another thirty seconds or so, I cleared my throat.

"Excuse me, sir, I don't mean to be rude, but I've got to get to work. If you're still deciding, do you mind if I jump in? I know what I want, so I'll be super fast."

He turned halfway around and regarded me with a smug expression and raised eyebrows. His brown hair was a mess, he had dark circles under his eyes and his face was gaunt, and he had a stubbled beard that said he likely hadn't shaved in at least a week.

"I bet you do," he said before turning back to the counter and staring up at the menu like I assumed he had been since the beginning of time.

"Excuse me?" I asked as I reached forward to tap him on the shoulder. "You bet I do what?"

"Know what you want," he said, and winked.

My face twisted in complete awe at this douchebag, and I rolled my eyes. "You know what? I'll get coffee later. Have a nice life, dude," I said. I turned on my heels fast enough to whip him with my ponytail just a little bit and sauntered away. That wasn't my best behavior ever, but that dude was a serious jerk.

By the time I'd gotten to my floor, my sour experience was pretty much out of mind.

UpAndComing was still a fairly small company, and the office atmosphere was an interesting one, hardly resembling a professional workspace. I was in the visual arts department, helping small businesses refine their logos and branch out their visual marketing opportunities. My office was in the corner, with glass walls on all sides.

The owner of the company, Alan Walker, believed in total transparency between co-workers, and this belief was reflected in the building's design. Literally. Every wall within the office that separated us from one another was glass. This helped keep us all honest and made it much easier to communicate with each other.

The moment I had clocked in and started going through my list of "to-do's" for the day, one of my two best friends came strolling into my office.

"Morning, cutie!" she shouted, tossing a bright yellow envelope on my desk.

"Good morning, Nessa," I replied. "Looks like someone had a date last night."

I gestured to the hicky on the side of her neck that she had tried, and failed, to cover up.

Her hand instantly shot right to the spot and her eyes widened.

"Ah, shit! Is it that noticeable?" she asked.

She leaned anxiously against my desk.

"If by noticeable, you mean huge, painful looking, and so obvious you could see it from space, then yes. I'd say it's definitely noticeable." I grinned at her as her crystal blue eyes bulged.

"Shit!" she cursed again. "You've got to help me. Can I borrow your scarf?"

I rolled my eyes and removed the silk scarf I put around my neck this morning.

"You're lucky I love you," I grumbled as I tossed it across the desk and into her freshly manicured hands.

"Oh, thank you, thank you, thank you!" She blew me a kiss before diving her hand into her pocket and pulling out a compact mirror. "Damn, that thing really is noticeable, isn't it?" She clicked the mirror shut and shoved it back into her pocket before tying the scarf around her neck and turning the knot to the side across from the hickey. I had to admit, the scarf really did look good on her, and it accented the pink pearl earrings that hung barely visible through her curled, shoulder length, mouse-brown hair.

"No kidding."

"Thank you, my love. Once again, you have saved me from Mr. Walker's wrath. How shall I ever repay you?"

"Um... buy some scarves of your own, maybe?" I said. "Or stop dating vampires."

She laughed and waved her hand at me, dismissing my comment.

"Why would I do such a thing when I can always borrow yours?" She ran her fingers over the silk material dramatically and turned to leave my office. A few minutes later, I got a phone call.

"Hello?" I answered.

"Me again, cutie."

"Vanessa? Why are you calling me? Why not just walk down the hall and come see me? You were literally just in here."

"Nonsense, I'm very busy," she said, sighing through the phone.

I craned my neck to see her office at the end of the hall.

"Nessa, I can see you from here. You're painting your nails."

"Like I said, very busy. I just wanted to call and remind you about dinner after work. We're meeting at Mallorie's, remember?" she asked. From across the building, I watched her blow on her hands.

"Sure, I remember. Mallorie's tonight. Now get some work done before you really get into trouble!" I hung up the phone without waiting for her reply.

For the rest of the day, I worked on a small business account I had been building for a local up-and-coming restaurant. They already had some great ideas for marketing their business, and it was up to me to make sure that the art that went with those ideas caught the attention they were looking for. I spent the later part of my shift sketching ideas with the box of oil pastels I kept in my desk.

Getting paid to draw all day? Yep. I had a pretty great job.

As I was getting ready to leave the office later that afternoon, I passed Mr. Walker's office, and he called me in to see him.

"Miss Morgan," he said, waving his hand through the glass door. I peeped my head inside.

"Yeah?"

Alan Walker was a short, borderline stubby man with premature gray hair and black rimmed glasses. He was kind and always did his best to let his employees know he appreciated them in various ways. This appreciation was often shown by surprise office parties, all-expenses-paid team retreats, random balloons, bonuses, and good old-fashioned pats on the back.

He was a great man to work for, and I was lucky to have found a job with such a nice boss.

"I just wanted to let you know that I got those sketches you sent me. I have a meeting with the firm to discuss them tomorrow, but I think you've done an excellent job, as always." He nodded, and his hair bobbed a little bit in the front.

"Thanks, Mr. Walker. I'd love to hear what the owners have to say about it. You'll let me know, won't you?"

"Of course." He nodded again and folded his hands on the top of his desk. "Miss George told me to tell you to get straight down to Mallorie's, and not to forget."

"Got it. Thanks again," I said, turning to leave.

"Oh, and Miss Morgan," he called again. I looked over my shoulder at him. "Thank you for making her look presentable again today. It does not go unnoticed. Oh, and please tell her again that, although I may not act as such, I am her boss. I am not a carrier pigeon."

Mr. Walker made a sour face as if he'd just bitten into a lemon and then smiled. I laughed.

"Sure thing. Have a good night, Mr. Walker."

As usual, Mallorie's was packed.

There weren't many bar restaurants as tasteful as this one in town, and everyone knew it. Vanessa and I were lucky that Lici had gotten off work early and reserved us a booth. She sat with her elbows on the table, lips glossed and pouty, black hair straight and gorgeous, large gold hoop earrings dangling almost to the bottom of her neck.

"Chikas!" she shouted when she noticed us, throwing her arms out in a hugging gesture, though she didn't actually get up from the table, knowing it would be snatched up immediately if she did.

Felicia had caramel brown skin with black hair and eyes so dark they appeared to be black.

Although she was adopted and had no idea where her birth parents were from, she was positive she was of Hispanic descent, and despite not speaking hardly any Spanish, she snuck in as much of it as she knew into her speech as often as she could.

"Hey lady," I said. When we reached the table, I bent over to hug her. Her sequined black tank top sparkled in the restaurant's dim lighting.

"How was work?" she asked both of us.

Nessa eagerly flagged down a server, who came to our table promptly despite the obvious dinner rush.

"Hi there. My name is Jeff, and I will be serving you this evening. Do you know what you would like?" said the lean but muscular man in a black uniform and matching apron.

As we did every time we went to Mallorie's, we went all in. This time, we ordered their eighteen-inch supreme pizza and three strawberry margaritas. The server turned away with our order in hand, and Lici smiled at his backside.

"Great, for me," I said, continuing answering Lici's question. "I think I'm really getting somewhere with this new restaurant account," I took a roll from the center of the table and tearing into it without even buttering it.

"And for you, Ness?"

Nessa fanned out her hands in front of us and stretched.

"Work was okay."

"Just okay?" Lici asked.

"Yeah, well, I almost got in trouble again today. I swear, Mr. Walker is always on my ass about something."

"Well, maybe if you did more work at work and less talking on the phone, he might adjust his attitude," I said, smiling. Nessa stuck her tongue out at me.

"I'm the receptionist for that department. I'm supposed to be on the phone," she spat back.

"True, true," Lici butted in. "But I think you're supposed to be on the phone with customers, not co-workers."

"Or friends, or boyfriends," I chimed.

"Yeah, yeah, I get it. My work ethic sucks. I don't want to die working my little tail off like the two of you. I just need to find a man so my dad will finally let me be about working." Nessa frowned at the two of us.

Lici raised the water she'd been sipping in agreement.

"Amen, mi hermana."

I was about to argue that Lici wouldn't stick to one man if her father offered her a fortune, but I was reminded of Nessa's not-so-inconspicuous hickey.

"Hey, speaking of finding a man, want to tell us about that date you had last night?"

Her eyes widened as the server approached the table.

"Ugh, I can't wait for that margarita," Nessa said, adjusting the strap of her purse on her shoulder and turning both our attention back to her.

"Oh, no you don't!" shouted Lici. "No way you're changing the subject. Tell us about that date, girl!"

Nessa sighed dreamily.

"Oh, guys, I really feel like this could be it. Wesley and I... we just connected, you know? Right off the bat. We went out for coffee and talked until the shop closed. About everything. It was amazing. I've never felt so in touch with someone before."

Felicia smiled mischievously, and I knew before she opened her mouth what she was going to say.

"Mhmm," she said. "Bet the sex was amazing, too."

Again, Nessa's eyes widened and her pale face turned pink.

"What?" she gasped.

I burst out laughing as she looked around us to make sure no one was listening in.

"How else would you have gotten that monkey bite on your neck?" Lici asked, pointing to the spot on her neck where the scarf had slipped down. "Don't think I didn't notice."

Nessa covered the dark mark with her hand.

"Busted," I said as the server returned with our food.

"Thank you very much, mi amor." Lici flashed a flirtatious smile at the server, who smiled back with heated cheeks before leaving the table once more.

"God, you guys! Between the two of you, I don't think I can keep up," I joked, taking a huge bite of the steaming, delicious pile of cheese, pepperoni, and various vegetables. "There's so much sexual tension at this table I think I might have to call my mom and get permission to be here."

"Oh, puh-lease," Nessa said, taking a large bite of her own slice of pizza. She may have been dainty and elegant in the presence of her suitors, but this was ladies' night, and the three of us were ready to pig out.

"Yeah," Lici agreed. "Don't act all high and mighty, now. Just because you don't share it as openly does not mean you don't get freaky. You're about to be married, and we know you aren't going to walk down that aisle all in white for anything but a fashion statement."

She pointed her pizza at me, and it drooped as she swung her hand around to emphasize her point.

I almost spit my food out as a bout of laughter took me by surprise.

After about fifteen or so minutes of more juicy girl talk, our server returned.

"How is everything tonight?" he asked, clasping his hands together and bowing slightly as many servers do when working for their tip. He studied Lici, who eyed him like he was the main course. Perhaps this particular waiter was working for something more than just a tip.

"Fine," she said, making no attempt to hide the fact that she was obviously checking him out.

"Oh, jeeze," Nessa said, pulling a pen and notebook out of her purse. She tore a corner off one of the pages and scribbled on it before passing it across the table to Jeff. "That's her number. We'd like a couple more 'ritas please, just like the last ones."

Jeff smiled at Nessa, the pink in his cheeks turning a dark crimson, but he tucked the piece of paper into the pocket of his black apron.

"Three strawberry margaritas coming right this way." He retreated, and the three of us let out a series of giggles.

"Dude," I said, covering my mouth with the back of my hand, trying not to get any pizza grease from my fingers onto my face.

"What?"

This time, it was Lici's turn to stand against our scrutiny.

Nessa spoke up before I could.

"That's just gross. You're never going to find a decent guy flirting the way you do."

"What can I say?" Lici sighed, glancing my way. "I found my soul mate already. He's been deemed untouchable."

"Please," I said. I rolled my eyes and stuffed another large bite of pizza into my mouth.

Lici and I had known each other since middle school, and as long as I'd known her, she'd been interested in dating my younger brother, Jeremiah. When we reached high school and she really started getting into boys, I told her he was off limits.

"I can't even think about you doing... the things you do, to my baby brother. Trust me, he'd be ruined. You're too much woman for him to handle."

"That may be so," she sighed again, more dramatically this time, and pretended to blot tears from her eyes with her napkin. "I guess we'll never know, though, will we? And just think. You probably blocked your brother from the most passionate lover he'd have ever known."

Nessa and I made gagging noises that stopped abruptly when we realized Jeff was back. After giving Nessa and me a look that showed he clearly thought we were insane, he smiled at Lici.

He placed the margaritas on the table one at a time, then slipped a skinny black folder onto the table after them, more toward Nessa and me than Lici.

"Here's your check, whenever you're ready. Thank you for coming to Mallorie's, and I hope you all have a wonderful night."

Before either of the other girls could, I reached my hand out and snatched up the bill, making an awfully loud banging sound that shook the margarita glasses.

"Woah, hold on," Nessa said, pouting. "It's supposed to be my turn tonight, isn't it?"

"Now, now, Vanessa dear," I said, holding the check high above my head so she couldn't try to grab it from me. "Yes, technically it is your turn, but I have an announcement to make to both of you, and I need the leverage." I winked.

My two friends were silent for a good ten seconds before Lici blurted out, "For God's sake, woman, spit it out!"

"Well..." I began, looking from one to the other. "Adam and I are officially moving forward with the wedding plans, and I would like to ask the two of you to be my bride's maids."

I couldn't help the grin on my face as my two best friends in the whole world squealed in excitement over my offer.

"Damn, lady!" Nessa said, grabbing my hand. Her pearl bracelet clinked against the charm bracelet I wore. "You didn't have to take the check to convince us for that one!"

"I know." I beamed. "I just wanted to do something nice for my ladies."

"Color us happy," Lici said.

"Absolutely," Nessa agreed. "What are you thinking for outfits?"

"Well, I want to do something that signifies our relationship. You know the feeling you get when you watch a really beautiful sunset?" My girls nodded. "That's how I always feel around Adam. Like we're in those last amazing moments before night takes the day away, burning and bright, but sweet, too. I wanted to do red and orange to symbolize that. What do you think?"

"Are you kidding?" Lici shrieked. "That's incredible. I'm all in, and you know those colors would just look great with my skin tone." She ran her fingers along her tan arms.

"Oh, that's so romantic, and if anyone could pull that off, it would be you," Nessa said, resting her chin on the back of her hand. "I'm in."

"Great. I already picked out the dresses I want you to wear. They're gorgeous. I was hoping you two would be free this weekend to try them on?"

"Hell yeah!" they shouted together.

"Awesome. Adam and I have that wedding on Saturday, and I'm pretty sure it'll be an all-day thing. I was hoping we could go on Sunday?"

"But wait," Lici said. "Doesn't your madre have that barbeque planned?"

"Yeah, I was thinking we could go after that. The dress shop doesn't close until seven on Sundays, and I already called ahead. They said they'd be happy to stay open later for us if we need it."

"Sounds like a plan to me."

After dinner and drinks, I rode the bus home from Mallorie's and walked to the apartment from the bus stop. I hadn't had much to drink, but I was a lightweight, so already I was feeling a little tipsy and off balance. I felt so good, though, and it had nothing to do with the alcohol. I was marrying the most incredible man, and I had my family and two best friends to do it with me.

"Yoo-hoo!" I called out as I stumbled into our apartment.

I dropped my bag and jacket on the floor as I tried to wiggle my key from the lock. I clicked the door closed and placed the keys on the counter before making my way to the bedroom, leaving a trail of various clothing items behind me.

"Hey, baby," Adam said, switching on the bedside lamp. His voice was gruff from sleep, and he rubbed his eyes.

"Did you have a good time?"

"Absolutely," I slurred.

I plopped down on the bed and slipped out of everything else I wore but my bra and underwear.

"I'm glad," Adam said. He sat up and pulled me close to him. I moaned as my eyes closed, and I wanted nothing more than to curl up with him.

"Wait!" I yelled suddenly. I jerked my body back into a sitting position. "I have to brush my teeth."

I stood and wobbled my way to the bathroom. Catching my reflection in the mirror, I smiled.

I still looked pretty nice.

The green makeup I'd put around my blue eyes that morning before work was still surprisingly intact, and my hair was still pretty neat. I brushed my teeth, washed my face, and pulled my hair into something that resembled a bun before going back to the bedroom.

"Did you take the bus?" Adam asked when I returned.

I nodded. "Yup."

He sat up and patted the bed beside him.

"You could have called me, you know. It's one thing to ride the bus during the day, but to ride it at..." He checked the alarm clock by the bed. "Eleven-thirty at night after you've had a few drinks... You know it freaks me out."

"I'm good! Besides, you were sleeping," I said, sitting beside him and caressing his stubbly face.

"Well, I'm awake now. Next time call me, okay? A beautiful woman like you should not be riding the public transportation system alone late at night."

"Oh, all right," I relented. I was in no state of mind to argue with him. Instead, I crawled under the covers with him and pressed as close as I could against him. I gave Adam a big, sloppy kiss before placing my head on his chest. Wrapping his arm around me, he gave me a squeeze and kissed my forehead.

"Goodnight, kid," he whispered through the darkness.

Chapter 3: *An Event to Remember*

THE BRONSON'S WEDDING WAS BEAUTIFUL, JUST AS ADAM'S DESIGNS had indicated they would be. The decorations were fabulous, and the brick red and baby blue flower arrangements were to die for.

During the ceremony, the lovely couple shared their self-written vows and mixed blue and red sand in a large clear bowl to signify that they had become one. I squeezed Adam's hand and peeked over at him as they shared their first kiss as husband and wife. He was smiling, and I wondered if he was just as excited as I was by the thought of us being up there soon.

Several people in the audience cried, and I thought that whatever brought these two people together must have been big for so many people to be so moved.

The music during the reception was lively, and the guests were pretty much all dancing: another success on Adam's part for coordinating. Two or three groups of people throughout the event had stopped by to ask him if he had any business cards on him. He refused to bring cards to his events, so I made a habit of stashing some in my purse. I passed the cards around to those who asked for them, beaming with pride.

Toward the end of the night, the two of us were dancing to a sweet old love song when the bride and groom danced their way to our corner. Most of the guests had already left, and it looked as though Mr. and Mrs. Bronson were about to do the same. As he always did, Adam planned to stay behind and clean things up after the event was over.

"Excuse me, Adam," the young woman said, clinging to her new husband's arm. She smiled up at him as though he were the only person in the world she could have ever wanted. "My husband and I are going to leave for the hotel now. We just wanted to thank you so much for this amazing night. We couldn't have done it without you."

Adam smiled modestly and waved away her remark.

"It was my pleasure. And thank you for inviting us. You two really are a lovely couple."

Mr. Bronson reached out his hand, and Adam took it.

"We've been thinking about what you said, and Alison and I have agreed that, just in case one of us should die, we're both okay with the other moving on. It's more important to have been happy with each other while it lasted."

My jaw dropped, but I didn't want them to notice, so I quickly closed it while they were still looking fondly at Adam. I gritted my teeth and loosened my grip on Adam's shoulder, letting my hand slide to his elbow.

Mrs. Bronson looked at Mr. Bronson with pure adoration, and then whispered, "Okay, honey, we should get going now. The hotel, remember?"

He nodded and placed a small kiss on her cheek.

"Thank you again. Have a good night, you two," Mr. Bronson said as they turned, arms wrapped tightly around each other.

"Congratulations!" I called after them as they—and the last few remaining guests—exited the building. Once they were gone, I turned and stormed silently away from my fiancé. I busied myself gathering bundles of blue and red tulle in my arms.

"Kalli?" Adam asked, rushing after me.

I ignored him.

"Kalli, come on."

"Really, Adam? You talked to them about this? They're not even your friends! Was it before or after you tried convincing me?" I spun around and shoved the tulle into a big canvas bag.

"Actually, we were discussing their plans for the wedding, and they brought it up. Before I asked you. I told them what I thought, and it looks like they really considered the answer I gave them."

I said nothing. I was too busy chewing the inside of my lip. My eyes burned and began to water, and I turned away from him before I could start crying. It was all hypothetical. I didn't know why I was so emotional about this. Chances were that he and I would have a long, happy life together, but something about it made my heart ache.

Adam stood behind me. I could feel his eyes on my back. I grabbed a chair, cringing as it slid loudly against the floor. I climbed onto the seat and started unhooking lights.

"Baby?"

I closed my eyes.

I couldn't be mad at him for this forever, could I? I was already beginning to feel the anger slide out of me, and I suddenly felt exhausted. I took a deep breath and looked at the floor, turning my head just enough so I could see him out of the corner of my eye, working to keep my balance.

"Do you think you're going to die or something?" I shot the words at him like a bullet.

"No, I just want to make sure we have everything in order before we get married. I want to make sure we don't leave anything unsaid. You know me. I need to be prepared."

"I just got you," I said. "And I know you're a little on the fence about it, and you joke, but I really do believe we will have a chance to be together after we die. Why would I want to screw that up by getting with someone else?"

The tears finally broke free and rolled down my cheeks, likely smearing thin trails of foundation and mascara as they went. I was glad no one else was around to see it.

"Okay, baby," Adam said. His tone was soft and sweet, and he rubbed the back of my arm just above my elbow. His hand lowered and he pulled on the skirt of my lime green, paisley printed dress. I climbed off the chair as gracefully as my strapped, open toed high heels would let me, and he pulled me into his embrace. I breathed in the scent of our laundry detergent mixed with his cologne. He smelled clean, sweet, and just a little bit like lemons.

"Hey, okay," he whispered, nuzzling against the blonde hair that hung in loose curls over my ear. "You don't have to move on if you don't want to, okay? I won't bring it up again."

"Promise?" I asked. I hated the whine in my voice... the need in it. I sniffled.

I didn't know if I was asking him to promise that I wouldn't have to move on, or that he wouldn't bring it up again. Either way was perfectly fine with me.

"Cross my heart," he said.

I braced myself for the next words in the common phrase, but they never came.

Chapter 4: *A Family Gathering*

THE NEXT MORNING WAS A BLUR OF EVENTS.

After a quick breakfast, a shower, and a run to the grocery store, Adam and I drove over to where my mom lived across town. Mom and her girlfriend Nancy had already taken care of the meats, buns, and condiments, Lici and Nessa were in charge of desserts, Granma called dibs on prepping a fruit salad, Dad was assigned the task of rounding up chips for everyone, and Adam and I were on drink duty.

The moment Adam pulled into my parents' over-crowded gravel driveway, a group of neighborhood kids swarmed around his car, waiting anxiously to see what crazy soda flavors we'd brought with us this time. The folks in the neighborhood weren't technically invited to the barbecue, but that didn't mean they couldn't all stop by for treats anyway; and they did—every time. Everyone in the neighborhood knew that the Morgan household was a place where all were welcome.

"It's a good thing these kids want to rot their teeth out," Adam commented, shutting off the engine and unlocking the car doors.

"Oh yeah?" I asked, raising an eyebrow at him. "Why is that?"

"Makes it really easy to bring all this pop to the backyard in one trip. We bring extra, give them each a can for carrying a box. It's a convenient system." Adam said, smiling at me when I let out a snort of a laugh.

"Oh, I see. Convenient."

He was right, though. The moment we unbuckled and opened the car doors, the kids eagerly opened the back, and the six twelve packs of miscellaneous, soda pops were carried to the backyard without either of us having to touch a single box or ask for help.

"Hello, sweet pea," Granma said, holding her arms wide open as we entered the backyard. I adjusted the strap of my burlap purse and readied myself for the huge bear hug that was sure to come. As expected, the second she was close enough, Granma enveloped me in her tiny yet surprisingly strong arms, overwhelming me with the smell of her lavender and citrus perfume.

"Hey, Granma," I squeaked out through the pressure she was applying to my torso. I hugged her back as best I could. "You're kind of crushing my lungs."

"Well, it's your fault, you know," she murmured into my neck. "Making me wait two whole months to see you. It's just cruel!" She rocked me back and forth for a few seconds before backing away and squeezing my elbows. She eyed Adam, who stood just behind me, smiling like a maniac. "You're up next, kiddo," she warned.

"Bring it on," he said, planting his feet on the lawn. "I'm ready."

"Oh!" she gasped. "Speaking of being ready, I'm so glad you two have finally decided to actually plan your wedding. How are things going? Have you set the date yet?"

"Actually, we have! We were thinking about September fifteenth," I said. My mom walked up with Nancy right behind her, and Dad followed right behind Nancy.

"The fifteenth!" Granma shouted. She finally let go of my arms and tackled Adam in his own too-tight bear hug. Mom and Nancy came next, teaming up to wrap me in a big hug. Mom's purple hair was cut short and choppy, and it curled against the middle of her neck. I remembered the first time I had commented on her crazy hair colors when she first started showing gray.

"*Hey,*" she had said. "If I'm going to look old, I might as well look a little insane, too."

I couldn't argue with that then, and I adored her for it now.

"Hello dear," she said as she pulled away from me and took Nancy's hand.

Nancy was the tiniest woman I'd ever seen in real life. She stood barely over four-foot-eight, though she swore up and down that she was at least four-foot-ten.

"Hey Mamma, hey Nance. It's good to see you. Are you guys still okay to come with us after the barbecue?" I turned back and looked at Granma so she would know she was included in the "you guys."

"Of course!" Nancy said. "Wouldn't miss it."

"The fifteenth of September is coming up pretty close," Dad said, bringing me into his own one-armed version of a bear hug. I couldn't remember the last time he hugged me with both arms. That was just his way of hugging, I guess. But he always, *always* kissed my forehead before he let me go. "We're moving our way pretty steadily through August, now. It's a good thing you guys have been putting this off so long. At least I had the presence of mind to plan ahead of you and start saving a while ago."

Although they had been divorced forever, and mom had been with Nancy for just about all of that time, my parents were still super close, and my dad still wore his wedding ring as a symbol of how happy he was with the time he got with her.

Dad reached out for Adam's hand.

"Good to see you, Adam."

"Come on, Charley," Mom said, bumping him with her shoulder. "Leave her alone. We started saving for her wedding before she was even born."

My dad put his head down as though he'd just been caught stealing the last cookie from the jar.

"All right, all right." He put his hands up in surrender before turning and walking back to his station at the grill.

"Let's go, kiddos," Granma said. "Hot dogs are already done."

I tried to contain my excitement as we followed her to the table, but I couldn't help licking my lips and rubbing my hands together greedily.

Several of the neighborhood kids already had their own hot dogs in hand as they played a game of tag on the back lawn.

"You know what those things are made of, right?" Adam asked me as I prepared two hotdog buns with ketchup, mustard, and dill relish for myself.

"Yup. Every bit of nasty truth, and there's no way you can turn me off of them." I smiled up at him, bumping him with my elbow as I placed the only two charcoal-black hotdogs—made especially for me the way I liked them—into the buns on my plate. I moved down the line toward the chips and drinks.

Adam chuckled and shook his head. He grabbed a plate of his own and prepared himself a hamburger bun as I picked up one of the now complete hotdogs from off of my plate.

"Get in my belly!" I shouted at the hotdog and took a huge, totally *un*ladylike bite. My condiment concoction squished out of the bun and covered the corner of my mouth. Smiling, I offered him the partial hot dog. "Want some?"

"Gross," he said, but a wide grin exposed his white teeth.

"Still love me?" I asked after swallowing my oversized bite.

"Um..." he started, "I think I've got to go..."

"Not so fast!" I said, grabbing his hand and almost dropping my heaping paper plate on the ground. Letting go of him, I flung my left hand through the air and wiggled my fingers, causing the sunlight to bounce off my engagement ring in every direction. *That would be a really cool picture to paint,* I thought, and I made a mental note to try it later. "We're already engaged. Can't back out now!"

"That... this poor fella didn't know what he was getting himself into?" he said.

"Nope. You've had me almost five years, my love. No one would buy it."

Adam let out a dramatic sigh and rolled his brown eyes. "Darn. I guess I'm stuck with you, then."

He entwined his fingers with mine and grabbed a napkin, wiping the mess from my face. I felt like such a baby that I let out an obnoxious laugh, grateful that I had already swallowed my food. I covered my mouth as my eyes widened and Adam's grin grew even wider.

"Dude, you really are a pig," my younger brother Jeremiah said as he jogged up to us, having witnessed the whole ordeal. "You decide to leave her yet?" he asked Adam as they bro hugged.

"Can't," Adam shrugged. "I think I missed my window. Stuck for life now, I guess. Kalli says you guys would be onto me."

Jeremiah seemed to think about that for a moment. Then, he nodded.

"You're right. If you backed out now, you'd have to flee straight to Canada in the night before any of us could catch you. That's your only chance of making it out alive. And you know Kalli would be leading the pack." Jeremiah smacked my arm, and I let go of Adam's hand and pushed my brother playfully.

"Dang straight, I would. Do you know how hard it was to find this guy?" I said.

"Hola, mi familia!" Lici interrupted, emerging into the backyard and drawing everyone's attention to her as she always did.

Jeremiah's eyes scanned the length of her body.

He made his way back to the grill to steal food from the pile Dad was working to create.

Lici wore a maroon tank top with a low neckline that was more purple than red, and tiny, frayed navy-blue shorts. Her dark hair was pulled back in a messy bun that looked absolutely stunning on her.

Nessa was with her, as I had expected. Nessa's brown hair was down and curled, and she had little tiny sparkly pins throughout the top. She wore a white cami tank top with a transparent, light pink blouse over the top, and a cute pleated gray skirt that hung about four inches above her knees.

"Hey girl!" Nessa said as the two raced up to me as if they hadn't seen me in months instead of days. I let out a girlish squeak and licked the ketchup off my fingers before giving then a hug with one arm, still trying to balance my plate of food with the other.

"What's up?" I asked.

"Well..." Nessa began, raising her eyebrows and nodding her head in Lici's direction. Lici just smiled.

"Damn it, guys. What?"

"Remember that server at Mallorie's?" Nessa asked me.

"Yeah, so what?" I asked, but then I saw the smug look on Lici's face. "You guys hooked up *already?*" I asked. I was actually surprised. Usually, she made them wait for at least a week to go out with her. Lici opened her mouth to tell me all about it, but my mom interrupted.

"Now, ladies. Keep it PG. This place is swarming with impressionable ears," Mom said. She carried a watermelon, and her blue eyes glanced nervously at all the running kids.

"Sorry, Liz," Nessa said guiltily. Lici's tan face actually turned slightly pink.

"All right," Lici said, lowering her voice so that just the two of us could hear once my mom had reached the party table. "We'll discuss my dirty deeds later. This is a family gathering, after all." She eyed Jeremiah from across the yard, who was now discussing something of great importance with Adam, judging by the dramatic flailing of the two men's arms. "My, my, sis. That man is muy caliente!"

"Dude. Family gathering," I reminded her, looking around to make sure there were no little kids within earshot. "Besides, he's off limits, remember? Always has been, always will be."

"Fine, fine. Off limits. Whatever." She pouted.

"Good." I nodded. "Now go get some food before it's all gone."

"Yes, your majesty." Lici gave a little curtsy, and Nessa just rolled her eyes.

I nodded my approval and said, "Thank you. You're dismissed."

As he typically did on occasions such as this, Jeremiah disappeared for a moment and reappeared with his guitar.

Although he was twenty-two, only seven years younger than me, he still insisted that someday, perhaps someday soon, he would be noticed for his talent and go big.

Now, I'm not going to lie.

He was great. His large hands made it easy to play the more difficult chords and challenging solos, and he had the perfect voice to be a rock star. I always thought he wasn't pushing himself hard enough with all the acoustic songs he wrote, because he definitely could have made it big in the rock industry.

"Hey Mi! Have you written anything new?" I asked, smiling at my little brother. At this point we had all gotten comfortable on the grass and awaited his performance. Lici, Nessa, and I all sat together, of course, with Nessa in the middle of us. From the other side of her, I heard Lici whisper.

"Damn, that boy is *fine.* Guitar or no guitar."

I had to lean over way too far so she could see me around Nessa, who giggled when I mouthed the words, "Dude. Off. Limits," in the direction of my friend, who continued to stick out her bottom lip.

Jeremiah had, in fact, written two new songs, and he played them beautifully. The notes resonated within the acoustic guitar's beautiful body, and the melody bounced out to his audience of cheering neighbors and family members.

I spoke with my brother once, maybe twice a week over the phone. During those conversations, I always made a point to ask him if he'd written anything new, and when he did, he always invited me over to be the first to listen to them. I guessed it was payment for all the times the other kids in school would tease him for being a music nerd and I stood up for him, threatening to knock their lights out if they messed with my little brother.

These two new songs, however, I had not yet heard.

They were beautiful. Sad and sweet, but still full of my brother's totally addictive energy, and the lyrics were absolutely stunning. Sitting there listening to those two songs plus a few of his older, more polished songs, watching him play with a passion he had only for music, I couldn't really blame Lici for wanting to be with him. He was awesome. And she'd seen it all—she had watched him develop from a little dork to this talented musician before us.

And, okay, he was decent looking, too, for a brother. He had darker blond hair than I did, and much darker skin, but his eyes matched mine almost perfectly, and the silvery blue of his irises contrasted with his darker features in a way that made him look almost inhuman to the ladies.

After everyone had eaten and a good majority of the guests had already disbursed, although I was definitely the kind of person that got disgusted if my dishes had anything on them, I volunteered to do the dishes for my parents. The three of them deserved a break. As I washed, my eyes kept wandering out to the backyard, where Adam, Jeremiah, and my dad talked, and my two friends very conspicuously eavesdropped.

Chapter 5: *The Dress*

DRESS SHOPPING REALLY WAS A BLAST.

We got to the dress shop just after six o'clock. My mom, Nancy, Granma, Lici, Nessa and I had all decided to carpool, and we all stumbled over each other to get out of my mom's minivan. My mom's ancient van didn't have air conditioning, so despite the fact that it really wasn't a long drive, by the time we got there, we were all covered in a layer of sweat and sang praise to the tiny breeze that blew outside the dress shop.

"Oh, thank the *lord!*" Nessa said, fanning herself with her sparkly pink handbag.

"Amen," Lici agreed. "I thought I was going to die in there. Liz, you have to get that fixed. For the sake of every passenger you'll ever have, please, fix your AC." Lici also fanned herself as beads of sweat dripped down her forehead beneath her shining black hair.

My parents had had the AC problem in that van since they bought it used back in my freshman year of high school. Aside from that, and the thirty or so other problems the vehicle had, the van was great, but I was very much used to getting out of the car with my clothing stuck to my skin with perspiration. I silently thanked myself for deciding to take the bus everywhere since I started college. Yes, I had my driver's license, but thanks to this van, I had pretty much decided that owning a car would be more hassle than it was worth. The bus I rode was well maintained and always had fabulous working air conditioning.

Nancy whirled around and slapped her thigh in exasperation.

"See?" she asked Mom before turning back around to face the girls. "I've been telling her that for years now. I never go anywhere in this van if I can help it."

"Well, I don't see a problem with it, and neither does Liz," Granma piped in. "Maybe you girls just need to stop being a bunch of girls about it. Right, Kalli?" Granma looked to me for support.

All eyes turned to me now, and my cheeks began to burn. My eyes widened as I threw my hands up, palms out, in defense against the mob of raised eyebrows.

"Hey, hey, I'm on my own side about this," I said.

"What do you mean, 'your own side'?" Lici asked. "There's clearly only two sides here, and only one of them is logical." She held her hands out on either side of her torso. Then she raised one and said, "Keep the car hot as Satan's bedroom, *or,*" she raised the other hand as high above her head as she could reach. "Fix the god-damned air conditioning."

From Mom, I heard a quiet, "Oh, come on."

"Well," I said, reaching out and taking both of Lici's hands in mine, making them perfectly level with one another. "I'm used to it, and I don't really mind the heat. Buuuuuut, I also really enjoy not having my clothes stick to my body like I went swimming in them every time I leave the house."

Granma rolled her eyes.

Before I could say anything else, Nancy pointed at the front of the dress shop, just in time for us to see a short, thin bald man exit through the glass front doors.

The man met us outside the dress shop and waved both hands dramatically at us. His excitement and high energy brought a wide smile to my face as I pulled the bottom of my sweat-soaked tank top over my fraying belt.

"Hello, hello ladies!" he practically screeched. Although I'd only ever spoken to him over the phone, he greeted each of us with a hug and a very European-style kiss on either cheek. "Which one of you is the beautiful bride?"

Before any of us could answer, he put his hands up and physically seemed to stop our words before they could escape our lips.

"Wait, don't tell me."

His hazel eyes narrowed as he scanned the six of us. His eyes widened when they fell on me, and he rushed to me like I was his all-time favorite celebrity. This man was beautiful. He kept himself meticulously groomed, and his smile was contagious. He wore a black, form-fitting shirt and thick, navy blue rimmed glasses.

"It must be you." He pointed one long, skinny finger at me before clapping his hands together. "Oh, aren't you just *adorable!*"

"How did you know?" I asked, smiling, totally surprised.

"I read your energy, of course," he said, as though it were totally and completely obvious, like I asked him if he breathed oxygen on a regular basis. "I'm Vance, by the way." He reached out his hand, and I shook it.

"My energy?" I asked. Although I didn't look at her and she hadn't said anything yet, I could feel the tension in Granma at this absurd statement, and I made a mental note to thank her for not saying anything to this nice man about it.

"Oh, darling, you are absolutely *radiant* with love! I'm going to find you a wedding dress without comparison." He turned and ushered us inside, and my girls and I exchanged some enthusiastic expressions as we entered the store. This guy was *definitely* getting an invitation to the wedding. Someone this passionate about love must be good luck for a couple just starting their marriage.

Once inside, Vance led us into a beautiful room with dark speckled gray carpet, off-white walls, beautiful crystal chandeliers hanging from the ceiling, and an octagonal stage in the center covered in the same speckled carpet. Three large body-length mirrors surrounded the stage, and little stage mirror lights hung around the edges. Behind the mirrors were two white doors that led into classy, comfortable-looking dressing rooms. On the wall hung several white robes, and above them sat a sign with large, elegant, printed letters that spelled out:

> *Feel free to wear these robes in between dresses.*
> *They are washed after every visit!*

Lici, Nessa and Nancy sat on one of the three large plush benches that faced toward the stage on the wall opposite the dressing rooms, but Mom, Granma and I were all too busy taking in the view to sit yet.

Vance circled around me before taking a good, long look at my face. He frowned for a moment, then his eyes brightened, and he clapped again.

"Got it!" he whispered. He turned to leave the room and then pivoted on the heels of his black dress shoes to face back in our direction. The smile on his face brightened the room. "Wait right there. I've got a couple of dresses in mind that I think you are really going to like!"

When he left the room, the six of us looked blankly at each other.

Granma whispered, "I thought they were supposed to *ask* you what you wanted before they went out to grab it."

Mom's purple hair bounced as she smacked Granma's arm. Granma let out a gasp and scowled, but Mom just shook her head.

"Oh, come on, Mom. He already knows what she wants. He read her energy!" She said the last sentence as if she was proclaiming that the man had won the lottery.

I had always found it interesting that Mom was so open to the other worldly stuff and Granma never bought it. She shot a disbelieving look at Mom, and I stepped in between them as I put one hand on each of their shoulders.

"Mom, Granma, we'll see if he really does know when we see what he brings in. Let's try not to argue about it before then, 'kay?"

I looked back at my two best friends, who rolled their eyes in sync. The only difference between their reactions was that Lici's eyeroll was accompanied by a quick shrug, and Nessa stifled a giggle with a manicured hand. Nancy just smiled.

A few minutes later, Vance came back in with three wedding dresses folded delicately over his arms, hangers dangling over the side. He hung them up on three empty hooks that sat on the wall across from the robes.

"Now, these two are fantastic, and nobody ever really seems to want them," he said, pointing to the first two dresses that he hung up on the left.

One was a long, cream wedding dress with swirling white flowers sewn in heavily at the bottom that faded as they got up toward the bodice. The bodice was fitted with two straps that crossed in the back, and two thick tank-top sleeves that would cover the space between my shoulders and my collar bones.

The second dress was a shorter one with a tulle skirt that puffed out like a flowing tutu. The top had short sleeves that were split in three spaces, so when I tried it on my shoulders would still be exposed through the slits.

The third dress was my absolute favorite. It had a shin-length skirt that was made of a silky ivory colored material. It flowed beautifully from the waist, but it didn't puff out like the other dress did. The bodice was also a light ivory color, embroidered with lots of not-quite-identifiable swirling designs that faded out as the skirt began. The top of the bodice had a sweetheart's neckline that faded from the thicker ivory material to sleeves made of a soft lacy material that had the same patterns embroidered in them and reached just past the elbows.

I ran my hand over the third dress as though I'd never seen or felt something so incredible. The other girls were chatting in the background and paid me no mind, but Vance noticed.

"That one's my favorite, too." He smiled and leaned against the wall with folded arms.

"It's amazing," I whispered.

"I know. I thought you might like that one. Now, this is your day, and I am at your service. If you'd like, I can grab the bridesmaids' dresses we discussed over the phone so those two lovely ladies can try them on, or I can bring you more options."

"No, this one is absolutely perfect. Just the bridesmaids' dresses, please," I said, and my eyes returned to the dress I was still running my fingers over.

When he returned for the second time with the bridesmaids' dresses in hand, the rest of my party broke up whatever they'd been talking about. The room was quiet for a fraction of a second, and then both Lici and Nessa ran up to snatch the dresses from Vance's hands.

The bridesmaids' dresses were each a deep, beautiful crimson red with a sunset orange laced neckline that went over the red silk material that reached up to wrap around one shoulder.

"Oh my god. Wow. These are gorgeous!" Nessa squealed, jumping up and down like a sixteen-year-old who'd just been asked to the prom.

"I'll say, Kalli, these dresses are asombrosa! I'm so glad you're not the kind of bride that picks out ugly dresses, so her gals won't be as pretty as she is." Lici showed off her white-toothed smile to the entire room as she danced around with her dress in hand.

Nessa held her dress up against her face.

"Okay, guys, are you going to make out with the dresses, or would you like to try them on?" I asked.

Mom and Granma took their seats on one of the fancy-looking benches, and Nancy joined them. Nessa and Lici chased each other into one of the dressing rooms. Vance peeked his head into the room and cleared his throat.

"If you need anything at all, I'll just be in the office, okay?"

"Thanks, Vance," I said. He nodded and disappeared around the corner.

"All right, chikas! Are you ready for this?" Lici asked. Before any of us could answer, my friends re-entered the room, walked around the back of the stage behind the mirrors, and strutted up the steps.

"What a grand entrance!" I clapped obnoxiously. "Encore! Encore! Give us more!"

"You joke," Nessa started.

"But we expect your entrance to be just as fabulous." Lici flipped her long dark hair over her shoulder. They really did look amazing.

The red and orange went perfectly with both of their skin tones, and they looked like goddesses.

"Man, do I have good taste, or what?" I asked, and every person in the room mumbled their agreement. I had chosen well.

"So, sweetheart, did you like any of the ones he brought in?" Mom asked me. I'd been waiting for it, and I gave her a big toothy grin and nodded my head hard enough that my hair fell in front of my eyes.

"Yep. I know which one I'm going with."

As I expected, everyone looked at me like I was nuts.

I reveled in it.

"What do you mean, honey? You haven't even tried any of them on," Granma said.

"You'll see what I mean when I show you." I turned and grabbed the dress from the hook it was hanging on and rushed into the dressing room Lici and Nessa had used. I guess they started to follow me, because Mom shouted for them to stay on the stage so she could get a picture. I slid into the wedding dress I felt was made just for me, and it felt amazing against my skin. It was like hugging a cloud and taking a warm bath all at once.

"Okay guys, I'm coming out!" I hollered through a crack in the door. Cheers found me from the other side of the room. As my friends had, I walked around the back of the mirrors, climbed up the steps, and stood in the center of the stage.

The room was silent.

Holding onto Nancy's hand, Mom put both of her hands up to her mouth. I could tell from where I was standing that she had started to cry.

"That's it," Granma said, and although I couldn't be one hundred percent sure, I thought she might be tearing up as well. "That's the one. No question about it."

"Granma, are you feeling okay?" I joked. It was weird, hearing that from her. Lici spoke up, and Nessa was fanning herself again.

"No, love. She's right. If that dress isn't completely and totally *you,* I don't know what is."

I frowned at her, and she just shook her head and pointed at the mirrors behind me. I turned, slowly, because all of a sudden, I felt more nervous than I had felt since Adam had first proposed. I closed my eyes and made the rest of the turn to face the mirror. I took a deep breath, and then I opened them.

And that was it—no question about it. I had found the perfect wedding dress.

Chapter 6: *A Beautiful Moment*

"I WANT BUBBLES."

Adam looked up from his planner like I'd just said the most bizarre thing ever.

"Bubbles?" he asked, putting his thumb flat down over his spot on the page so he would know exactly where to come back to when we finished our conversation.

We were sitting on the couch in the living room about two weeks after I'd picked my dress. His half of the throw pillows had been stacked neatly on the floor beside the couch, and I had just kind of squished in between all of mine. I wiggled around in them and tucked the largest one that said *live laugh love* on it over my lap.

"Yeah, bubbles. A lot of people think they're super cheesy, but they're so magical. I don't get why people have that stupid attitude toward bubbles, anyway," I huffed, momentarily setting my sketchpad on the pillow in my lap. I was supposed to be working on a logo for a new publishing house opening up in town, but I couldn't get my mind off the things I wanted to do for our wedding.

"Okay, I guess we can go get you some bubbles. Do you want them now?" Adam asked, obviously *not* getting what I was trying to tell him. I adjusted again. I appreciated the fact that despite how insignificant this conversation may have seemed to him, his eyes were still on me, thumb still holding his spot on the page.

"No, silly. I want bubbles for the wedding."

"You want bubbles for the wedding?" His eyebrows shot up toward his neat hairline.

"Yeah!" My eyes brightened and I straightened my shoulders.

He eyed me like I was crazy, but then his face relaxed, letting show his pearly white smile and straight teeth. "All right. What kind of bubbles would you like? Something that comes out of a dispenser?"

I pondered that question for a good, long moment.

"Hmmm... A dispenser would be cool, because then there would be a continuous flow of bubbles, which would be fantastic. But... I also want our wedding to be fun, and what's more fun than blowing bubbles like you're five years old again? So... I'm really not sure."

My shoulders slumped. Decisions, decisions.

"What about both?" His smile was now a full-on grin as bright as the sun.

"What?"

"Why don't we do a dispenser *and* let people blow their own?" I suddenly felt like a kid in a candy store, a princess, a *goddess,* all at the same time. My eyes squinted into almost nonexistent slits as I beamed my joy at him.

"Really?" I asked, not believing someone so wonderful and so generous just happened into my life the way Adam did. Outside, the sun sank low on the horizon, casting the most vibrant colors of the entire day across town in a final attempt to touch the world. A gentle breeze filtered in through the five-inch gap in the open window, and our sheer tan curtains danced with it.

"Really," he said. His brown eyes twinkled at me. "And you know what? We could take it a step further, too."

"What could possibly be a step further than both kinds of bubbles?" My jaw dropped as I waited for him to say that after the wedding, we would ride a unicorn into the sunset.

"Well..." He gave me five seconds of drum-roll worthy silence as my anticipation climbed up my chest, out my mouth, and through the open window. "What if we had the dispenser filter through clear bubbles, and we handed out red and orange bubble containers with the party favors?"

"Oh, that would be so cute! Then the containers would match the rest of the wedding," I said.

Adam shook his head and a few strands of his dark hair flopped onto his forehead.

"Nope. The *bubbles* would match the rest of the wedding."

"Wait," I said. I thought I heard my anticipation morph into excitement and burst the ozone layer. "There's no way that colored bubbles are a thing."

"They are a thing. Yes way."

"Oh my *god!* That would be effing *amazing!*" I shouted at him.

Adam leaned across the couch, set my now forgotten sketchpad on the coffee table, and pulled me over to his side of the overstuffed piece of furniture. My side of the couch crumbled in an avalanche of tumbling throw pillows that crashed onto the white fur rug. Laughter racked my body, and in that moment, I swore I had to be the happiest woman on the planet. Colored. Bubbles.

My excitement made me think about Vance from the dress shop and how excited I had been when he brought me the perfect dress right away. Leaning against Adam's chest, I looked up at him and batted my eyes.

"Adam, there's one other thing I've been wanting to talk to you about," I said. He did his best to see my face, but I was tucked up under his chin, so he could probably only see the top of my head and shoulders.

"What's up?" he asked. His hand came up and started combing through my hair.

"I was thinking... I really liked the guy who picked out my wedding dress. He was great, and I think you would have loved him if you were there. I'd like to invite him to our big day, since he was the one who brought me the perfect dress."

"Oh?" he asked, staring at the ceiling.

"Yeah. Is that weird?"

I felt self-conscious asking if we could invite a stranger to our wedding for being a cool guy, but I also felt like asking was the right thing to do. Adam was quiet for a minute. Then he shrugged beneath my head.

"Part of what makes you the woman I want to marry is your weirdness. This is your day. I'm already getting what I want, so if you want to invite someone who helped you find your dress, go for it. Whatever you want."

"Yay!" I said, wrapping my arms beneath his torso and giving him a big squeeze.

"I love how excited this gets you," he whispered into my ear through a forest of straight, blonde hair. There was really nothing else for me to do. I melted into his embrace. I felt like I had every time he'd held me since we first got together, and I had a quick and fleeting sense of guilt for having pushed him when we first got engaged to plan the whole ordeal out so quickly.

Just think, I silently scolded myself. *If you had gone through with it back then, you wouldn't have been able to experience this moment with him now.* And for the first time in a while, I was totally stunned by my relief that we'd decided to wait on the whole wedding thing until now.

"Hey," I whispered back to him, trying – and failing – to turn my head enough to see his face. I couldn't help thinking of a wide-eyed, cartoon owl turning its head all the way around. I repressed the laughter that wanted to escape me.

If I had to explain the reason I laughed, it would likely have taken the romance out of... well, pretty much every piece of the moment I wanted to hold onto.

I got up and turned my whole body to face him. I had one leg on either side of his body, and my hair draped down around us as I met his gaze. I studied the face I'd grown to adore so much.

"Come with me."

I had already started getting off of the couch when he pulled me in to kiss him. The kiss deepened, and soon we were in full-on make-out mode. In one clean swipe he stood, scooped me up, and began to carry me—not so gracefully—in the direction of the bedroom. We quickly changed course, however, when Adam's shoeless foot collided with the bottom of the coffee table.

"Shit!" he said, sucking in a bunch of air the way everyone pretty much does when they stub their unprotected toes. Rather than dropping me—or throwing me, as I would have done in his place— Adam tightened his grip on my body as he lifted his foot off the ground. Within seconds, his lips were on mine again.

"Are you okay, baby?" I asked between kisses.

"Yeah, I think so," he mumbled against my lips. "That hurt like a sonofabitch." We never made it to the bedroom. In fact, due to the toe-stumbling incident, we ended up being redirected toward the front door and settled on the kitchen.

I'd never had sex in a kitchen before, but it was one of the best experiences in that department I'd ever had in my life.

When we were finished, equal parts satisfied and exhausted, Adam crawled, totally naked, across the hardwood living room floor and grabbed a surplus of pillows and carried them back to me. We made a sort of bed out of them and lay there with Adam on his back and my head on his chest for the rest of the night.

I felt like bubbles. I felt totally a part of my surroundings, as though I wasn't actually a physical being at all, but one with the air, with the pillows and the floor, with Adam.

I sent a wish out to the universe that this feeling would never have to end.

I opened my eyes the next morning and let out a long, exaggerated yawn as I rolled over on my bed of endless throw pillows. The morning sun crept into our apartment through the open living room window, across the floor, and almost to where I lay in front of the kitchen island.

Taking my time sitting up, I took in the view of the main part of our apartment. It looked like a completely different world from down there, and I noticed so many things. I noticed how the cracks in the kitchen floor beneath the island were full of old crumbs and mop water—the one place in the apartment that Adam seemed to miss.

The paint along the bottoms of the walls had dripped in places onto the floor before it had dried, and there was a piece of old, rock-hard yellow chewing gum on the bottom of the countertop. Because Adam and I were the first tenants to ever rent this space as an apartment, I wondered if this single piece of gum was left by one of our guests, or if it had been stuck on by one of the guys who installed the counter in the first place.

Either way, I was appalled by the idea that anyone outside of middle school would stick gum under a piece of furniture like that.

I gave a good stretch and shook off the thought, smiling as Adam came into the room with a toothbrush in one hand and his cell phone pressed against his ear with the other. He was already almost fully dressed in a pair of gray slacks and a pinkish button up shirt that was still partially unbuttoned, and a silver and black striped tie hung untied over his shoulders.

"Hey baby," I said, covering my mouth as another monstrous yawn escaped it.

"Hey, you," he mouthed at me.

I stood and began picking up the throw pillows and returning them to their rightful place on the couch.

"No, Mrs. Waxley, those colors would be fine. Whatever you and your husband would like should work out just fine."

Adam looked at me and made a frustrated gesture at his phone with his toothbrush. I did the classic shoot-yourself-with-your-fingers gesture, and he nodded and pretended like he was going to throw his phone.

This action resulted in a loud bout of laughter from me that sounded more like a squawk than an actual laugh, which resulted in him covering the mouthpiece of his cell to block out the sound of his own laughter as he exited the room once again.

After I'd finished cleaning up the bed we'd made last night, I took a quick shower. I got ready for work and found Adam, still on the phone, in the studio/weight room.

"Hey love, I've got to go," I whispered to him from the doorway. He looked up at me and covered the mouthpiece on his phone again.

"All right. Sorry, the Waxley's can't make up their minds about whether or not they want to cancel their dinner party. I've got to get it all straightened out. Are we still good for cake tasting tonight?"

I smiled.

"Come on, Adam. It's cake. I'll be there."

"Great. I can't wait." His smile lit up the room, and he kissed my forehead. "I'll see you tonight, 'kay babe?"

"No problem. You do you, fabulous man. I love you!"

I grabbed my purse and house key from the counter by the fridge and got a silly idea at the last minute. I reached into the top drawer on the island and pulled out a brown napkin and a black permanent marker.

I jotted a quick note and turned it around on the empty island so Adam would see it before he left.

I laughed out loud as I made my way through the front door, down the steps, and to the bus stop.

Chapter 7: *The Missed Call*

IT WAS AN ABSOLUTELY GORGEOUS DAY.

The bright sunlight shone through the fluffy white clouds and made me think back to the night I'd just had, with my bed of soft, fluffy throws. I felt at least ten pounds lighter than I was, and I practically skipped for the last half of my trip to the bus stop. It was still warm out, with early September clinging to those last bits of summer, but there was a cool, gentle breeze that brushed against my skin as I waited on the bench for the bus to arrive.

I pulled a miniature sketch pad from inside my purse and drew a person lying on the clouds. Beneath the image, I wrote the caption: *best bed ever.*

A familiar groaning and sighing grew ever louder as the bus approached and stopped in front of me with a loud hiss. I waited for the creaking of the door sliding slowly open before shoving the sketchpad back into my purse. I hopped up and climbed aboard.

When I got to work, I saluted the bus driver. I was never really sure why I did that, but I did, every day.

Entering the building in which I worked, I grabbed a vanilla crème coffee from the lounge and headed up to my office on the second floor, remembering briefly the jerk I'd encountered a couple of weeks ago. When the elevator doors slid open and I strode into my totally transparent workplace, I couldn't help but notice once again what an amazing day it was, and the memory of that guy with the bad attitude was already gone.

Everyone in the office seemed to be affected by the tremendous weather as well: Every single person was smiling or chatting. A couple of my co-workers from website design whose offices sat just across from mine were dancing.

"Hey guys, what's up?" I asked as I approached them.

I was sure my wide grin exposed just about all of my teeth, their cheery dispositions contagious.

Jim, the taller of the two web designers, adjusted his thin metal rimmed glasses on his slender nose.

Mac, the shorter, stubbier one pulled up his pants. He really might have been cute if he didn't insist on pouring a whole gallon of gel into his brown hair and plastering it to his head in a god-awful comb-over every day.

"Just got off the phone with Aspect Technologies. They want us to design their entire website. From scratch!" With each word, Mac's voice raised an entire octave.

"Nice, congrats! That's going to be a *great* account!"

I laughed as they high fived a second time. I got the feeling they'd been doing that all morning.

"Damn straight!" Mac said, grabbing my arm. "And guess what else! Just you guess!"

"There's something else?" I asked, raising my eyebrows at him.

Jim nodded so much he was beginning to look like a bobble head, but Mac was the one that actually answered my question.

"They requested you personally to do all of their advertising design. Logos, backdrops, anything art-related, they want *you* to take care of it."

My eyes darted back and forth between my two dorky co-workers. My face felt strange. My forehead held a frown, but my mouth was still smiling. There was no way these two would lie about something like that, right?

"No way..." I began, hesitant. Yes, I'd been requested once or twice, but they were always fairly small marketing projects... I'd never been requested to do a project this big by myself. The responsibility was an honor, and the fire that lit in my chest told me I was ready to take it on.

"Way! They called you by name and everything. I guess they've had their eye on your work for a couple of months now," Jim stated, finally finding his voice, puffing out his chest through his green striped polo shirt.

"Wow, uh, I don't know what to say..." I stammered, stumbling over the words in complete surprise.

"Say you'll take the job." Mr. Walker's voice rang out from behind me, and I turned around to see the widest smile on his face, crinkling his eyes behind his oversized glasses.

"Yeah, damn it!" Nessa said as she, too, arrived at the office. She wore a navy blue scarf over her hair, sunglasses that totally blocked her eyes from view, and had bright red splotches on her cheeks that she'd tried—and failed—to make appear normal with way too much blush. "Take the assignment."

Nessa adjusted her sunglasses on her perfectly straight little nose, and I thought I saw her give the lightest little sniffle, which meant I had about sixty seconds until she went on full emotional breakdown mode.

I turned to Mr. Walker. Of course, I was going to take the job. I could turn it down, but this was an amazing opportunity, and I needed to take it. I also needed to get my friend to a private space, and soon.

"Thank you, Mr. Walker. What do I need for this?" I asked as I grabbed Nessa's hand.

"Well, they said it'll be a few weeks until they're ready to start the project, and they are already familiar with what you do. I would take that time to do your research, see what you're working with, and put together your very best work into one of those neat portfolios you love to make," Mr. Walker said. "You can probably get started right after the honeymoon. Until then, all of your smaller projects will go to someone else in your department now that you're finishing up the last big project I assigned you."

That last bit of news came with a twinkle in his eyes, and his smile twitched at the edges: A surefire sign that he would smile even bigger if it wasn't already at full capacity.

I set my coffee down on someone's desk. I wasn't sure whose desk it was; I just set the coffee down quickly.

"Awesome! Thank you." I smiled back and grabbed Nessa's arm, already turning her toward the elevator—the only semi-private area of the building within a thirty-five second walking distance. "Sorry, Mr. Walker, I forgot something downstairs. It's super important, and Vanessa agreed to help me with it. Is that all right?"

He nodded in my peripheral vision, but we'd already started our trek to the elevator. The voice of some British robot played in my mind, letting me know that we had *twenty-nine seconds remaining*. We got inside as a group of three or four women from administration walked out, chattering about God knows what. I tapped the toe of my ballet flats on the floor as I waited as patiently as possible for them to stop moving like freaking turtles. By this time, Nessa's entire face was that blotchy red, and we were at *eleven seconds*.

I pulled her inside and pushed the "close door" button about a million times. *Nine seconds remaining*. The doors began to close.

Mac and Jim started making their way to the elevator, surely to celebrate this great new opportunity with me. They both waved at me to hold the doors. *Six seconds*, that voice in my mind reminded me. *Damn it, why do these doors have to take so long to close? Five.* I pushed the button ten more times. *Four.* Almost there. *Three.* Nessa sucked in her breath and held it. *Two.* Finally, the doors had closed all the way. I turned to face my friend. *Zero.*

Blast off.

You see, I knew Vanessa. I knew her break up sunglasses. I knew those red splotches. I had her "I'm going to have a fit" countdown to a science. Right on cue, she fell apart, leaning into my arms just as an ocean's worth of tears broke through her and spilled onto my perfectly clean black button-up blouse.

I thanked the universe that I'd chosen this awfully dark and depressing but super absorbent top that'd been just sitting in the back of my closet. It could have been worse. I could have been wearing white, and yes, Nessa can cry enough to completely *soak* a shirt.

"Hey honey, what's wrong?" I murmured to my friend, who was now sobbing hysterically and clinging to my blouse as though she'd never be able to let go. "What happened?"

Her voice was thick with excess saliva and tears.

"How the hell did you get so damn lucky?" she asked.

"What?"

"You and Adam. You're perfect. *Perfect.* And you didn't even have to try! It's so fucking unfair."

"Hey," I soothed. I ran my hand over her silky brown hair and textured blue scarf. "Things didn't work out with this one, either?"

"No!" she choked the word out. My hand moved from her hair to pat her back between her shoulder blades. I clicked the button again, just to be sure the elevator doors would remain closed.

"I don't know, I... Things were great. I thought he was really it. We had amazing sex, and then we were lying in bed together and he started telling me about his baseball team growing up, and I actually thought, this is it. I love him."

I sighed, and my hand found its way back up to her hair.

"Oh, Ness. You didn't tell him that, did you?"

She was quiet for a second, and I almost thought she didn't hear me, but then her entire body stiffened like petrified wood. Before I really knew what I was doing, I had my hands on her shoulders. I pushed her back so that my arms were straight between us.

"Vanessa, how many times do I have to tell you? Most guys don't work like we do. You can't, can't, *can't* tell them you love them like that so soon. *Especially* right after sex..."

She whipped her arm to her face and brushed away one of a thousand tears.

"Well, it felt right at the moment! You know, he was opening up to me... and I didn't tell him I *love* him, I told him that... if we ever had kids, you know, I would want them to like the same team."

My jaw unhinged and fell to the elevator floor. I pressed the button again. I didn't know how long those things were supposed to stay closed for, but I was pretty sure we were going to get in some kind of trouble for taking up the elevator and not going anywhere.

"But after that," she continued, "he was up and out the door before I could blink, and I was left smelling him on the sheets and thinking about him watching baseball!"

My cell phone rang. I put a finger up and pulled it out of my purse, which I still hadn't had the chance to put down yet.

I didn't recognize the number, so I cancelled the call and shoved the device back into my purse.

Despite another round of overwhelmingly dramatic sobs, I scrunched up my face.

"Baseball, eew. No wonder it didn't work out, honey. Your guy was a baseball fan, for crying out loud." I was only half joking. I seriously never understood what could possibly be so entertaining about watching people hit a ball with a stick and run around in circles. Playing it? Sure, I could see how that might be fun. Watching it? Blech.

Nessa laughed, but soon her laughter morphed into a series of uncontrollable hiccoughs. Some old, instrumental version pop song played quietly from the elevator's speaker system. *Funny, I hadn't even noticed there'd been music playing this whole time.*

Nessa's face held that same awfully sad expression it had before.

"I just don't understand. I have everything: Money, good job, good car, good family, great friends, decent looks. Why can't I find love like you did? That's the only thing I want!"

My phone rang again, but I didn't even bother checking it this time. Whoever it was could talk to my voicemail. Once again, Nessa broke into a streaming waterfall of snot and tears.

"It's all right, it's okay. You'll find it. I promise. Maybe it's just taking so long because you already have everything else. You can't have your entire life fulfilled before you're thirty, right? That's just asking for an early death sentence." Sure, that made enough sense.

Nessa nodded and sniffled against my chest, and I heard her murmur a quiet, "Mhmm."

"Or not, you know? Maybe love is only for the ugly and underprivileged. Maybe that's *our* one chance at happiness."

This time, she pulled away. I pushed the button one last time, as I knew the conversation was coming to a close.

"Okay, that's a heap of bullshit. You may not have money, but you're hella pretty. And besides, my momma and daddy have the best relationship ever, and they're both rich and smoking hot, even now."

It was true. Both of Vanessa's parents had been born into wealthy families, and even in their mid-sixties, they were still the most attractive people I'd ever seen, and their affection for each other had always seemed genuine.

"Well, all right, then," I relented. "Maybe you just haven't found *the* guy yet. Maybe the reason you're taking so long is because he's still in the process of perfecting himself for you."

"You really think so?" Nessa rubbed her eyes with her hands like a toddler, smearing mascara all over her cheeks. I did my best to wipe it all away.

"I sure do. You'll find your guy."

She sniffled and wiped her runny nose on the back of her hand.

"Okay?" I asked.

"Okay," she said.

After soothing my friend, I let the elevator doors finally open, and it felt like I hadn't had a breath of fresh air in forever.

As we exited the elevator, I checked my phone. I had three voicemails. I hoped to check them after I got the chance to settle in a bit. I'd been to work for a good fifteen minutes now and still hadn't had the chance to set my stuff on my desk. What a day.

Nessa slumped and found her way to her desk. I stepped away from the elevator and walked to the corner of the room where I would be out of the way and, hopefully, less visible. I called Lici.

"Hey cutie," I said when she answered. "You might want to call Ness and make plans to get Mallorie's."

"Breakdown again, huh?" From the other end of our phone call, I could hear my friend sighing. Like I said, we were used to this by now.

"Yep. Full-on monster-tears mode." I looked out the window and smiled at the clear blue sky. Lici sighed again, blowing an annoying amount of static through my earpiece.

"It's kind of pathetic, you know?" she said.

I had a feeling she was referring more to Nessa's love issues in general than this particular elevator debacle.

"Give her a break," I said. "She's never had to work for anything else in her life. She's doing her best."

"Yeah, okay, whatever. Three seats at Mallorie's, then?"

I picked at my cuticles and made a mental note to go see Ness's nail lady before the wedding next week. My mom called, and I sent it to voicemail.

"Nah, Adam and I have cake testing later tonight, and there's still so much to finalize. Rain check?"

"Sure, sure. Awe, you guys. Word to the wise? You can never go wrong with chocolate, chocolate, chocolate."

"Duly noted. Hey, I've got to go, Lici. I need to call my mom really quickly and then I have to call this weird number back and get to work before they fire my ass. Have fun tonight, and go easy on her."

"Duh," she snickered, and I could basically hear her eye roll through the phone.

"Good." I scanned the office for Mr. Walker and found him on the other end of the building, just ushering a group of clients into his office.

"Love you! Adios, chika!" Lici said.

As soon as I was off the phone with Lici, I called my mom back. It rang twice before she picked up.

"Kalli, oh, thank *God*," she sighed.

"Hey mom, guess what!" I touched my cool fingers against my flushed cheeks. What a crazy, crazy day.

"Oh, honey, I'd love to hear..." My mom's voice trailed off. She sounded so sad, and in her pause, I heard Nancy talking softly in the background.

"Mamma, what is it?" I swear my heart stopped beating as I waited for her to tell me what was wrong. The clock on the wall by the window ticked quietly, but eternity passed by in those two seconds.

"Baby, it's Adam. There's been an accident."

Chapter 8: *At the Hospital*

My entire body went numb.

My phone fell out of my hand, and I scrambled, barely catching it against my chest. Shaking, I brought the phone back up to my ear.

"Uh... I... Wha—what?" I asked. My tongue felt numb.

"He's hurt, bad. The police couldn't get a hold of you, so they called Jerry and Alice, who called me since they don't have your new number. He's... he's really hurt, Kalli."

"Where is he?" My voice was rough, and the artificial mango scent of the office was clouded by the stinging in my nose. My vision blurred.

"They took him to Springworth General about fifteen minutes ago. You should go see him, baby. They're going to do everything they can, but you might want to—"

I didn't hear the rest of what she said because I'd already put my phone in my purse without hanging up and was headed to Mr. Walker's office. I bumped into someone's desk and almost spilled their coffee, but I couldn't focus enough to worry about that now. I had no idea how I was able to walk. My knees kept locking up, and I almost fell with each step I took.

Mr. Walker was in a meeting. It didn't matter. I opened his door, and as three strangers turned around to look at me, I realized I must have looked as awful as I felt, because they dropped whatever it was they were doing, and Mr. Walker stood up behind his desk, bumping over his #1 BOSS pencil cup. The clatter of rolling pencils could be heard all throughout the office, and several people stopped mid-task to see where the commotion had come from.

I hid my shaking hands behind my back and cleared my throat.

"I... I have... I need to leave." I stumbled over the words, but at least I got them out. "I need to get to the hospital."

Mr. Walker seemed to understand everything all at once, and he nodded.

"Do what you need to. Call me when you can," he said.

"I will." I meant for the words to carry across the room loud and strong, but they left my lips barely even a whisper.

"I'll call Vanessa to drive you. You can take the rest of the day off."

"Thank you, Mr. Walker."

By the time I'd turned around, Mr. Walker was already on the phone, and down the hallway in Administration, Vanessa packed a handful of things into her huge, pink leather purse.

If she said anything to me on the way to Springworth General, I didn't hear it. When we parked in the emergency NO PARKING zone, I suddenly felt so cold, stiff, like I couldn't move. I didn't want to move a muscle, terrified of what would happen if I went inside.

Nessa pulled me out of the car, however, and dragged me inside to the information desk. A woman with dark chocolate skin shot a 150-watt smile at us.

"What can I do for you ladies today?" the woman asked.

Nessa elbowed me, and I cleared my throat.

"Um. Stephens. We're here to see Adam Stephens."

"Mr. Stephens is still in Intensive Care. If you'd like, you can have a seat right over there with his family, and I will have somebody inform you when he's moved."

"Thank you," Nessa said when I couldn't force myself to respond.

We walked over to the orange, green, and brown spotted hospital chairs. Within them, Adam's parents sat, eyes filled with tears. They looked exhausted.

Nessa brushed my arm with her gentle hand, murmuring that she was going to grab a seat.

When I saw them up close, I found my voice.

"What happened? Is he okay? Did you see him?" Questions burst out of me before I could give Adam's parents a moment to answer, but they just kept shaking their heads.

"They told us he was in a serious accident," said Alice, pulling a nearly empty plastic package of tissues out of her purse and rubbing her already raw nose. "I guess a car turned too sharply too quickly and... and wiped him out."

Adam's dad patted her back as she sobbed, a faraway look drawing his attention to the chair closest to him.

My knees buckled beneath me, and Jerry reached out, catching me just in time. I clung to his thin sweater as I struggled to get my legs to work well enough to sit beside them, where Nessa had chosen to plant herself.

After a while, I could tell that Nessa was getting anxious. "Is it just me, or does every receptionist have really great nails?" she asked.

I slumped further into the chair, ignoring her question, then I leaned forward and dropped my head in my hands as a deep groan bubbled out of my chest. Nessa's hand rubbed big circles on my back as she chattered nervously. My stomach tightened until I could swear a rock had grown in its place.

"Oh my God," I said, digging my palms into my eyes.

"Hey, do you know anything?" Nessa's voice was gentle, but her back rubbing picked up its pace. "Did whoever called you give you any information?"

"Not really... Oh, *God!*" I felt like throwing up. Or running away. Or both.

"Well, it's all right. We'll wait until we hear something, and if it's really bad, then we'll worry when we find out, okay?" she said. "I'm right here, and Lici will be here too as soon as she can. Okay?"

I couldn't find any words to reply with, so I just nodded, listening to the of Alice's quiet sobbing beside me.

Two hours passed before a young-looking med student in black scrubs shuffled over to us. By that time, Lici and practically my entire family had gathered with us in the waiting room.

"Are you folks here for Mr. Stephens?"

My hands dropped to my sides, and I jumped to my feet in a millisecond.

"Yes, yes. Is he okay?" I asked.

My voice sounded totally foreign to me.

"He's out of surgery... that's all I can tell you. The doctor will be out soon to tell you the rest."

What the hell? We'd been waiting for hours, and that person clearly knew what was going on, but we had to wait for the *doctor* to tell us?

Lici, who'd arrived an hour and twenty minutes earlier, had been chasing down any uniformed employee she could find to try and get an update on Adam's situation. She stood up and tossed her purse aggressively over her shoulder.

"Wait a second. That's it? We wait forever for you to come and tell us to keep fucking waiting? What the hell are you even here for, dude?"

This comment startled Adam's parents, but they stood also, silently backing her argument.

I had to give props to the med student, because he hardly showed any fear at her anger, and I would have been shaking in my seat if she'd been yelling at me. Instead, he basically ignored her and turned his attention from Adam's parents to me.

"I'm so sorry. It won't be much longer now."

At that, he spun on his heels and disappeared through a wide, heavy door.

Lici and Nessa were mumbling under their breath about the service in this hospital. I ignored them, too. Something about how the med student looked at me before leaving totally haunted me, leaving my core feeling cold and empty. I got up and started pacing.

Please, please, please. I prayed to the universe for good news, prayed that Adam would be okay, prayed to see his face again soon. The medical student was right: It really wasn't long. About ten minutes after he made his retreat, an older looking gentleman with gray hair and white patches in his neat beard entered the waiting room. A nametag that said, "Dr. Martin Chang" stuck to his lab coat.

I met him in the middle of the room. For one reason or another, my friends and family stayed back this time, though I could tell from my peripheral vision that Adam's parents were just as anxious as I was.

"Doctor?" I asked. There it was, that stranger's voice again.

Dr. Chang looked at me directly, disregarding the rest of the people waiting for the news. His eyes were green, almost yellow, and incredibly sad.

"Are you the wife?" he asked.

His question struck me like a bullet to the chest, and I swallowed past the lump in my throat, blinking away tears as I replied. "I'm his fiancé. We're... we're getting married next week."

He nodded solemnly as if that statement deeply upset him. He looked over to the group, and Adam's parents approached, nervously joining the conversation as the doctor shared what he could.

"Are you the parents?" he asked them.

"Y-yes," said Jerry, he and Alice locked arms and squeezed each other tightly, holding each other up. I wished Adam was beside me to do the same as I stood on wobbly legs waiting for information as the doctor continued. "Mr. Stephens was in critical condition when he arrived at the hospital. His skull was fractured, and he had an excessive amount of internal bleeding."

Silent tears streamed down my face as he spoke, and I realized I'd been holding my breath. I sucked in as much air as I could and nearly choked on it, because the tightness had spread from my stomach to my chest and blocked out the air.

"Damn it, man! Tell her where her fiancé is already!" This time, rather than storming the forces, Lici muttered the demand from across the room, and although I didn't look back at her, I could hear in her voice that she was crying.

The doctor shook his head, but when he spoke, he could no longer hold my gaze.

"I'm so sorry, Mr. Stephens... well... He didn't make it. We... we all did everything we could." A heartbreaking squeak tore itself from Alice's chest, and my heart shattered. My knees buckled, and I grasped Jerry's shoulder, which shook behind his own silent sobs. As another man with dark hair and a solemn look on his face approached, the doctor continued. "Mr. and Mrs. Stephens, your son was listed as an organ donor. It's crucial that we work swiftly. As of right now, he is still on life support. Dr. Jean here would like to go over the organs that are still in healthy working condition and go over options with you."

Suddenly, the tightness in my chest and stomach wrenched upward, and without saying anything, I fled the building. As I ran, stumbling over legs that felt like wet spaghetti, my mouth filled with thick, hot saliva. The moment I broke into the parking lot, the need to vomit resurfaced, and that morning's few sips of vanilla crème coffee reappeared, transformed before me.

I puked and puked until all that came up was bitter, yellow bile, but my stomach wouldn't settle. Hot tears stung my cheeks and neck, and I continued dry heaving above a steaming, slightly sweet-smelling puddle.

It wasn't until I felt a hand on my back that I realized I had an audience. Mom, Dad, Nancy, Jeremiah, and Granma stood around me with tears on their faces, and sad, solemn looks piercing me from all directions.

I vaguely thought that Adam's parents were probably still in the building. They'd lost their son, after all, and would now be going over what organs would be harvested from his body. I felt a quick pang of guilt for leaving, but it disappeared behind a wave of sadness as Nessa approached.

Slowly, and with a hand that shook like I was having a seizure, I wiped the remaining bodily fluids from my mouth and looked at each of them. I could tell that my eyes were wide, too wide, because they felt like they were millimeters from popping out of their sockets.

I expected someone to make a joke, to tell me that this was all an elaborate prank gone too far, but no one said anything. They were all silent, all staring at me.

When my cell phone started playing my cheesy, Ode to Joy ringtone, the trance was broken. I blinked hard twice, reached into my purse, and pulled out my phone. The caller ID on my screen said, "Galleyway Bakery – wedding cakes."

The reality of the situation hit me like a heat seeking missile. I stumbled backward and regained my balance only to crumple onto the asphalt.

I looked at Mom, who rushed immediately to my side. I held my hands out, my horrified expression making my eyes even wider. *This is it*, I thought. *This will be the end of me.* The screen went black as the call went to voicemail, but no voicemail was left. I took a shuddering breath. A few seconds later, the same jovial tune erupted the silence, and the same name flashed across the screen. Terror struck me then, and I sucked in air as if I couldn't get enough.

"Mamma?" My voice didn't crack; it shattered. "What do I do? I... I can't answer it."

When she saw who was calling, I knew she understood. Faster than my mind could follow, she snatched the phone from my hand, pressed "talk" and walked away with the cell phone pressed to her ear.

"Hello?" I heard her say. She was silent for a moment while she listened, and then, "No, this is her mother. Listen... there's been..."

At this point in the conversation, Mom had walked out of earshot, so I wouldn't hear her tell the bakery that we would not be coming to our cake tasting. I shied away from the concerned looks from my friends and family members, I stared intently at an orange ladybug on the grass a couple of feet from where I sat in the lot. The ladybug had reached the end of a tall blade of deep green grass and was reaching desperately into empty space for something to grab onto, something to keep it going.

"Okay, thank you."

When I looked back up, Mom had walked back to us.

She pressed the end button on the screen and passed my cell phone back to me. Nessa waited anxiously a few empty car spaces down from me.

"Kalli, the doctor wants to move Adam and get him prepped... he needs to know what you want to do. Lici's in there stalling, but I don't know how long she can keep it up."

Even for Nessa, the tone in her voice was too gentle, too careful, as though I were a bomb that would go off at the lightest touch and she were some idiot trying to defuse me.

I somehow managed to get myself to my feet. I wiped my face and in a voice that sounded much more like my own, I said, "All right."

I led my family back into the emergency waiting room, where Lici really was stalling like a madman. I tuned out whatever it was she was saying and approached the confused looking doctor.

His eyes studied my face. Within them, I found kindness.

"I'm so very sorry for your loss," he told me, and I felt like he truly meant the words. "It's critical that we move him as quickly as possible, but I thought you and his parents might want to see him for a moment before we do. His parents are in with him now – they should be back here any moment."

"I can see him?" I squeaked.

He nodded. "Of course."

He led me to the room where they'd temporarily transported Adam to while they awaited permission to move him. The area was so small and exposed it may as well have been part of the hallway. His body was covered with a white hospital sheet, but two nurses' assistants folded the sheet back as I slowly walked up, clenching my fists and trying to prepare myself to see my fiancé... for the last time.

Chapter 9: *Goodbye, Mr. Sunshine*

The day of Adam's death.

MY HEART THREATENED TO BEAT RIGHT OUT OF MY CHEST.

In the worst way possible.

In the background I heard the faint beeping noises of various medical monitoring devices, talking doctors, nurses, assistants; but above it all, my heartbeat thrummed fast and loud in my ears. Now, as I reached the man I was set to marry in less than a week, all those noises faded away, and all I could hear was my own, deafening heartbeat.

"Adam?" I whispered, as if he could answer me, and I honestly expected him to.

I stood at his left side, so at first, he looked pretty normal, aside from the machines hooked to his body and the oxygen mask on his face. He was pale and motionless, but still, it almost looked as though he was just sleeping. But then, as I got even closer, I saw the bandage on his forehead covering the area they'd performed their surgery in their attempt to save him, and worse, the side of his face that had apparently hit the road.

The entire right side of his face was covered in road rash, with holes in his skin where tiny pieces of gravel had stuck into his cheekbones and along his jaw. The top part of that side of his face was badly dented. I knew right then that it was no small miracle he'd lived long enough to reach the hospital.

"Honey?" I said. Once again, my voice sounded foreign to me, and as disoriented as I was, I looked around me to see who it was that had spoken. "Ugh, idiot," I muttered under my breath when I realized that, oh yeah, it was me.

Standing beside my fiancé, seeing his face, there was so much that I wanted to say, but I couldn't.

Nothing would come out, so I just stood there flapping my silent mouth like a fish out of water. I grabbed Adam's hand, hoping that through this one small action he would be able to know how much I loved him.

A group of nurses came in to roll him away. If they said anything to me, I didn't register anything – my eyes were glued to Adam. His hand slid upward across the bed in my grip, then dropped over the edge as I struggled to keep up.

Then it was gone, out of my grip, out of my reach, and I was trying desperately to find my voice to tell them to wait, that I hadn't said anything yet; but my body froze, and my voice still refused to come.

I leaned back against the tan and green wall and then slid down onto the floor, clutching the gaping hole in my chest, forehead pressed deep into my knees. I cried there for a long time.

Eventually, though, I was joined by my party, which had grown significantly as Adam's grandparents and two cousins that had been close enough with him to be sisters had joined us. His two cousins had makeup all over their messy faces, but at the moment, they were no longer crying.

Jerry rubbed his wife's shoulders. His eyes were dark and sunken into even darker red circles around them. Alice sobbed hysterically – she was the reason I noticed that they had all joined me. But I realized very quickly that they weren't looking at me out of shock or pity or even grief, but instead out of curiosity.

Where was Adam?

Somehow—too late—I found my voice again.

"They – they took him away." That was all that I could get out, but it was more than I'd been able to say since laying my eyes on Adam.

Alice's already heartbreaking cries turned into ear-piercing wails as she acknowledged the fact that her son really was gone, now rolled away to be operated on. We slowly made our way back to the waiting area, as if we were all still hoping that he'd come waltzing back out to see us again.

After a little while, one of the ladies from the information desk walked cautiously into the center of the group. She cleared her throat to get our attention, and the wailing subsided.

"Excuse me, I don't mean to bother you folks, but I wanted to let you know that they'll be finishing up shortly. Mr. and Mrs. Stephens, they'll be sending him over to Springworth Mortuary, as you requested. They may let you see him again before they embalm his body, if you'd like. Sometimes they do that. If you hurry, you can probably catch him before they start their process."

Alice stifled her sobs and nodded.

"Yes, thank you," Jerry croaked.

With that said, Adam's dad helped me to my feet, and we all bustled through the hallways to the parking lot.

The mortuary smelled too strongly like those wax air fresheners – apple, with an undertone of biology class during a dissection lab, as if the owner of this business was trying desperately to make this experience pleasant. I scrunched up my nose and wished I had some menthol cream to put on my upper lip to block out the reminder of what would soon happen to Adam.

I fell behind the group as they went in to see Adam's body before the professionals started their work. My family and friends turned around, inquisitive looks on every face.

"Um..." I started, trying hard to talk over the thick lump of emotion in my throat. "You guys go ahead. I'm... going to wait here."

"You don't want to see him again?" Adam's mom asked.

I could tell she meant no harm by it, and she said it gently, but the words sent icy spikes through my heart. Tears welled in my eyes, and I choked on words that again refused to pass my lips. I shook my head. My sweaty blonde hair bounced around my face.

My family, as well as Lici and Nessa, stayed behind with me while Adam's family went in to see him. An awkward silence filled the room like a toxic gas.

Most of the time our eyes stuck to the black and white speckled flooring of the mortuary's lobby, but there were a few times where I looked up only to catch Lici staring at Jeremiah, or him staring at her, or someone else staring at me.

I wanted to curl up into a ball under the chair. I wanted to get away from the eyes that reminded me I wasn't going to be able to hear Adam's voice or feel his kisses or run my fingers through his soft chestnut hair ever again.

I made a tiny squeak deep in my throat as I choked back the emotions that threatened to flood the whole room.

Normally, I would have said something to them, given them crap or told them to mind their own damn business and keep their eyes to themselves, but my voice was quickly proving to be worthless and unreliable. So, I turned my eyes back to the floor.

Keeping my eyes downcast, I leaned over.

"Hey Lici?" I asked, testing the waters. Two words. Okay, so far so good. Just in case, though, I cleared my throat before I continued. "Would it be possible for me to stay with you for a little while? I don't really want to go home..." Without Adam, I almost said.

Surprise filled her dark brown eyes. I'm sure she, and everyone else, expected me to stay with my parents, curled up in my old bedroom. But I couldn't go back there, either. I had too many memories of Adam in the home I grew up in as well, and I didn't trust myself not to break down if I thought of any of the times he came over and mingled with my family.

"Are you kidding?" Lici replied, recovering quickly from her surprise. Although her eyes were filled with tears, they twinkled. "Of course, girl. My place is always open to you. Besides, it's been forever and a day since we had a sleep-over. Why don't we have Ness over, too?" I could tell how hard she was trying to make this sound like a normal thing, but the faux cheer in her voice just hurt.

I nodded. Her place was the only place I could stay where I wouldn't immediately be bombarded by memories of things I could no longer have. Adam and I had visited her home a few times over the years, but she had mostly come to us.

"Okay."

Just as I agreed, my mind was filled with thoughts like, *Just wait until I tell Adam. We'll have foursome and pillow-fight comments for days.*

Except... this time Adam would say nothing. Adam was lying lifeless on a cold, stainless steel table just rooms away from me. He would never say anything, ever again.

I picked nervously at the edges of my phone case, checking the time every thirty or so seconds. What was I doing? I groaned, slipped my phone into a pocket deep within my purse and zipped it closed. What was I waiting for?

When Alice, Jerry, and the rest of Adam's family all re-entered the room, I was overcome with a sense of dread I couldn't shake, and I stated my worries aloud.

"I don't know how to plan a funeral." I said those words with all the fear, sadness and anxiety I felt, but when they left my throat, they had a strange, monotonous quality to them that made me shiver. Despite Alice's tendency to take matters into her own hands, much like her son always had, it was Jerry who put his hand on my shoulder and spoke.

"Alice and I will take care of the funeral arrangements. But you knew him in many ways better than we did, and I want to do things right to honor him. Would you mind if we called you to help with details? Do you think that would be all right?"

Again, my chest ached, and my bottom lip began to quiver uncontrollably. I bit down on it hard enough to draw blood, and I nodded.

Lici stopped at my apartment on the way to her place and ran in to grab enough outfits to last me until World War III while Nessa and I stayed in the car and listened to some guy on the radio talk about how the good weather we'd been experiencing would soon be broken by a heavy autumn rain.

"Better go out and get yourself an umbrella and some goulashes, now, 'cause we won't see Mr. Sunshine for a while!" the man said.

"No kidding," Nessa mumbled, and I watched in the rearview mirror as she put her forehead against the window in the back seat.

"I don't think Mr. Sunshine is ever coming back," I whispered, and my comment was followed by another thick, heavy silence.

Lici's house growing up always smelled like grapes and fresh, hot chocolate chip cookies – a scent that had followed her into adulthood and into her own home.

Walking into that scent was like a warm bath. It brushed against my skin, sunk into my hair and clothes. I breathed it in and slowly set my purse on her unfinished wooden coffee table as I took in her apartment.

The living room walls had been painted – again – this time an orangey tan on top, yellow on bottom, with forest green trim separating the two colors. The walls were decorated with pictures, mostly of us girls and her closest family members, but also with loads of fruit. Paintings of fruit that I'd done, plates with fruit delicately painted on, sheet metal cutouts in the shapes of various fruits, and several arrangements of plastic fruits in bowls that looked so realistic almost everyone that visited was tricked into trying to eat one.

Lici liked fruit: she thought that having it around livened the place up, and I usually agreed with her.

Her couch, where I would be sleeping, was a large, cream colored, embroidered couch with green stripes and purple and red flowers on it. Its cushions were heavenly, and I sat, slowly sinking into them.

"It's so weird to me that you insist sleeping there when I literally have *three* bedrooms you could choose from. Why is this, again?" Lici asked. I rolled my sore eyes and plopped against the back cushions. This was as close as I wanted to get to a bed without Adam.

"I love this couch," I mumbled.

"End of discussion, Lici, as always," Nessa said.

"All right, whatever you say," Lici said, placing a hefty black garbage bag full of my clothes on the floor. "Do you need anything?"

Her perfectly plucked eyebrows raised, and Nessa busied herself grabbing ramen noodles from the pantry in the kitchen.

"Anything to drink?" Lici pressed when I didn't answer.

"No, thanks. I'm pretty tired. Can we rain check for tomorrow?"

"You got it, babes. Let me grab you some stuff."

I ran my fingers over the tiny bumps on the couch's embroidered flowers and thought back to what the weatherman had said. I wondered if it might rain forever.

"No need," I called hoarsely down the hallway while she dug through the linen closet. "This'll work." I pulled down a striped crocheted blanket from the back of the couch and lay my head on one of her overstuffed, red corduroy couch pillows.

The last thing I remembered before falling asleep was the sounds of the coffee table being slid across the carpet, and a clinking glass as Nessa served up the ramen she'd made.

Chapter 10: *Those with the Best Intentions*

One day after Adam's passing.

IN THE MORNING, I AWOKE TO A BIG PLATE OF FRESH-OUT-OF-THE-OVEN blueberry muffins.

"Good morning, honey," Nessa said.

She placed the plate on a stool she apparently had pulled out of the closet last night because she couldn't live without her dying cell phone, and the charging cable wasn't quite long enough to reach the floor, despite the fact she had slept right by the plug.

I sat up, rubbing my eyes harder than I should have. I felt like someone had dumped a bucket of salt on my head.

"Oh, hey girl. You're up!"

Lici entered the room in one of her many pants suits that she wore to work. It wouldn't have fit her personality at all if it wasn't embellished with silver stripes and a peach-colored silk tank top that flowed like water beneath her jacket.

Needless to say, her realty customers never complained about her professional dress, but they always got to witness a little bit of her sparkle.

"Listen, I couldn't get work off completely today, but I can probably get off after my first two showings this morning, and then we can do anything you want. Make a list." She placed two large rose gold hoop earrings into each ear. "The place is yours, so do what you want, okay?"

"Okay," I said through a yawn. I must have slept at least ten hours, but my entire body felt like someone had flipped the "off" switch. There was a deep, hollow pain in my chest waiting just beneath the surface. It felt like I was suffocating.

"And we're *both* on call if you need absolutely anything, okay?" Nessa popped the last bit of muffin she'd been eating into her mouth before reapplying her lip gloss. "I also called your mom. She's ready to come over whenever you call so you won't have to be alone."

"Thanks guys... I don't know what I'd do without you."

As nice as it sounded to have my mother over, I really didn't want it. Maybe because I knew she would automatically start talking about how my soul needed to heal? Maybe because I knew she wouldn't let me just hide under the covers all day?

The three of us shared a tight hug, and then my two friends left for work. The moment they left, darkness creeped in and hung over me. I grabbed a muffin, picked the top into microscopic pieces, and dropped it back onto the plate. My chest ached so badly that the thought of eating made me feel like I'd puke my guts out all over again, even though I hadn't eaten in the last twenty-four hours.

I flicked the remaining crumbs off my fingertips as a storm brewed within my rolling stomach.

My chest constricted, and before I could register what was happening, I was overcome by a fit of racking sobs I hadn't realized I'd been fighting.

I pulled the heavy crocheted blanket over my head and thought of Adam's sweet face as I forced myself back to sleep. It was difficult, because I couldn't relax without thinking about him, but if I acknowledged those thoughts too much for me to take, I would be reminded that he was gone, and that was too much. It didn't feel real, even though part of me knew that it was.

The world felt empty without him.

I woke up around one thirty in the afternoon to five missed calls and six new messages.

Two missed calls were from wedding vendors curious as to why Adam and I hadn't called to make any final arrangements.

I ignored them. I knew that sooner rather than later I would have to call them back to cancel everything, but I just couldn't face it today.

One call was from Adam's lawyer. He left a brief message about needing to get in touch with me, but I couldn't even think about it.

The fourth missed call was from my mom. She didn't leave a voicemail, but instead sent a text message that read:

> **Hey sweetheart. I just wanted to check up on you. Whenever you can, let me know you're OK. I love you baby girl. Pay attention to the world around you. I'm asking the universe to keep you safe.**

The next message read:

> **Don't forget to eat. I know how you get when you're upset. <3 Mom.**

The one voicemail that I did actually respond to without automatically deleting was from Jerry.

"Hello, Kalli. I'm sorry if it's a bad time... well hell, it's a bad time for all of us. It's a God-awful time. But Alice and I have started on funeral arrangements..." His voice broke, and I listened to a grown man trying his hardest to compose himself for about five seconds. "It's best to do this as soon as possible, you know. Um, anyway, we had some questions about what kind of food you think Adam would have wanted, and... if you would be all right with us setting the funeral for Friday. We know that's only a day before the wedding..." Jerry trailed off again, choked up that he'd never get to see his son get married, probably. "But it's best not to wait too long before we... we bury him. Call me back when you get this, okay? Bye."

Bury him... Tears stung the corners of my eyes as they rolled over my temples and into my ears. I let them run.

I had three text messages from Lici and Ness just checking in to make sure I was still alive.

I patted down my body. Yep. Unfortunately, I was still alive, which made the horror of the last twenty-four hours real.

The last text message was from my boss.

Good morning miss Morgan.
How are you feeling today?

I dropped my phone on my face and struggled beneath the blanket to pick it back up.

"Shit," I muttered. Rubbing my forehead with one hand, I dialed my boss with the other. It rang five times before he answered.

"Good afternoon, this is Alan Walker of UpAndComing Advertising. How may I help you today?"

"Hey Mr. Walker, it's Kalli."

"Oh, miss Morgan! Hello. I should have checked my caller ID. How are you holding up?"

"I'm... fine." The lie made my head pound and my heart ache. "I'm... I'm sorry I didn't call in this morning; time just... got away from me, I guess." My voice was dry and emotionless, though I felt like my chest might implode.

"Please, don't worry. Miss George told me about your situation this morning. I am so terribly sorry for your loss. I have always thought you two were such an incredible couple," he said, and then silence filled the room as I tried to think of what to say.

I swallowed past a brick in my throat. "Thanks, Mr. Walker."

"Listen, Kalli," he said. I could tell he was serious by his use of my first name. "I'm going to give this new account to someone else. You've definitely earned it, but I want you to focus on yourself right now."

My heart dropped clear down to my pelvis. I bolted upright and threw the blanket off my head. My mess of blonde hair flew into the air and stood straight up from the static that I caused by the abrupt movement.

"No. Mr. Walker, please don't give away this account. I've worked so hard for this. Please."

"I don't want to overwhelm you in any way..." He trailed off, but then he took a deep breath like he was about to say something else. I didn't want to hear it. I threw my hand up as though he'd see it through the phone, as though it would stop him.

"Mr. Walker, I need this. If I can't cover this account, I won't have anything. I can handle it. I *promise.* And if it turns out to be too much – which it won't – then I will find someone who can finish it, and I will personally coach them through the process."

My entire body shook as I awaited his answer in silence. That silence stretched all the way around the world and back to me.

"All right," he said.

I let out the breath I was holding.

"Thank you. I won't let you down."

"I believe you. I've got to go, miss Morgan. But please, let me know if you need anything. You already have the next few weeks off. Keep them and keep me in the loop."

"I will," I said, and hung up the phone.

I breathed a heavy sigh of relief and felt the tightness in my chest ease just a little. I plopped back against my corduroy headrest. As Jerry's last comment rang inside my mind, I had put myself to sleep again.

Bury him...

I dreamt of Adam's body, slowly rotting away in his wooden box. I dreamt that I had died, too, and my ashes flowed through the wind over his grave, swirling and reaching out for him, but the breeze carried me away before any of me could touch the ground he laid in.

Chapter 11: *The Last Note*

A week after Adam's passing.

THE FUNERAL CAME FASTER THAN I EVER EXPECTED.

It came fast enough to spread vertigo like the plague between all those who had been touched by Adam's amazing love. I had spent the entire week barely moving from my spot on Lici's couch—barely existing.

It had been a closed casket visitation: Jerry, Alice and I had decided it would be best if people didn't see him the way he looked after his accident. Instead, we put up all our favorite pictures of him—pictures in which he was happy, and healthy, and very much alive.

I sat and silently sobbed throughout the whole speech before they laid his casket in the ground. I didn't even hear the speech because my heartbeat thrummed so loudly in my ears.

Throughout the entire burial process, I couldn't get myself to open my eyes. I just couldn't watch that decorated wooden box go into the ground. I even threw a handful of red and orange rose pedals onto his casket without looking.

By the time it was over, and I finally did open my eyes, I was so dizzy that the cemetery started to spin, and the light stunned my eyes so harshly that I almost passed out.

The wake was hell and a half. It was held at Jerry and Alice's home, the house that Adam grew up in—the house he didn't leave until he graduated college.

I was able to carry myself into the home dressed all in white like everybody else – a detail I'd fought with Jerry about a great deal over the last few days until Alice finally agreed with me. Adam planned celebrations for a living. He'd loved it. He would want his life to be celebrated with the brightest of colors, not mourned in dreadful black.

A quiet murmur rose above the clinking of glass and silverware, over the hushed cries that spread throughout the home. I took my shoes off and walked in my socks on their soft tan carpet to the first row of seats that filled Alice and Jerry's large dining room.

A number of people remarked about Adam and the effect he'd had on their lives. There were friends, neighbors, family, clients. All of them were changed by the opportunity to have known someone so amazing, and I was by no means the only person whose whole world brightened every time he had smiled.

Part of me wanted to feel bitter about all of these people commenting about Adam and his life. They hadn't known him like I had. But the largest part of me allowed them to feel what they were feeling without getting upset about it. After all, he did have a way of touching lives.

Jerry stood and shared the memory of teaching his son to ride his bike. As he did, I recalled the time that Adam found out I'd gone an entire twenty-four years without ever learning how to ride a bike myself.

"What? No way!" he'd said, totally exasperated. He'd pulled out that cute little notebook of his and then wrote step by step instructions, which did nothing to help me in the moment. He'd had this romantic plan in his head, but it actually turned into a huge disaster. I wrecked big time and split my knee open.

The most memorable part of that date was the fact that he'd lifted me up into his arms and carried me inside, leaving his thousand-dollar bike on the sidewalk.

"Are you okay?" he'd asked. His forehead was wrinkled with worry and sweat beaded in through the cracks. "Oh my God. I need to take you to the ER. You need stitches! What a stupid idea! I'm going to call an ambulance."

"Um, hell no," I'd replied, taking his blood-soaked hands in mine. "Do you have any super glue?"

He'd looked at me like I was completely insane. "What?"

"Super glue?"

He had obliged, patting my knee as he got up to search for the glue. It'd stung, and I sucked in a deep breath.

"Oh my God! Sorry! Sorry!" he had said, flapping his hands as he went to search the closet in the hallway.

By the time he got back into the bathroom where I still sat on the toilet, I had cleaned myself up. I snatched the superglue from his hand and put myself back together before he could object. I held my wound together for a minute and then, putting the cap back on, I raised my arms into a shrug.

"Ta-Da. All better."

Absently, as Adam's dad told the story I'd already heard a hundred times, my fingers traced the puckered, three-and-a-half-inch scar.

I scoffed when Jerry smiled at how much Adam had loved riding his bike. *Yep,* I thought. *He loved it to death.*

Then it was Alice's turn. She talked about how hard it had been to potty train him. Although I'd also heard this story once or twice before, she told it in such a way that really brought the memory to life and had the whole room laughing despite the darkness that lurked in every corner. I was laughing too, but it didn't feel like my laugh.

Finally, it was my turn. After a long silence, I stood. I pondered at the numb sensation that filled my legs, and I swore I could feel my heartbeat in every part of my body, and my face flushed. Could I do this? Slowly, I padded up to our makeshift podium.

Standing up there, staring at all of those tear-streaked faces looking back at me, I wanted to cover up. I had this huge, gaping hole in my chest, and I was sure that everyone could see right through my ribcage.

I pulled my white cardigan over my chest and crossed my arms.

"Hi everybody," I said, testing the waters. I tried to smile, but it felt foreign on my face. All those people were hurting too. "Adam was... he was... everything." I sucked in my breath in one huge, ridiculous sounding sob. "Um. Excuse me," I croaked.

As it turned out, I couldn't do it.

I rushed from the podium and hid on the stairs by the garage. I was followed by my friends and family, and they patted my head and rubbed my back and murmured nice things to me, but I couldn't unbury my face. I couldn't show them the tears I felt I would drown in. It didn't matter how many people said they missed Adam. Talking about him like that was useless. It wasn't going to bring him back.

He was never coming back.

After a while, they all backed off. They ate, they comforted each other, but they stayed close enough to watch me, just in case. I could hear them in the room as I tried to squeeze my eyes closed tightly enough that they wouldn't produce any more tears.

Alice was the first person to approach me on her own without someone else tagging along to check on me.

"Kalli, can I sit with you for a minute?" she asked.

I shrugged, still refusing to lift my head off my arms.

"You don't have to look up, but I have something I want to say to you, and I want you to know it's damn hard for me to say."

I did lift my head then, because Alice never, ever swore. My eyes probably looked as big and red as dodgeballs, but hers did, too.

She took a deep, calm breath and her light brown hair hung wildly around her face. She looked exhausted. When she exhaled her shoulders slumped and she rubbed her already red eyes with the backs of her hands.

"I loved my son," she said, her voice wavering. She swallowed, and I sympathized. I'd been swallowing past a throat lump of my own for the last several days. "*Loved* him." Her "I" in that sentence had been quieted – practically inaudible.

I nodded. My eyesight blurred even more. "I know," I whispered.

"To be a mother... who loses her son, her *only* child... I—" She took a moment to clear her throat and compose herself a little. "I can't even begin to tell you how that feels."

Both of our bodies shook with silent sobs as we huddled together on the stairs.

"But..." she continued. "For you to lose your *soul mate?*" She shook her head. Her hair flipped angrily around her face. "You, Kalli, loved my son like no one else could. Not even me. You were going to be partners in life. Your life together had barely even started, and I got to spend his entire young life with him."

Not even Adam's own mother understood what I was feeling. Her words comforted me some, but they also accentuated my sadness.

I went home the night before we were supposed to be married, after the funeral. Lici dropped me off.

"Do you want me to come in with you?" she asked.

She put her hand on my lap.

Her nails were painted black with white and silver sparkles over the top. Her lipstick was smeared, but I honestly thought nothing of it, because her mascara had been smeared, too, as if it'd run and she'd wiped it away. I thought it was simply due to the fact that she'd been crying. Hell, I knew I was a hot mess myself. I didn't even want to *think* about looking into a mirror, so who was I to judge if her makeup wasn't perfect?

"No, I'm okay. I really think I need to do this alone," I said.

"Okay, okay, but if you need anything. Even if it's two A.M., you call me. Got it? I'll keep my running pants on."

Her kindness filled my eyes with another round of stinging tears. God, I didn't think I could even cry this much. I crinkled the bag of clothing in my lap.

"Sounds like a plan. Thank you, for everything," I whispered.

She shrugged. Her shiny, straight black hair rolled on her shoulders. "Sure."

We hugged awkwardly over the center console, and I let myself out of the car. I swung the black garbage bag and my purse over my shoulder.

"I'll see you later," Lici said. Her fingers fluttered in a graceful wave, and then she made a phone with her hand and mouthed the words, 'call me.' I nodded, turned, and didn't look back at her until I was through the first level doors and up the flight of steps to our apartment door.

My apartment door, now. God.

There was no point in looking back. I knew Lici was going to be there, staring at me with those sympathetic eyes. I shook off the thought, adjusted the bags on my shoulder, and wiggled my key into the doorknob.

When I got the door open, I busied myself getting the key out of the lock. I closed the door and turned around. The smell of our apartment was stiff and thick in the air and it hit me like a train. The air closed in around me. A *clunk* sound echoed through the room, muffled only by a loud crinkle when my belongings slid from my grip and hit the floor. I clenched my fists and tried breathing again, this time with purpose.

With this attempt, breathing came a little bit easier, though I felt like a Sumo wrestler sat on my chest. I went straight to the fridge. I don't know why I did that, because I hardly ever went straight to the fridge. But hey, grief does weird things to people, I guess.

Even weirder, when I got into the fridge, I pulled out all the things Adam ate and I never really wanted. Two-week-old potato salad, a disgusting looking green smoothie that he must have made the day he... um...

The day I saw him last.

I gathered the bucket of protein powder that he kept in the fridge into my arms, along with some other things I really didn't bother to look at. I dumped my armfuls of miscellaneous foods onto the counter, closed the fridge, opened the cupboard beneath the island and pulled out the blender.

Without thinking or planning or doing anything smart or rational, I began throwing all of the random food items into the blender and held down the "pulse" button until everything looked mixed. Popping the lid off the blender didn't give me the same satisfaction it always had before, but that observation was fleeting and left me quickly.

I grabbed a tall glass water bottle from another cupboard and poured the majority of the blended concoction inside before taking a huge swig. This, of course, was every bit as nasty as it sounds, which sent me vomiting into our large stainless-steel kitchen sink. I sat there shaking for a few moments after I finished, then I washed my hands and my face and cleaned out the sink.

I took another drink. Maybe, I thought, if I could gather together all of the things he ate, I could bring him closer to me. It was better going down the second time and tasted slightly less repulsive. I secured the water bottle's lid with the thick brownish liquid still inside, and started cleaning up my mess, putting all of the strange items back into the fridge before wiping down the counter tops.

As I wiped away the last of the smoothie mess, I accidentally sent something fluttering off the counter and onto the floor.

"What?" I said aloud. I made my way around the island to the other side where a brown napkin had fallen. I was sure I hadn't seen it when I got home, but I was also sure neither of us had put any napkins inside the kitchen appliances. I scooped it up.

On the side that faced me was the note I wrote that last morning before I went to work. *Looks like you missed a spot...* When I flipped the napkin over to look at the back, a note was written in Adam's neat handwriting.

Oh! Looks like I did. Don't worry, love.
I'll clean it up when I get home tonight.

I hadn't realized until I set the note down that I was holding my hand over my mouth so tightly that it ached when I let go. Overwhelmed by my curiosity, I laid down on the floor and looked for the spot I knew would still be there. Sure enough, there it was. Right where I had left it.

I'll clean it up when I get home tonight...

But he never came home. He would never come home again.

Who was going to clean up that spot now?

Suddenly taken by a round of hideous sounding, body-wracking sobs, I grabbed the note, my water bottle full of health smoothie trash, and dragged myself to the bedroom. I crawled into bed, pulled the covers clear up to my cheekbones, and I looked around the room. Across from the bed, hanging on the closet door, sat my wedding dress in its forbidden orange dust cover. I fell asleep still sobbing, still staring at the dress hanging on the door.

Chapter 12: *Going to Therapy*

Three weeks after Adam's passing.

I PAINTED.

I spent the entire two weeks that were supposed to be my honeymoon painting to release all the grief I was feeling, and the entire time, I retreated into myself.

I ignored countless phone calls and deleted voicemails from Adam's lawyer without ever listening to them.

I didn't want stuff. I didn't want money, or whatever else Adam wanted to give me.

I wanted Adam.

I painted Adam – how I remembered him, not how I saw him last. I painted a ridiculous amount of sunsets. Sunsets at the beach. Sunsets over country sides. Sunsets over cities. Sunsets over sunsets. All of these, I threw away.

Strangest of all, I painted monsters.

These weren't your typical monsters—these were full-blown nightmare fuel: twisted, bony, misshapen things with eyes that were too big and clawed fingers that were too long.

I painted and sketched about twenty pictures like this before I realized I might need some serious psychological help.

I realized I had hit rock bottom when I found myself sleeping beside the toilet in the late afternoon with yet another disfigured creature-sketch in my arms. *That's it,* I thought. *I need to see somebody about this.*

I spent that evening after work searching online different combinations like "best grief psychiatrist," "death of a loved one counseling," and "am I possessed or just grieving?"

Finally, I found a small office somewhat close to my work and decided to call and make an appointment. I wasn't sure how to do so, so when I called and got the reception desk, I froze.

"Hi, um. I need a shrink, I think."

"Is this an emergency? If so, would you like me to call 911 for you?"

This slapped me out of my anxiety a bit.

"No, no. It's not an emergency. God, sorry. I've just... never done this before."

"No problem. Thank you for clarifying. What kind of counseling will you be requesting?" the woman asked, and I wondered how often she had to ask people if their reason for calling was an emergency.

"My... my fiancé recently... uh... well, he died... and I guess I kind of want to talk to someone about it."

"I'm so sorry for your loss," the woman said, with real, sincere empathy in her voice. "Let's get you on the schedule."

So, after answering a few questions on the phone, I decided to create myself a new beginning... sort of. I scheduled my first appointment for my first day back to work.

That first day was much easier than I had expected, and much harder, too.

It was easier because my new client hadn't decided quite what they wanted me to start with, so I spent the majority of the day doodling ideas (and a bunch more starving nightmare creatures) and going over our staff list looking for someone who could be my backup if things went south and I couldn't handle the project alone.

So, I filled eight hours with not a whole lot of work, which made things so, so much harder than they would have been if I'd been busy. Despite the fact that I busied myself with my drawings and my determination to find someone as dedicated to my work as I was, the day passed in an eternity, and thoughts of Adam filled my mind with every free millisecond I had.

A few times throughout the day, Nessa came to bother me. She'd check in, ask how I was holding up, which was, by the way, becoming my least favorite question on the damn planet.

She'd fiddle with the scarf around her neck—which I wasn't sure if she'd purchased herself or if she'd borrowed it from someone else in her department—and smack her lips the way she always did when she tried on new lipstick.

Eventually, though, when I ignored her for long enough, she took the hint and went away with an exaggerated, very Vanessa type sigh, leaving me to my doodles.

"Thank you," I said to the universe, looking up at the sky I couldn't see through the ceiling.

On my way out of the office at the end of the day, I stopped in Mr. Walker's doorway. He was eating a chocolate cupcake that was left over from the huge welcome back party they had thrown me. I'd had my own cupcake, but overwhelmed as I was, I licked the cream cheese frosting off of it and threw it in the trash.

"Oh, hello!" he said, swallowing the large bite he'd taken before setting it carefully down on the napkin that sat on his desk. "Leaving for the day?"

"Yes sir. Have you heard anything more about the Aspect Tech account?"

"Not a word. I'm hoping to hear their ideas by the end of the week, but the meeting has yet to be scheduled. I will let you know when I do hear something, though," he said. Although he kept things professional as always, he looked at me like I was some sad creature left to rot on the side of the road.

I nodded, and some of my hair fell out of my loose ponytail.

"Oh, miss Morgan?" he said when I turned to leave.

"Yeah?"

"I would love for you to sit in that meeting as well. I know I usually do a one-on-one meeting with you folks after I've had a previous meeting with the client, but you've earned your presence in there, and

I really think it'd help them come to an agreement if they could see some of your ideas."

I actually smiled, though an anvil of guilt dropped onto my chest immediately after I realized I was smiling. Why was I smiling when my reason for happiness was gone?

"Wow, Mr. Walker. Thank you so much. I'll do my best."

"I never expect anything else," he said.

Outside, rain poured ferociously, beating down on everything it came into contact with. Honestly, I was glad for it. I don't think I could have faced the sun. The bus stop had an enclosed waiting area with a heated bench and a roof, but I waited outside, letting the rain wash over me, soaking my clothes, my skin, my hair, and my soul. The bus sighed to a stop and let me in. I realized I must have looked crazy: soaking wet, makeup running, hair sagging, climbing onto my source of public transportation when there was a perfectly dry waiting area.

I didn't give a single shit.

Not one.

I kept my head down as I passed the normal, dry, concerned looking passengers and made my way to the back. I had about a fifteen-minute ride to the therapist's office, and I didn't want to soak anyone else.

Three or four seats from the front of the bus stood a guy with his back to me. I remember thinking that he desperately needed a haircut, and he looked like a zombie when I passed him, but he wore a collaged superhero backpack that, although he was obviously too old for it, I thought was super cool. *Weird*, I thought. I felt like I'd seen that backpack before. I tried not to be a stalker, but my eyes wandered back to that backpack for about eleven minutes, until he got off. By that time, the rain had pretty much stopped, and I was no longer soaking wet, but that almost sticky, in between wet and dry kind of wet, thanks to the bus's off-warm air conditioning vent being right beside me.

The entire bus ride to therapy, my stomach was in knots. I dreaded talking to someone about what I was going through. I was afraid they were going to tell me I was grieving wrong, or I was crazy, or even just tell me I was normal. Everything felt like it would be something I wouldn't want to hear.

Dr. Jacobi's office was well maintained. The sidewalk was recently swept, or the rain had washed them clean, the hedges were trimmed, and beautiful bunches of red, yellow, and orange flowers dotted either side of the pathway.

I hated them.

I wanted to rip them out of that expensive looking soil, but I didn't, of course, because I hadn't *completely* lost my mind yet.

Dr. Jacobi's secretary was the same sweetheart I had spoken with on the phone, and his office building smelled like apples and cinnamon.

The apple scent twisted the wrench in my heart, reminding me of how the mortuary smelled. Thankfully, this was a much more natural scent, and the cinnamon helped to quell some of my nerves.

On each of the square glass tables that made a corner out of his comfortable, plush waiting chairs sat a bowl of dried apples and real cinnamon sticks.

Looking over some pamphlets on the table, I picked up one that had a picture of a woman smiling and shaking hands with a very stereotypical shrink-type person. In big blue letters was written the question: *Is private practice therapy right for you?*

I honestly didn't know. I flipped through the pages, but my eyes refused to focus on anything, so I set the pamphlet back down.

I pulled out my damp sketchbook with the intention of adding to the ideas I'd started coming up with for my newest client, but those designs quickly took a turn for the worst and became gruesome, terrifying creatures. I'd just finished an entire page of these creepy things when Dr. Jacobi's secretary called me back to see him.

I felt like throwing up, and after stuffing my sketchbook back into my purse, I wrung my hands red.

His office, like the rest of the building, was well managed and smelled fantastic. I noted a bookshelf to the right of Dr. Jacobi's desk that had four shelves completely filled with psychology books. Some of the books had white rectangular stickers on the spine, and others were left blank. Dr. Jacobi stood when I entered the room. He wore a green v-neck sweater over a collared, button up shirt and some very nice dark blue jeans. He looked to be in his late forties, with silver hairs reaching into the brown around his ears and just above his forehead, but he was overall a fairly good-looking, kind-looking guy.

"Good afternoon, Kalli. How are you feeling today?"

I wanted to say I was fine. My first instinct was to look at him and say, "Oh, you know, I'm great." But then I thought about the drawings I just finished, and the whole reason I came here, and I decided to go the honest route.

"Well, no offense, Dr. Jacobi, but I feel like crap."

"Please call me Will. The 'Dr.' there is just to let you know I've done my homework, but I've found that it's kind of hard to trust people if you can't call them by their first name. Wouldn't you agree?"

I thought about that for a second before realizing how right he was. Maybe he had done his homework, after all. Still, I'd never met anyone with a doctorate degree that didn't give the whole, "I didn't go through graduate school to be disrespected. Call me Dr." spiel.

I nodded. "I guess. How about Dr. Will, then?" I gestured to the bookcase. "What are the stickers for?"

His gaze followed mine and found what I was talking about.

"You're the first person to have asked that. Funny. Well, the stickers are a reminder for me that I've had the chance to read those particular books. The ones without the stickers are ones I have yet to check off the list."

"Oh. Organized." Efficient. My thoughts immediately turned to Adam. He would have loved that idea.

I felt like punching a wall because he would never be able to hear about this doctor's tactic, and I wanted so badly to curl up in bed with him and tell him all about it.

Dr. Will shrugged as tears welled up in my eyes.

"It helps me remember, that's all. So, shall we get started? I don't want you to pay for any time we don't spend helping you. Now, Alisa tells me that your reason for coming here is an issue with your recent drawings. What is it you've been drawing, Kalli?"

I sighed and ran my fingers through my still wet, tangled mess of hair. "You're going to think I'm some kind of freak."

"Oh, I highly doubt that," he said with raised eyebrows. "Did you happen to bring any of these drawings?"

I scoffed, reached into my bag, and pulled out my sketchbook. I flipped open to the page I was working on in the waiting room and passed it to him. "Sorry it's still wet. Rain, and all." I felt naked, vulnerable.

"No problem," he said. He studied the page with a furrowed brow, and I studied him. His hair was a caramel brown color, with a few white hairs sprinkled in on top of his head and in his trimmed beard and eyebrows. He started flipping backward through the pages, and I got uncomfortable just standing there and shifted my weight. It was strange to me that we were both still standing. In the movies they always asked their patients to sit first thing, didn't they?

"Interesting..." he mumbled, and then said more clearly, "Kalli, I'm amazed by your attention to detail here. You've got astonishing talent."

"Oh, thanks," I said dryly. "Now if only the art I made didn't scare anyone who saw it – myself included..." I let the sentence drop as I really didn't know how to finish it.

"Why don't you have a seat and tell me when all of this started."
Ah, there it was.

He gestured to a super comfortable looking chair across the room. I sat, and he sat across from me in one of those fancy spinning office chairs. I took a deep breath. There was no way this man would be able to help me if I wasn't honest with him.

I really wanted help. I wanted to know if there would ever be a time I would feel happy again.

"Well... I was engaged to the most... incredible man. I mean it. He was amazing. But he died... just a few days before we were supposed to get married. I loved him more than anything, and I miss him like crazy. Like... every second. But I think I'm broken, and I don't think I'm grieving him the way I should be. I guess that's maybe why I started drawing these things. Maybe because... I'm not handling this right?"

I felt like bawling then, telling this stranger that I'm not grieving my dead fiancé correctly, stating the things I'd been too afraid to tell anyone else about.

If anyone could help me, it was him, and that gave me enough strength to keep the tears at bay.

"What do you mean, you're not handling it right? Is there a right way to handle such a loss?" he asked.

"Isn't there?" I asked.

"Is there?" he replied. Great, now I was genuinely confused on top of everything else.

"Isn't there supposed to be five stages of grief I'm supposed to go through? I'm all over the place. I didn't even cry when I found out he was gone... I just... puked in the parking lot."

He crossed his ankles, and his pants wrinkled at the bottom.

"There are five stages of grief that we all have in common, but there are more than that, too, and to go through them in order works fine in theory, but that's just not how it goes. We don't all grieve in the same way. We label those five stages of grief because they are the most commonly experienced, but in truth, everybody faces grief and death and loss differently. Puking in the parking lot may have been your way of processing the information you were given. Processing your loss."

Man, I've got to tell you, I had been beating myself up for the last three weeks over the way I reacted in the hospital. But what he said made me feel just a little bit better, and I let myself relax a little.

"So, I'm not a terrible person? I mean, I've cried more than I thought was humanly possible, but it's been at the weirdest times, and I guess I've just felt like I've been grieving weird in general."

"Grieving *weird* is perfectly normal," Dr. Will said. "I don't think there's anything wrong with you for reacting the way you have. Now, why don't you tell me more about these drawings? Did you start creating them the day he died? Or was it before? Or did they only start after the fact?"

"Um..." I picked at my fingernails. "It didn't really start until after. For the first week I stayed with a friend. I guess it didn't really start until after I went home."

"Did you live together? You and your fiancé?" he asked.

"Adam. Yes. We lived together for just shy of two years."

"I see."

We talked a little bit more about that, about the different ways I had been reacting to different thoughts about Adam, about how badly I hated the universe for taking him away from me. When my hour was up, he asked if I had any questions, and I said I didn't. He told me I could always call him if I did and handed me a business card with his number on it. We both stood.

"Kalli, it's been wonderful getting to meet you. I only wish it had been under better circumstances. Listen, losing a loved one is just about the hardest thing that can happen to you in your life. Especially one so close to your heart, and especially since your life together had scarcely begun. I know it may seem impossible, but you will heal. It will never go away, but it will get easier to manage as time goes on."

"Okay... I hope so," I said. "Can I come back, or is this all you can do for me?" I hoped he would say I could come back soon. I felt so much lighter after talking with him.

"Oh, yes, please do come back. I'd like to see you once a week for the next month or so to see how you're doing. Maybe I can assist you through this process, and then you can set the schedule from there if you feel I've helped. Sound good?"

"Yeah, I think so," I said. "Thank you. Would it be all right if I kept the same sort of schedule we had today? I can plan an hour after work every Monday."

"Actually, I'd like to schedule you for an hour and a half next time, but I won't charge you for the extra thirty minutes. I'd just like to do what I can."

"Wow, you can do that?"

Dr. Will shrugged.

"It's my practice. I sure can. I'll see you next week."

Chapter 13: *A Big Fight*

Still three weeks after Adam's passing.

From my appointment, I took the bus to my parents' house.

"Hey Mom," I said as she answered the door. My hair was frizzy from drying without being brushed, and my clothes were officially dry, but they were starting to smell.

"Hey baby cakes. How was your first day back?"

She held out some plates for me to set the table with as I told her about work, which sucked with everyone's sympathetic glances all day, and my appointment, which actually didn't. "All in all?" I said, lifting two stacks of plates in a shrug. "Meh, it was a day."

"At least it was good enough to be a day. God knows you've had a lot of non-days lately," Dad said as he came into the kitchen. He kissed the top of my head and ruffled my hair. "Hey kiddo."

As I set the table, Dad washed his hands and helped Mom serve up mashed potatoes, spicy chicken enchiladas (chicken free, of course, since it was Mom's night to cook and since she and Dad got divorced, her sexual preference was not the only thing that had changed). I was most excited for what came after the enchiladas: pumpkin pie. Granma came in, and I noticed that we were one place setting short.

Dad still lived with Mom even after Nancy moved in; they just slept on opposite sides of the house to give each other some personal space. Granma did not live with them, but she was only about a five-minute drive away and so was practically there all the time anyway.

"I thought Jeremiah was going to be home this weekend. Did he change plans?" I asked.

"Nope," Granma said. "He's changing. He'll be right down."

Now you may be thinking, duh, your mom just forgot a place setting. No big deal – just go get another one. But some things had never changed about my mom, and her serious attention to all-things-mealtime was definitely one of them. For as long as I could remember, she always made a huge deal about how eating is one step to your soul's quintessential happiness. Without food, you'll never be truly happy, so it was important to do it right.

"Oh. Where's Nancy?" I asked. It wasn't like Nancy to miss dinner like this. When she and my mom got together, she quickly adapted to my mom's mealtime obsession, and she was just as much into these family functions as the rest of us. As Mom served the steamed carrots, I picked one off my plate and tossed it into my mouth. Mom frowned; Dad gave me a wry smile for eating without sitting down at the table, but his smile quickly faded.

Granma gave her uh-oh face, pulled out a chair, and sat down.

Dad avoided eye contact with... well, everyone as he loaded up everyone's plates.

"What?" I asked.

I seated myself. Mom followed. Dad stuffed a serving-spoonful of chicken-free enchilada in his mouth. Granma just looked at Mom, now wearing her don't-start face.

"Honey," Mom began. "Nancy is with her daughter, Melody."

I tried not to make a face. Poor girl. That was my one real qualm with Nancy: She named her daughter Melody. The girl wasn't even that into music. After pushing aside my urge to cringe at the name, I realized the weirdness in that statement.

"Wait, doesn't she, like, *hate* her daughter?"

"They don't *hate* each other," Dad said, swinging his fork around in the air and finally taking his seat. "They just hate each other."

"Ah, I see. Thank you for clearing that up for me. Much better now." I turned my attention back to Mom, thinking about what Adam would say if he were here. "You were saying?"

"Dad's right. They haven't spoken in years."

"So why now?"

"Melody was pregnant," Mom said. The grim expression on her face told me the woman hadn't just popped out a baby.

"Was?"

"She... she miscarried, hon."

Granma sucked in a breath.

She pushed her plate just a little farther away than it was before.

"Oh, wow. That's awful. I'm so sorry to hear that." I didn't know what else to say. Apparently, Dad and Granma didn't either.

"I know. It's a tragic thing, really. And the doctors don't think she'll ever be able to get pregnant again without the risks being twice as high. She's too old."

I stared at my dinner. All thoughts of pumpkin pie vanished as I thought about how awful it would feel to lose a baby – both physically and emotionally. After everything I'd experienced lately, I didn't think I would ever be able to go through something like that. I would crumble like a tissue in a rainstorm. Thinking about that... having this conversation without Adam here beside me, I felt like I'd swallowed a boulder.

"Actually, hon," Mom said cautiously. "Since Nancy found out earlier today, I've been meaning to talk to you..."

"Elizabeth. Not now," Granma said, her tone like steel. Mom seemed oblivious to the fact that Granma had said anything at all.

"The same thing could happen to you."

"Mom, Melody is almost six years older than I am. That's more than half a decade," I said slowly.

"I know that, but they say having a baby after thirty can be detrimental or even fatal to a mother, the baby, or both, and in this family, eggs start dying ten years early. At your age..."

I interrupted her, dropping my fork on my plate, sending droplets of carrot juice onto the tablecloth. "I'm twenty-nine, Mom."

Mom put her hands up and just repeated her last argument.

"At your age, you're already at risk."

Through gritted teeth, I said, "And?"

She scoffed as if *I* was actually being the unreasonable one.

"Well, don't you want to start trying?" she persisted. I could tell she was trying to be gentle, but she may as well have tried beating me with a baseball bat that said *Who cares about your dead fiancé? Get knocked up.*

I swear, time stopped. We all sat completely still and in total silence. I narrowed my eyes. Finally, I spoke.

"That would be kind of hard *now*, wouldn't it?"

"I know, I know. I just... don't want you to miss your chance. I'm not saying you try moving on right away, but these things take *time*, you know?"

"Are you *serious* right now?" My heart was pounding. Sweat tickled my palms. My fork was magically back in my hand, and I gripped it so tightly that my knuckles turned white.

"Kalli," Mom said quietly.

"Liz," Dad warned.

"No," I said. "You're seriously asking me to move on? The love of my life died *three weeks ago.* Does that mean nothing to you? I wasn't sure I wanted kids before he died, but now? I don't give a damn if you *ever* get grandkids. Why would you say something like that? How insensitive can you be? He *just* died, Mom. And... and now—"

Mom blinked back the tears that pooled in her eyes.

My own eyes stung with the threat of tears, and I swallowed against them.

"I'm sorry I brought it up. Really. I just... I... I just don't want you to have any regrets about missing your shot to have kids. I'll just drop it and we can finish up our dinner. I've made pumpkin pie."

I pushed my plate into the center of the table and shoved my chair back. The sound of it scraping against the floor seemed only to punctuate the anger I felt fuming off my body like heat waves.

"Suddenly I'm not very hungry," I growled.

Jeremiah's footsteps came rumbling down the stairs as he pulled a t-shirt over his tank top. "Hey everyone. Sorry, I had to finish up a call with someone. What did I miss?"

"I'm out," I said, throwing my hands into the air, shooting a disgusted glance at Mom before storming through the kitchen to the door. I grabbed my stuff and turned to open the door, only to be interrupted in the foyer by my dad.

"Hey, kiddo. She means well. I get that you're upset, and you have every right to be, but just... don't hold it against her, okay? She does know what you've been going through."

"Mmph," I replied. He kissed me on the forehead. I heard Granma lecturing Mom from the dining room as I closed the door behind me.

When I got home, I was so tired and so upset that when I finally got my keys out of the door, I called out, "Adam?"

I wanted to tell him everything. I wanted to say, "You wouldn't believe what my mom said tonight..." But my reality hit me with a vengeance, and I fell to the floor in a heap of uncontrollable sobs.

The next day I kept my head down and ignored everybody. I still did my work, of course, but I refused to acknowledge that anyone existed on the planet except myself, except for when I had to greet my boss, but I think by the time I'd finished my sour hello he knew I was better left alone. I was still absolutely *furious* that my mother had been so completely insensitive, intentionally or not. Even if I wanted to have kids, my partner—the person I would want to have and raise them with—was gone.

By the time I got on the bus to head home, I was pretty sure someone could have roasted marshmallows over my body I was that heated about it. Move on, like it was nothing. Like *Adam* was nothing.

The bus seat sent a whisper of air up as someone sat beside me.

"Hey there," that someone said.

I glanced up from my shoes, which I had been glaring at for some time now. It was cool backpack guy, and boy, he looked like he hadn't seen the sun or had a decent meal in his life.

"Hi," I grumbled.

"What's up?"

Lamely, I looked up at the ceiling of the large transportation device and shrugged. "Metal and stuff."

"Ah, a literal joker, nice. I'm Seth," he said.

I nodded as though that would be a polite enough response to this stranger I didn't want to talk to. Apparently, it wasn't.

"What's your name?"

"Kalli."

"As in California?"

"No. Just Kalli."

"Huh. Cool. Nice to meet you, Kalli," the guy said. Was this guy hitting on me? *No*, I thought. *He must just be trying to be friendly.* He extended a hand for me to shake. I considered biting it, but I had no particular desire to go to jail. So instead, I shook it.

"Hi," I said again, hardly trying to mask the irritation in my voice. I thought he would find another seat, or at least take the hint and leave me alone, but he continued without a care.

"So... I know this may seem forward, but I think you're beautiful," he said weakly, covering his mouth to let out a breathless cough before clutching his chest like he was trying to hold it together. "I've noticed you on the bus a few times, and I swear to God I've met you before..." *Really, dude?* I was a tea kettle that someone had left on the stove. I started to boil. I tapped my fingers on my jeans to try and distract myself from my flaring temper. "I've actually started riding this bus pretty regularly. I've been meaning to ask... could I get your number?"

There it was. Perfect screaming temp.

"Dude, oh my God. Seriously? If she put you up to this, I *swear* I'm going to lose it. Where did she even find you?" I held my hand up to stop whatever his response would be. "It doesn't matter. I suggest you listen to me *very* carefully.

I do *not* need to move on, so I suggest you leave it alone."

The bus route could not be timed more perfectly. As we pulled to a slow halt, I ejected from my seat and got off without taking a second look at the guy I was sure needed to pick his jaw up off the floor.

By the time I walked to my apartment from the bus stop, I was still fuming. I stared at the orange bag that contained my wedding dress. It was just sitting there, night after night, taunting me. Filled with an anger I couldn't explain, I swung it off the hook, tossed it over my shoulder, and walked back to the bus stop, dress flopping wildly behind me.

If I had to look at this dress for one more second, my heart was going to explode.

My chest restricted as I rode a new bus to the dress shop. Over the last three weeks, I'd been able to work up the courage to cancel all wedding planning folks who kept calling. I managed to get through it all with a lot of tears and even more pizza, but I got through it. This one, however, was a real depression causer.

I didn't want to get rid of the dress I'd loved so much, but I couldn't really have it taunting me every time I walked into the room. Maybe I could get some money back from it, if it wasn't too late. As if money mattered at all to me right now. I took a deep breath when the bus stopped down the block from the dress shop, and trying not to hit anyone with the bulky material, I exited the bus. My ears were thrumming as I hoped I could find someone who could help me.

When I got inside, I looked around and was instantly spotted by Vance. He dropped the customer he was working with a light pat on the arm and a charming smile, then he rushed to me.

"Hey, girl! I got your invitation, but I never got a call back when I tried to RSVP. Is everything all right?" he asked.

My lip quivered, eyes watered, and suddenly my voice box felt rusty. I shook my head, and my messy hair bounced against my face.

"I..." I started, finding my voice again after clearing my throat and taking a deep, shaky breath. "I won't be needing this. My fiancé was... killed. In an accident." I took a moment to clear my throat as a look of complete shock washed over his face.

"Oh, but you *loved* that dress," he said as he pulled me, almost a complete stranger, into a hug.

I snorted/sobbed and nodded against his small shoulder, covering my mouth with my hand. "I really did," I said.

Slowly, he pulled away and took my arm, leading me to the same computer I'd checked out with when I bought the dress.

"We can still give you a return on it," he said, blinking away tears of his own. I nodded and set the dress on the counter, but when he reached for it to scan the tags – which were still secured within the neckline – my fingers clasped tightly on the bag and wouldn't let go. I suddenly felt that if I released this material from my grasp, I'd lose the promise I was about to make to Adam forever.

My heart stopped beating and my eyes widened.

What the hell am I doing?

I'd already cancelled everything else; this was all I had left.

Vance seemed to understand my craziness, and he nodded. "You sure you want to return this, sweety? You don't have to. Who says you need to have a wedding to wear a beautiful dress?"

The way I looked at him must have been the same expression I would have used if he told me Adam was back from the dead.

Tears spilled from my eyes yet again as I choked out, "You really think I can keep it?"

Vance put his hand gently on my shoulder from across the counter. With a voice like cotton, he said, "Really truly. Keep it, hon."

So I kept it.

That night, I wore the dress around the apartment. It fit a little more loosely than it did when I bought it, but I loved it just as much.

Chapter 14: *The Zombie Gets a Makeover*

Three months after Adam's passing.

I SPENT THE NEXT COUPLE OF MONTHS JUST BARELY GETTING BY.

I continued going to therapy, which seemed to help with the panic attacks I started having after losing Adam and forcing myself to take some distance from my family.

Outside of therapy, I did my work, rode the bus home, and that was it.

One Friday night, I curled up in bed, pulled the comforter (which I hadn't washed since before Adam's accident) clear up to my chin. I was lonely as hell, and furious.

Throughout the week, my mom had called me eight times. I had ignored her calls successfully seven of those eight times. The first time she called I had just gotten to work on Wednesday and my coffee hadn't kicked in yet. I'd almost forgotten I was still mad at her until she opened her mouth and blurted out, "Kalli, I'm sorry I said all that when you came over for dinner. It's been months, hon. I wasn't trying to undermine your feelings, but—"

Aaaaaand "click." I didn't feel like listening to whatever argument would come after that "but." I was still upset. Who was she to tell me that I needed to move on? Didn't she know that there was no replacement for Adam? She still lived with my dad years after their divorce!

I knew that if she got the chance, she'd bring up my high school and college boyfriends, which were fairly great the entire two minutes I had dated each of them. But those relationships *hadn't* lasted. I had never come *close* to feeling anything for them like I did with Adam.

And then the encounter with the dude with the backpack on the bus... ugh, it had just turned out to be an overly irritating couple of days, which lingered into the next two months. *Replace Adam...*

No, it just wasn't possible. I started thinking about how Adam looked the last time I saw him, lying in the hospital the way he had been. My chest ached like a dump truck had fallen on it.

"Okay..." I said aloud to the darkness between painful gasps, clutching the comforter until my fingers were numb. "Okay, think of something else. Anything else... Think of... something good."

With great effort, I steered my thoughts toward my last vivid memory of Adam. The morning of the accident came to mind.

He was on the phone. I left for work. Oh, God. If I'd only stayed with him, if I'd just asked him to ride the bus with me... NO. I shouldn't do this. I can't do this. What came before that?

I fell asleep thinking about our last night together on the kitchen floor, holding Adam's pillows close against my body.

As I had since the accident, I woke up several times throughout the night. At one point I jolted upright in bed from a dream I had that I couldn't remember the very second my eyes opened. This frustrated the hell out of me, and I couldn't go back to sleep for ages. Finally, however, it must have happened, because I woke up for good with sunlight glaring in from the balcony window.

Saturday... Oh, I forgot it was Saturday. I wiped both hands across my face and sighed. Maybe, I thought, I could close my eyes and sleep again until it was time for me to go back to work on Monday.

But of course, it didn't work that way. Within five minutes, my legs pulled me out of bed. Without even attempting to make the bed, I zombie-walked first to use the bathroom, then to the kitchen.

I made myself a pot of coffee and took the entire pot into my studio with me.

I painted three new creepy, grotesque pieces that I was sure my new shrink would find interesting, and I masterfully ignored five more calls from my mother.

By the time I was finished with the third piece, Lici called me. That call, I did answer.

"Hey lady," I said with half as much enthusiasm as I used to.

I used a dry rag to wipe the oil paint from my hands and face and brushed a loose strand of hair behind my ear.

"Hey babe," she said. Listen, Ness and I want to go out today. Catch up. I've been hella busy with this new property closing, but now that's finished, I've got mucho moolah burning a hole in my gorgeous denim pockets. You wouldn't believe how many people are buying houses right now! Anyway, it wouldn't be a date without you. Do you have plans?"

I picked at the paint beneath my fingernails.

"Oh, yeah. I'm totally booked up."

"I see. So... you're sitting at home, unwashed, still in your pajamas, locked in your studio, huh?"

It was scary how accurate her description was. I wasn't that gross, was I? I lifted an arm and sniffed, then started coughing because I really did smell. "Yeah, pretty much."

"Thought so. Come on, hermana, it's been *decades* since we've seen you. Please, come out with us!"

"I don't know... my dishes are stacking up, and I really don't feel like it. Besides, I think I'm coming down with something. There was a lady on the bus yesterday who coughed all over me. And Nessa sees me literally every day."

"She told me you've been avoiding her. That doesn't count as seeing you."

"I really feel sick this morning," I said.

"Ugh, I hate getting that weekend flu," she said.

I did my best to ignore the dripping sarcasm in her tone.

"Yep. That's probably it. Maybe next week."

I heard her talking incoherently to Nessa for a few seconds before she came back on the line.

"Whatever. I'll talk to you later." Without another word, she hung up. Guilt gnawed at me subtly, but I was just glad she hadn't fought me more about it. I rolled my shoulders, doing my best to relieve some of the tension in my neck.

I sat back on my heels and stared at the new additions to what was looking to be a very dark collection.

I must have zoned out, because I came to fifteen minutes later to a knock on the front door. Well, I guess it was more like a rapid series of angry pounds on the door that continued as I got up and made my way through the apartment to answer it. I had a hunch who it might be before I even opened the door.

Sure enough, Lici and Nessa shouted their cheerful greetings at me when I pulled the door open. Their bright moods were sickening.

"Hey hon," Nessa said, letting herself in and setting an armful of bags onto the island. She turned and gave me a warm, too-tight hug.

"How did you get here so fast?" I asked.

"We already figured you were going to be a sourpuss," Lici began. She smacked her glossy lips at me.

"Yeah... so we kind of planned ahead. We were already on the way when we called you," Nessa added, shooting me an apologetic glance. "Don't be mad. We've just missed you like crazy!"

I let out a long, exaggerated sigh, putting my hands in my pockets. "I'm not mad... I guess I could use a day out."

My two friends clapped in unison.

"Great! It's settled then," Nessa said.

I looked around my cluttered coffee table. "Let me just find my purse... I swear I put it right here yesterday." When I turned back to them, Lici had a disgusted look on her face as she eyed what was once my coffee table. Nessa's expression appeared to be a mixture of concern and fear.

"Um..." Nessa started.

"Um... No." Lici's hand went up. "There's *no way* we're letting you out of the house looking like that. When was the last time you brushed your hair? Or took a shower?"

"I showered yesterday." I rolled my eyes. Leave it to Lici to make a bigger deal out of this than it was.

"Did you condition? Brush? Braid it? Anything?" she pressed.

I picked at my fingernails and stared at the ground in response. I'd washed it at least... Those kinds of things just didn't seem important to me anymore.

"Exactly," she said. "Don't you worry, my friend. We have everything you need right here." She did one of those cheesy super-model reveals where she spread her arms to show the bag-covered island behind her.

Thus began my two-hour makeover. While they washed, conditioned, styled, restyled, primped and prodded, we talked of little except my "on-the-verge fashion catastrophe." Sure, did I condition my hair the day before? No. Had I been wearing baggy pants, and even baggier shirt that I may or may not have pulled out of the dirty hamper to throw on and two mismatched socks when they showed up? Yeah, so what? It's not like I had anyone to impress anymore.

I actually made the mistake of saying that last part out loud in the midst of their conversation, which resulted in about three minutes of cold stares from Lici, and sad, awkward glances from Nessa. Lici opened her mouth like she was going to say something, but whatever it was, she kept it to herself.

When they finally got my hair and makeup just right, Lici had me slip on one of her hottest hookup dresses. It wasn't much, but the two-hundred-dollar piece of stretchy, shiny black material accentuated every curve of its wearer's body.

My eyes widened once I saw myself in the full body mirror that hung on the bathroom door (that I'd deliberately covered with dirty towels over the last couple of months).

"I can't wear *this!*" I said, covering myself up.

"Why not?" Nessa said. She was in the middle of digging through her silver sequined bag for accessories. She raised her eyebrows but didn't look up.

"It's sexy!" I squeaked.

Lici came and stood beside me, looking at me through the mirror. "It's black. You're in mourning. It's perfect."

Chapter 15: *Rejoining the Land of the Living*

Still three months after Adam's passing.

OUR FAVORITE RESTAURANT WAS TOTALLY VACANT.

For once, it was easy to get a table, and we had our pick of any booth we wanted. Our usual booth was empty, so we headed over and scooted in.

I had to keep one hand on the material at the back of my thighs to keep the stretchy dress from becoming a shirt as I sat down, slinging the jacket I insisted on wearing over the back of the booth.

I peered around the restaurant to check out the few people who were eating within the establishment.

Only a few small, miscellaneous groups were scattered through the restaurant, and the building looked sad and kind of pathetic without its usual one-person-per-square-freaking-inch crowd.

A group of very bored looking teenagers hung out at a booth toward the front windows and away from the bar. A man argued with his very angry looking lady companion about God knew what. He waved his hands manically as he followed her out the door.

All the other groups were boring looking normal types of people with nothing better to do with their Saturday afternoon than sit around in an empty restaurant.

"Man, it's dead!" Nessa exclaimed, then immediately sent an apologetic look in my direction while she nervously curled her silky brown hair around her index finger.

I rolled my eyes and looked through my menu. I did my best to hold back the sneer I wanted to shoot her way. Even at the word dead, my chest hadn't started hurting until she reminded me with that look. Thankfully, Lici came to the rescue before the silence could creep too far in.

"What do you guys want? I was going to order the pizza, but... I think I want something a little less greasy."

She looked at Nessa. Nessa smiled back. I flipped to the next page in my menu.

"I think I'll get something a little less greasy as well. It's important to look presentable these days, you know. Unwanted acne could give people the wrong impression." Nessa added, unwrapping her utensils.

"What impression is that?" I retorted. "That you're a female that's risen above the stupid expectations of the world we live in and eats how she wants to because she's beautiful regardless? Yeah, that *would* be a bad impression to give. I think I'll get their chicken noodle soup and some grilled cheese. Emphasis on grilled."

I snapped my menu closed and looked at my friends.

Nessa's mouth was open, jaw practically on the table. Lici's perfectly plucked eyebrows touched her hairline. Okay... I guessed that was a little unnecessary, but hey. After the day I'd had, listening to them continue their "search for perfection" rant did not seem like an option to me.

I should apologize... I thought. But I really didn't feel like it, so I turned my gaze to the table.

Soon enough, a nice-looking girl with red hair, zillions of freckles, and a nametag that said, "Sheri" skipped up and took our orders. I requested the chicken noodle soup and grilled cheese. Lici and Nessa both ordered a salad and a side of breadsticks, despite the very convincing argument I'd just made.

We talked about work for about half an hour. Five minutes or so of that half hour was spent with Nessa and me sharing minute details about events that had happened at our work recently. The rest of the time was taken by Lici explaining the housing market explosion that was happening at the moment and explaining to us that now is the time to buy because prices were ridiculously low but would only go up from there.

I thought about Adam. He had always talked about buying a house in the suburbs like where he grew up, but I had always wanted to stay in our apartment.

Then, the three of us sat in silence. Typically, this is when we'd start talking about guys: who Lici was having sex with, who Nessa was trying too desperately to hold on to... it was a thing. Then, for the past several years, we'd always defaulted to how lucky Adam and I were to be out of the "looking" phase of the dating game.

If the conversation ever lagged, we'd turn to family. We'd talk about Nessa's rich and emotionally stunted (except toward each other and their daughter) parents. We'd talk about Lici's biological parents, wherever they actually were. Lici just knew her birth parents were from somewhere exotic with centuries of rich, authentic Spanish culture.

We'd touch base about whether or not Lici was currently speaking to her adoptive parents, who loved her to death, but wanted too much to do with her life for her liking. Then, we would talk about my family. Lici would run her hands through her long black hair and tell me for the billionth time how hot Jeremiah was, and I'd tell her to back off.

Somehow, the conversation would always end up with dad and Granma, Nancy, and Mom.

That was the natural order of things. But I didn't want to talk like usual. Adam was gone, so he and I were no longer lucky in any sense of the word.

Lici was acting all weird, Nessa looked like a skittish rabbit, and I was still so beyond pissed at my mom, and therefore wanted nothing to do with her. So, we sat in silence and occasionally made feeble attempts at making small talk.

About fifteen minutes after the bearable awkward level had reached capacity, when we had completely exhausted every possible option for small talk topics, Nessa sat up and said she needed to use the bathroom. She stretched casually and not so casually made a face at Lici that said, "Hey dude, I have to talk to you, so let's pretend we have to pee at the same time."

Lici nodded and then to be nice, she turned to me.

"Want to come?"

At my decline, she did one of her dramatic hair flips and reached her hand with several dangling, sparkling bracelets out to Nessa. As soon as they wiggled out of our booth and turned away, I could pretty much hear them talking about me. Did it bother me?

Nah.

Let 'em talk.

A few minutes later they returned, and I noticed for the first time how totally out of place I was. I didn't belong here with these two wild women I had fit in so well with before. I stood and grabbed my jacket off the back of the booth with one hand and pulled the super tight dress down with the other.

"You leaving?" Nessa asked, trying unsuccessfully to hide the hurt she felt that I was ditching early.

"Yeah, I'm tired. Don't really feel up to this," I muttered.

Lici grabbed her purse.

"I'll walk you out," she said.

I gave Nessa a quick hug goodbye, and Lici told her to save their seats. Silence inched its way in as we walked, filling more and more of the space between us until it was claustrophobic even after we exited the building. When we cleared the exit, Lici spun on her heels and threw both of her hands to her hips. Her purse slid down from her shoulder and hung, swinging back and forth, from her elbow.

"Hey, I need to talk to you," she said, attitude thick and sticky in her tone.

"Not really," I mumbled. Whatever shallow thing she was about to say, I definitely did not need to hear it.

"*Excuse me?*" Lici's perfectly shaped eyebrows furrowed and her short, wide-ish nose squished up as she glared at me, but she took a deep breath, rolled the anger or frustration or whatever she was feeling off her shoulders and tried again. The icy December air blew in gentle wisps around us. I shivered and pulled my jacket more tightly around my torso.

"Listen, Kalli; I know you've been through a lot. Trust me, what you've been through since Adam... is beyond fucked up. But you've been really shitty about it. Yeah, I get it. It hurts, and you have every right in the world to be pissed off about what happened. But you're *not* alone in any of this, despite how hard you've tried to push every single person that cares about you away."

I should have been more understanding about what she was trying to say, but her little rant made me sick to my stomach with a sour rage that burned and twisted in my gut.

"And?" I asked. I shifted my weight and tried desperately not to roll my eyes.

"And it sucks! Nessa's found someone, and it seems to be sticking. They've been together almost two whole months now. That's beyond breaking her two-and-a-half-week record. But she can't tell you about it because A: You're so absorbed in your own self-pity you hardly look at her, and B: She's terrified of hurting you. She deserves to be happy, and she deserves your support. She deserves to be honest with you about her relationship. We both do!"

I opened my mouth to shout something stupid back at her, but I stopped myself.

"Wait, what do you mean, you both do?"

"Nothing." Finally, she looked away. She hunched up her shoulders and folded her arms, as if she finally felt the cold wind blowing in around us.

"No, you seem pretty bent on ripping me a new one, so let me have it. What do you mean?"

Lici shrugged, and much more quietly now, she said, "I found somebody, too."

I stepped forward. For Lici to get serious enough to call the person she was sleeping with a somebody was a huge deal. It had never actually happened before.

"Who?" I asked.

"What does it matter? You're too in your own shit that it wouldn't make a difference, anyway." Her voice was back, and she used it this time less as a weapon and more as a shield.

"Lici," I started, feeling like total crap. All the anger I had felt just seconds before had completely vanished. "Hey, I'm sorry. Really. Of course, it matters. Who is it?"

She stared intently at a crack in the sidewalk.

Barely audibly, she mumbled, "Jeremiah."

"Who?" I asked. Had I heard her correctly? Was the wind making me hear things?

"Jeremiah," she repeated.

I gasped, disbelieving. "Uh... my Jeremiah?"

She rolled her eyes and scoffed, shifting her weight like she couldn't wait to be done with this conversation. Hell, I couldn't wait, either. I wanted to take a bomb to this conversation and forget it ever happened.

"He's not *your* Jeremiah."

The rage rushed back almost instantly, and it boiled behind my cheeks, turning them a bright, furious red. All guilt and sincerity from the moment before was gone.

"Are you fucking serious?" I shouted, ignoring the few people walking by, who looked at me like I had lost my freaking mind. "Felicia, for *years* I've listened to every nasty sex story, every threesome, every experiment, and I've only ever asked you one thing. Keep your *habits* away from my *brother!*"

"Nasty? Habits? Really?"

My jaw dropped. Was that really what I said? I tried to think back to it, but those words bounced around in my head, allowing me to think of nothing else. I knew it was harsh, but I was still fuming, and there was no way I was going to take it back.

The bus pulled up, groaning as if it wanted to escape this argument as well.

I spared it a quick glance and then went back to looking at Lici.

"Well?" I retorted weakly.

"You know, I'm going to go back inside," Lici said, practically sneering. I could tell that her eyes were filling with tears as she adjusted her purse on her shoulder. "You'd better go. Don't want to miss your bus."

Lici turned and walked back inside with her arms folded, and I rushed to get on the bus.

I hoped that by the time I got home, I would be calmer. Maybe I could look at this thing from a different angle.

When I got home, I was just as mad, maybe even more so because my mind had had about half an hour to remember every horrible thing she'd ever said about the guys she'd had sex with. *How could she do this? Seriously.*

Since we were in middle school, I'd asked her to do only one thing: Pick anyone but my brother. Her relationships never lasted, and it was usually because she'd found someone more appetizing.

Now, Jeremiah was the center of her weird, twisted attention.

I locked the door behind me, went straight to the bedroom, and threw my purse and phone on the bed.

Then, with my jacket still on, I took an arm and cleared off everything that was on the long, stubby dresser (books, magazines, nail polish that I'd gotten out but never actually used, sketches for paintings, and piles upon piles of used tissues). After that was done, I went out to the living room and picked up the TV. Okay... the first attempt quickly failed.

I almost dropped it on my feet.

"Holy shit!" I whispered, sucking in air. "You're freaking *heavy!*" But of course, now that I'd gotten the idea in my head, I just HAD to move the TV. So, I bent my knees like any sane, reasonable person would do and tried again. I bumped the wall a few times in the hallway and almost dropped the TV on the floor when I got into the bedroom. I had to set the thing down and get a better grip on it at that point. At last, I got the TV to the dresser and hooked it up.

"We shouldn't put a TV in the bedroom," Adam said.

The room in my mind filled with light. At this point in our relationship, we were still figuring out what color to paint everything, so every wall of every room had three or four random swatches of paint on it. Half unpacked boxes littered the floor.

Adam stood in the doorway, rubbing the beard I'd begged him to grow that he absolutely hated. I stood toward the balcony, huge flat screen TV at my feet.

"Why not?" I asked. "It's already in here."

"Statistics have shown that having a television set in the bedroom has a huge negative impact on, well, bedroom activities..."

I snorted.

"Adam, you can say sex, you know. We've been at it for a while now. I'm not going to get offended or anything."

"The point is that issues in that area can quickly lead to other problems down the road. Do you want this TV to ruin our relationship?"

The room darkened again, and as the memory faded, so too did Adam's face. How long had he had that beard? It was funny... I loved that thing. I had actually counted the days he kept it. But now, I couldn't for the life of me remember.

My phone buzzed twice, and the screen lit up a small section of my bed.

A picture of Lici and me sticking our tongues out at the camera came up, along with a message that said:

> I get you're pissed. But we made that deal when we were 12. Don't U think it's time 2 let that go? We're all adults now. Besides... I haven't been this happy b4. Not w/ a guy anyway. I just wish ness and I didnt have to hide our crap from you. Anyway. Nite.

Damn. I sighed. Despite the gut wrenching, nauseous feeling I got at the thought of the two of them together, I didn't have a say in the matter. They were going to be together if they wanted to be. Lici was right; I really had been ruining the shit out of everything. I unlocked my screen to text her back.

> Sorry... I rlly do want to hear about it...

> RLLY?

I blew a raspberry at my phone as I struggled to resist the urge to say, "Of course not, stupid!"

> Yep. Rlly. Just... NO NASTY STUFF PLEASE!!!

The bubble popped up again. Disappeared. Popped up again.

> No nasty stuff. Promise. OMG I have so much I wanna tell you. Lunch? 2morrow?

> I'll see what I can do.
> Night.

After I sent that last text, anxiety swallowed my stomach whole. My chest imploded at my stomach's departure.

I dialed my therapist. It was like 9:00 at night, so of course no one was at the office, and I left a message.

"Hi, Dr. Will. I'm sorry to bother you on the weekend, and I know we have an appointment after work on Monday, but I was wondering if you could fit me in any earlier than that? I have some stuff going on, and I don't know if I can wait until after work. I'll pay extra, whatever it takes. Um... Okay, bye." I hung up the phone and let it fall to my bed. For hours, I stared at the TV I'd put so much effort into moving but now couldn't bring myself to turn on. Instead, I tried to picture Adam's face in that beard. The beard came fine after a while, but Adam's face seemed off, and I couldn't get it to look right.

Chapter 16: *Time to Stop Shutting People Out*

Still three months after Adam's passing.

I WOKE UP THE NEXT MORNING TO MY CELL PHONE RINGING.

I must have fallen asleep with it still on the covers, because now I had to dig through a mound of tangled pillows, blankets, and limbs to find it.

Finally, I got it. The person calling was my therapist, and I rushed to answer it.

"Dr. Will? What? I mean... I didn't think you'd call me back until tomorrow. It didn't say anywhere online that your office had weekend hours." Through the phone, Dr. Will chuckled.

"Well, technically we don't, but sometimes I like to escape the house early on Sundays and pretend I still have a purpose on the weekends."

"No offense, Doc, but that doesn't sound very healthy." I did my best to rub the sleep from my eyes and stifled a yawn.

"I acknowledge that. We've all got our issues, don't we? Some of us have just been trained to manage them a little bit better. Now, that message seemed pretty urgent. I'm here this morning, if you'd like to come on by."

"Oh, jeeze. Um, I don't want to make you work on the weekend. I really can come tomorrow if you've got the time to see me earlier than our afternoon spot," I said, rubbing the back of my neck.

"Nonsense," he said, and I could practically hear his hand waving through the phone. "My job is to help my patients when they need me, not to only be available when it suits my schedule. That's why I opened my own practice. I want to be available when it matters. Really, I insist. If you need to talk, come and see me. Besides, you'll be helping me fulfill that purpose I mentioned."

I shrugged.

"Well, okay. I just woke up, so I've got to get ready and grab a bus. I can be there in about an hour, if that's okay."

"Sounds great. I'll see you then."

I got up, attempted to make my bed for the first time in who knows how long, threw on some makeup and a pair of comfy, stretchy blue jeans. I was still wearing the dress from last night, but it had rolled up around my torso and honestly looked pretty cute as a shirt, so I kept it on, threw my hair up into a high ponytail, and left the apartment in time to catch the 8:30 bus.

Forty-five minutes and over ten stops later, I arrived at Dr. Will's office. The flowers I'd wanted to destroy on my first visit were long wilted. Their tiny, shriveled carcasses were covered with a thick layer of ice. I felt a tinge of sadness that they were so far gone, and that I'd wished for their demise.

Dr. Will opened the door shortly after I knocked. I was startled by this at first, but then I remembered it was Sunday, and his secretary was likely enjoying her weekend off. It makes sense he'd be here working with the door locked and answer it himself.

"Hey, Doc. Thank you for letting me come in today. Things are so messed up right now."

He motioned toward his office, and I followed him in, babbling away about things before we even reached the door.

"My best friend is doing my brother, and apparently I'm forcing them to be unhappy because they can't share it with me, and my mom and I are still in a fight, and everyone keeps telling me I need to move on, and I can't remember Adam's face!"

Once we were actually inside the office, he rushed to his desk and scribbled a few things down on his notepad, but he left it there as I sat. I plopped onto the couch across the room and pulled my feet up. I was wearing Uggs, which despite the name, I'd always adored.

"Brother, still fighting with mom, visualization troubles. Okay, that is a lot. Let's back up a little bit. You can't remember his face?"

I already felt my heart squeezing at the thought.

"No. Well, every time I think of him, I see the way he looked after the accident, all bumpy and bloody. That, I can remember pretty clearly. But when I try to remember how he looked before, I come up blank. I loved that face. I *adored it.* I probably looked at it five zillion times. Why can't I remember it?"

For the second time in twenty-four hours, my chest seized, and I dropped my head in my hands.

"Do you have any memories of him? Memories that resurface on their own?" Dr. Will asked.

"Yeah, sometimes."

"And in those memories, can you see him clearly?"

I thought about that for a moment. "Yes, but when I try to remember him after, I get nothing. The closest I get is an image of someone who definitely isn't my Adam."

"Have you been sleeping? Dreaming?"

Where is he going with this?

"Sleeping, yeah. Off and on. It's easier to stay asleep during the work week when I'm busy. And I do dream, I know I do, but I can't ever remember them when I wake up."

"Okay, that's okay," he said. "In my experience, it's not uncommon for people to struggle to remember their dreams normally, let alone in times of high stress or emotional turmoil. The mind does all kinds of things to help us when we're struggling. Now let's go back a little bit further. You mentioned that you and your mom still aren't getting along?"

Through ground teeth, I answered him. "No."

"You two have always been so close, from what I've gathered. You told me that the two of you got into an argument after our first session over an insensitive comment she made. Is that still the reason you're having trouble getting along?"

I nodded and told him exactly what she had said at the dinner table that night. It was something I should have done in our session after it happened, but it was still so raw at the time. Thinking about it in retrospect, it felt silly. It all felt so ridiculous, especially that I was now only not talking to her out of principle.

"I see. I can understand why that would upset you, especially so soon after Adam's passing. Even if she didn't mean for her words to be perceived that way, they must have had a difficult impact on you. I can see why you might still be sore about that. You said, Felicia and your brother are dating? When did that start?"

"I'm not sure," I answered. "I'm supposed to meet up with her later and hear all the grotesque details." I briefly wondered why he was jumping from topic to topic so quickly.

"You two have been friends for a long time, right?" he asked, shifting his weight from one foot to the other.

"Forever." I felt totally defeated at the word. It felt so foreign to say the word after barely seeing her for months, and after Adam... It had been all I could do to keep track of the days so I didn't miss work.

"Well, I understand that you're not happy with the situation, but old friends are hard to come by. I might consider keeping that in mind when you meet with her."

My shoulders slumped. "Damn it, why are you so right?"

He chuckled and shrugged, pointing the butt of his pen at his diplomas and certificates displayed on the wall.

"Years of schooling, remember?"

"Oh, yeah."

He chuckled again. All this time he'd been standing, and he now sat on the edge of the desk.

"You want to know what I think about all of this?" he asked, raising his eyebrows.

"That's what I'm paying you for, isn't it?" I asked.

"Of course. Well... I think they're right."

"What the *hell*?" I asked. I didn't mean to curse again in front of him. It just sort of slipped out with the shock of what he'd said.

"Remember, you asked for my opinion, so I'm going to give it to you, and we can chat more if you have questions or concerns. What you do with the information I provide is your choice," he said.

I rolled my eyes and relaxed into the sofa. "Sure."

"Thank you. They're both right. Your mother, and Felicia. It does seem that you've been pushing people away from you, whether the action is intentional or not."

"Okay, great. I suck. Lici was right. Now, how is my *mother* right about anything?"

"Well, look at it this way. Your memories of Adam come naturally, and you see him just fine. However, you keep trying to force yourself to remember him, and in fact, these efforts are actually making him increasingly difficult to picture. Kalli, it seems to me that you're not allowing your grieving process to happen naturally."

"I'm grieving plenty, trust me."

He sighed.

I folded my arms across my chest and pouted.

"Let me rephrase that. I believe you're not allowing your healing process to take its natural course. Hearing this, along with everything else you've told me thus far, I really believe it's time for you to consider moving forward."

I swear, my heart stopped beating. My eyebrows jumped way up off my forehead, and my voice could have burst an eardrum as I squeaked, "You *what?*"

Dr. Will put his hands up in defense. "I'm not saying you have to get married tomorrow. I'm not even saying you have to find someone new. But what I am suggesting is that it may be time to stop pushing people away. Being open to having people in your life could be a really positive thing for you."

"Really..." I did my best to process the information he was sharing. "I don't have to jump into the dating pool and mate right away?"

He shrugged again and did his best to hide a smile.

"Of course not. You don't *have* to do anything. This is just my opinion, remember. What you do is completely up to you. You don't ever have to be involved with another man again, though I wouldn't recommend going that route. All I'm suggesting is that you allow people around you to be a part of your life again. I would love to see you embrace your social life again, step by step.

"In our previous sessions, it has sounded like a very important piece of who you are. You flourish around people, and I think it's important for you to be around people you love that can be supportive. You can take matters of romance and intimacy or not as it comes up naturally."

I was quiet for a long while before I spoke again, letting his words seep into my heart.

"Huh... Okay, I think I can handle that. Thanks."

We stood and Dr. Will walked me to the door. When he opened it and I turned to leave, he stopped me.

"Oh, Kalli, this visit is on me, okay?" he said.

I frowned for a moment and opened my mouth to argue. He put his hand up before I could get a word out.

"Trust me, this visit was more to help me than anything. You've done *me* a favor, reminding me why I do what I do."

"Oh. Well, um... thank you again. Oh, by the way... when will you be able to plant more flowers by the walkway?" I asked, remembering how full of life those flowers had been when I first visited.

"We don't re-plant anything out there. They're perennials. They grow back on their own every spring and fall, even after winters as harsh as this one has been."

The short walk back to the bus stop felt so much longer than usual, probably because frozen snails would have moved faster than I was. But that slow pace was exactly what I needed to process everything that Dr. Will had said.

As I passed the flowers by the walkway, I was filled with a new sense of hope that lightened the dread I felt. If those little guys could come back to life after being frozen for so long, maybe I could, too.

When I got to the bus and climbed on, I felt pounds lighter than I had in months. *Okay. Be* open *to having people in your life*, I thought. *I can do that.*

I planned to meet Lici at Mallorie's at around one in the afternoon.

She was running a little late, and as I waited for her, I realized I really didn't want to go inside.

"Find coffee places near me," I said into my phone. After a moment, tons of results popped up on my screen. I flicked through them, reading reviews until Lici finally pulled up in her little black sports car.

Instead of waiting for her to get out of the car, I jogged up, opened the passenger side door, and got in. Her confused look quickly faded into a smile when she saw my screen. On it was a cute little coffee shop with a castle-style stone wall exterior. Above the door hung a sign that said, "The Happy Place."

"La café, huh? I'm down." She lifted a shoulder as we pulled up directions. She made a U-turn in the snow that I wouldn't have dared to even *think* about if I drove a car as nice as hers. A car like this would be treated like royalty in my possession. Well, if I drove cars at all.

When we got there, the coffee shop was every bit as adorable as it looked online. We walked in, and the tiny golden bell above the door twinkled to announce our arrival. A sweet little old woman with hair as white as cream peeked over the counter. I mean, she actually peeked *over* the counter – that's how tiny she was.

"Hello! Sit wherever you like. I'll be with you soon." She smiled and shuffled some things around behind the counter. "Banana pudding scones are 50% off today. All the menus are to your left."

We both grabbed a menu from a little cubby-like section that sat beneath a bulletin board that covered the entire wall. Pictures with miscellaneous pastries, yummy looking drinks, and random, happy looking people scattered the board three times over. We chose a small, round table in the corner by the window. The early afternoon sun sparkled off of the ice and salt that littered the sidewalk outside.

"So..." Lici said, drawing my attention away from the outside world and to the situation at hand. A smile stretched across her glossed lips. I sighed and repressed the urge to puke when I remembered what we were there to talk about.

"So..." I replied. Maybe if I put it off long enough it would just go away... I busied myself looking over the menu. I struggled deciding between the chocolate caramel swirl and the iced vanilla bean and cinnamon frappe. Both sounded absolutely marvelous, and I was relieved that this particular coffee shop kept the names of their drinks and pastries straight forward: there would be no guessing what was in something, and they had a variety of flavors that you could just toss into your drinks for free.

The entire world fell silent. We both pretended to study our menus intently, but I'm sure neither of us could actually focus. Finally, the little old woman skittered up to us, her tiny, old fashioned black heels clicking on the floor as she approached.

"Good afternoon, ladies. What can I get for you today?" she asked, her kind, wrinkled face glowing.

Lici ordered a double chocolate mocha, and I decided to go with the iced vanilla bean and cinnamon frappe after all, despite the cold weather outside.

"Back in a moment," the woman said. She nodded and scurried away.

I sighed. We were going to have to talk about this sometime today.

"All right let's hear it," I said, trying to hide my disappointment at the fact that the whole topic hadn't magically vanished.

Lici clapped her hands together like she was a three-year-old in the toy store and adjusted excitedly in her seat. "Oh my God, where do I even begin?"

"Well, when did all of this start?" I asked. I grabbed a napkin and unfolded it to keep my hands busy. This was bound to be painful.

"Oh. Um... at the funeral. We were talking about Adam, and you, and we just sort of hit it off. I swear, Kalli. Something's different about him. I've never had an in-depth conversation with a guy without wanting to cut it short and get down to business, but we talked for hours, about everything. Especially about you," she paused and waggled her eyebrows to make her point. "And I sure as *hell* have never wanted to take things slow before!"

"Wait, wait, wait. Are you saying you wanted to take it slow? *You* of all people?"

"Um, hello, that's exactly what *I'm saying!*

My eyebrows shot up. My jaw dropped. I waited for the punchline, but there was none. She was serious.

"Woah."

"Tell me about it," she said. "Taking it slow is for romantics and losers, and I am definitely neither of those."

The woman was back, and she handed us two oversized mugs of coffee and two strange looking yellow and brown scones.

"I didn't mean to eavesdrop, but I happened to accidentally overhear that one of you has found love! I was with my husband forty-three years before he passed away. Loved him 'til the very end. Here, these are my famous Banana Pudding Scones. Forget 50% off; these ones are on the house for you two today," she said, grinning and exposing long smile lines in her face.

"Thank you..." I tried to read the name on her nametag, but it probably had been faded for at least the last decade or so.

"Mel," the woman said, and curtseyed.

"Gracias, Mel. Seriously. You have no idea how weird this whole thing has been for me."

I looked at her in disbelief, but Lici looked straight at Mel.

"Well, being in love is a fabulous thing. It can change your life like *that*." Mel snapped her fingers, but they didn't make any sound. "Now, enjoy your drinks, and let me know if there's anything else I can do for you sweet ladies."

When Mel was gone, I turned back to Lici, who was eyeing her scones like they were going to bite *her*.

I grabbed one myself and took a big bite, and a sweet banana flavoring spread across my tongue.

My eyes widened, and I held it up.

"Dude. These are actually pretty good!"

She looked at me like I was nuts. When she didn't try one, I said, "You're really serious about all of this, aren't you?"

"As a freaking aneurism," she said.

"Wow. Okay." I filled my mouth with another bite of my scone.

"Okay?" This time, *her* eyebrows shot up.

"Yeah, I guess. If you really feel like it's *that* different with him, then... okay." Lici looked like she was about to cry. "So... I know we said no nasty stuff, and I *definitely* don't want the details... but... have you..." I trailed off, uncomfortable suddenly to even say it.

"Si," she said quietly and blushed. She actually blushed.

"Oh. Okay." I did my best to keep from making a face.

"After three months."

"Um... what? Three months?"

"I know! And since the funeral, I haven't even thought about seeing anyone else. Haven't wanted to. Are those really any good?" She was eyeing her scone as I scarfed the rest of mine down.

"Dude they're SO good."

She picked hers up and took a cautious bite, and she moaned at the taste. The two of us ate and drank our coffee, and I was so grateful that things felt so much more normal between us.

Chapter 17: *Opening Up*

Approximately six months after Adam's passing.

A FEW MONTHS PASSED AS I TRIED OUT MY NEW "LET PEOPLE INTO YOUR life" philosophy. At first it had been hard to open up and push myself to talk to people, but as the days progressed, it all got much easier.

I still wasn't speaking to my mom, still holding onto this grudge like my life depended on it, but being open to others helped me feel close to normal for the first time in forever.

This workday in particular had gone really well, and I plugged in my earphones – this time just for the tunes and not to stop people from talking to me – as I hopped up the stairs onto the bus. One of my favorite songs played quietly in the background.

On the ride home, I decided to get off a stop earlier than I usually did and walk the rest of the way home. The clouds were low, heavy, and thick with the promise of an early March snow. I'd decided to wear my super cute white leather jacket with the soft, fluffy interior, so I was ready for a nice, chill walk. As I strode from the back of the bus past rows of half-empty seats, I happened to notice cool backpack guy caught in the middle of a lengthy horror novel. When I got off, the huge, creeping metallic machine crept forward, only to stop again abruptly to let someone off. Out of the bus came backpack guy, practically stumbling down the steps as he tried not to drop anything. I shrugged and turned to start walking again.

"Hey," he said, racing up to me.

I turned back around. There was a light pink in his cheeks, and I briefly wondered if it was from the cold or from embarrassment. He wasn't exactly muscular, and his lack of breath showed he didn't exercise much, but he did look worlds better than he did the last time I saw him.

"Oh hey," I said.

A small gust of cold wind picked up, ruffling his dark brown, messy, curly hair. We both turned to face away from the cold.

"Hey," he said again. It was quiet for a moment, and I focused my attention on a small pebble on the ground at my feet. I kicked at it with my boots.

"I want to tell you something, but I don't want you to freak out at me, and I don't want to get yelled at again..."

Oh, yeah. I thought back to our last encounter. I'd forgotten all about the fact that I'd kind of exploded the last time we talked.

"Oh. Um, okay. Sorry about that, by the way. You kind of caught me on a bad day. It's Sam, right?"

"Seth, actually. It's fine, I figured as much. Uh. Okay," he said before taking a deep breath.

He opened his mouth to continue, but I interrupted.

"Hey, aren't you that guy I ran into at the coffee shop in August or something? Over at UpAndComing? I thought I recognized your backpack. Man, you were a real jerk that day."

He stumbled over his words a bit and actually looked super embarrassed. "Yeah... my bad. I'd been sick and was a real dick about the whole coffee thing. I'm sorry about that. It was definitely a me thing."

I nodded, raising my eyebrows as silence stretched between us.

"Anyway," he continued, "I'm not quite sure how to tell you this, so I'm just going to come right out and say it."

I remembered Adam saying how he didn't like it when I rode the bus alone because he never knew what kind of crazies might be waiting for me. And here was backpack guy, looking super freaked and nervous and totally sketchy. For the first time, I actually thought Adam might have had reason to worry after all.

I took a step backward.

"I don't ride the bus," he said, looking incredibly uncomfortable.

"Dude. I literally just saw you riding the bus," I replied, tone flat. Where was this conversation headed?

"Ugh, no. I mean, I don't *usually* ride the bus. I have my own car. But it broke down, so I started riding the bus until I could get it fixed. That's when I first saw you. *After* the whole coffee incident, I guess. I'd kind of forgotten about that." This poor guy looked absolutely miserable. He seemed cold and his arms were full of the materials he hadn't had time to put in his backpack before he got off the bus. On top of that, he seemed to be desperately trying to communicate something with me, but I was not getting it.

Okaaaay... I thought. I resisted the urge to tell him to get the hell on with it already.

He was clearly distraught, and if I didn't start walking soon, I was certain I would end up a statue until summer could thaw me out. I chose to be patient, however, and he moved on after a couple more seconds without being prompted.

"I've never been the kind of guy who wanted to go out with someone based solely on her looks, and it wasn't even really like that... but... I guess when I saw you, I wanted to get to know you right away. I kind of felt like I *needed* to be around you. If that makes any sense." He shifted the things in his hands so he could hold them all in one arm, and then he ran his free hand through his mess of brown hair. "God, I sound like a serial killer, don't I?"

For whatever reason, this comment made me smile, which I immediately felt guilty about.

"Only a little bit," I said. "Are you trying to ask me out?"

This time, *he* backed up, eyeing me warily. "Depends. Are you going to flip out on me again?"

My first instinct was to get defensive, to tell him to screw off because I wasn't interested, and I almost went there. But then I remembered how hard I'd been trying to let people in, and I thought of Adam. Despite the nerves that tied my stomach in knots, it felt warm. Something about this guy seemed familiar to me, and I wanted to figure out what it was.

"Okay, sure. But you don't get my number."

"Really? Great! How will I..."

I reached into my purse and pulled out a pen and ripped off a corner piece of paper from my sketchbook, handing the items to him.

"You give me your number, and I'll call you." As he wrote down his number, I continued before that guilty feeling could eat me alive. "And you have to meet me. There's no way in hell that you're picking me up."

"Okay, I can do that—"

I scooped up the paper out of his hands.

"And, it has to be a group thing with my friends in a public place. They need to meet you, too. Deal?"

"Do I have a choice in the matter?" he asked in a way that said he already knew the answer to his question.

"Nope," I said.

He had a very cute smile that stretched a little farther out and a little higher up on the left side of his face. He reached out his hand, and I shook it.

"Then, deal."

It was only after I turned away from him to walk the rest of the way to my apartment did the pain fully register. I'd just made a sort of date with a guy who wasn't Adam.

Chapter 18: *The Sort-of Date*

About a week later.

I SPENT THE NEXT COUPLE OF DAYS CHICKENING OUT, BUT I DECIDED that, even though I didn't feel ready to see anyone else romantically, I really was trying to get back to some version of my old self. My old self loved meeting new people and making new friends.

When I finally decided to call Seth, it was ultimately because I'd convinced myself that there was no way I could possibly fall for anyone else, so what could this hurt?

A few days later, I called Seth from the city's one remaining functional pay phone and gave him the details, which he seemed to follow well. I figured it was only fair that he have some kind of heads up about my friends, what they were like, and what the three of us could be like when we were together. We talked about their names, their quirks, and the things they enjoyed bugging people about. When the girls heard about my whole "kind of date" situation, they flipped.

We were on a three-way phone call, and hearing both of them scream on the other end made me really wish I'd just texted them with the news, but I had a feeling that, had I messaged them, they would have called me to scream about it anyway.

I'd wanted them to bring the people they were seeing, but both of them agreed that having their own dates would only distract them, and they needed to be on high alert with me having my first date in... well, a long time. Every time I thought about that, I pictured Adam, and then I wanted to throw up.

It was just Lici, Nessa, Seth and me. The girls and I took Seth to that same little coffee shop Lici and I had visited, which I'd been to about five times on my own since Lici and I went together. The girls and I decided that Mallorie's was a special place, designated now only for the three of us and dates that had been pre-approved by all.

We met at The Happy Place that Friday after work. Lici, Nessa and I showed up half an hour early to catch up and discuss the details, and Seth came five minutes earlier than we'd discussed over the phone. He'd taken an Uber (I guessed his car really was broken – if he had one at all), and the three of us went to meet him outside as soon as he stepped out of the vehicle.

Seth reached out and shook all of our hands one at a time, starting with Lici and ending with me. After that, he stuffed his hands into the pockets of his brown leather jacket. His comic book backpack, I'd noticed, was nowhere to be seen.

"Kalli, it's nice to see you again. Vanessa, Felicia, it's good to finally meet you."

Lici narrowed her eyes and turned to me. "You told him what we look like, didn't you? You totally tipped him off!"

I smiled, trying to quell the unease I felt doing this without Adam. "Yep. I figured coffee with the three of us was going to be complicated enough as it was. No need to make it any more confusing for him than it has to be."

Nessa gently pushed Lici's shoulder. "She's got a point. Besides, it was nice of him to address us by name. Thanks for that, by the way."

"Not a problem," he said. "Seems I've got to make an impression on the two of you if I want to see Kalli again." Seth grinned, showing the same lopsided smile I saw a few days ago. My two friends giggled like idiots, and I dramatically rolled my eyes and smirked. Now if I could just figure out why it was I hoped he would win them over...

"Yeah, if," I said. My heart was at war with itself, and I had no idea what to do about it.

Once we were inside, we all sat at one of the tiny round tables. It only had three seats as it was against the wall like many of the others, but after asking Mel if it would be okay, I moved an extra chair over for Seth, careful to set it just a few extra inches away from me. We'd just met, after all. As we waited for Mel to come take our order, I studied the people around me.

Lici was dressed in her usual pink and orange tones: A fluffy pink coat with fringes on the bottom, unzipped to reveal her tight cream-colored cami, topped off with a pink and neon orange glittery scarf that draped over her shoulders. Nessa wore a light blue, slim-fitting turtleneck sweater and a light gray scarf that made her blue eyes look even brighter than usual.

Seth wore a nice dark pair of blue jeans with just a little bit of fade along the thighs and calves. His leather jacket was halfway unzipped, and he wore a simple dark gray tee shirt underneath. Nicely dressed but not overdone.

My heart seized for a moment when I thought of how Adam had loved wearing a suit so much that it was pretty much all I could ever get him to wear—whether he was working or not. He was not the casual dress type by any means. Even his biking clothes were fancy.

The thought of Adam in his biking gear, of course, made me recall that was the last thing he ever wore. I swallowed past the baseball forming in my throat.

Thankfully, my dear friends distracted me from the ache in my chest when Mel came up to take our orders. Nessa started remarking about how she wished there were fancier names for the coffee in her household growing up, everything had a fancy, over complicated title.

Mel simply smiled and stated that she hated when coffee-houses tried to make things sound better than they actually were by giving them some over-the-top kind of label. After we ordered, the official interview part of the date-thing began. Each of us took turns asking

Seth questions—some nicer than others—and for the most part, his answers seemed genuine, yet casual.

"So, Seth, what's your favorite color?" I asked, figuring it was best to start things off slowly.

I knew the ladies would be brutal with their questions, not holding anything back.

"Hmm..." he started. "I've always really liked the color red, but there's a really specific color of blue that has been really appealing to me lately. What's yours?"

I smiled. This was something Adam and I had always disagreed on. I always said that my favorite color had changed from orange to green as I grew up, but he always argued that you couldn't change your favorite color once you picked. I think his favorite color would have remained a deep, vivid blue even if he finally relented that one is not obligated to stick with a single favorite color for life.

I cleared my throat and blinked back the stinging in my eyes.

"I like green."

"Um, excuse me, but *we're* running the interrogation here, Mr. Smith," Lici said. She actually looked at her hand, where she wrote down his name, and probably, her hard-hitting questions. "If you pass, you'll have plenty of time to ask her any questions you like, comprende?"

"Oh, sure, I guess. Sorry." Seth smiled sheepishly.

"Damn," Nessa began. "Why haven't we done this before? It's a terrific idea. If we'd done this before now, I wouldn't have been with half the assholes I've been with." The four of us laughed, and then Lici was up.

"Are you a serial killer, and have you had any violent charges or jail time in the past?" My eyes widened. She didn't even look at her hand for that one.

Mel returned when Lici asked this question, and she spent the next few seconds looking around us anxiously, as though she was trying to determine whether or not he was the serial killer type. She placed the drinks and various on-sale pastries on the table.

Seth looked Lici right in the eyes and said with a straight face, "Yes, but I only kill on the third Wednesday of every month, and I spent twelve years in jail before they let me out on good behavior. I got really friendly with the warden there at the end. Promised if she let me out, I'd send nudes twice a week and visit on the holidays."

Mel turned away abruptly when she heard the word "nudes" and retreated slowly back to the kitchen.

Lici smirked, her snark matched. Nessa's eyes looked like they were about to pop right out of their sockets. It looked like it took everything she had not to spit out the sip she'd taken from her drink.

"You're kidding, right?" she squeaked.

"Oh, no... that's totally true," Seth said. He winked at me before continuing. "Actually, I have spent the night in jail once for public intoxication when I took the garbage out and locked myself out of the house one night. Tried to break back in, neighbors called the cops, and I got a super comfy cell to stay in while they sorted things out."

"Damn," I said. "That's rough. I can't tell you how many times I got into my house through the window as a kid. Of course, my neighbors couldn't have cared less, and I was very rarely intoxicated..."

"Okay, okay, my turn!" Nessa said, finally over the idea that the man sitting with us said he was a serial killer. As usual, it took her a little longer than the rest of us to realize the joke. "Um... any big deal ex-girlfriends we should know about?" Seth pondered her question for a moment.

"I've had my fair share of serious relationships, if that's what you're asking. But none of them are a big deal currently."

"Huh. Fair enough," I said. "What do you do for work?"

"I'm a game designer," he said, leaning back in his seat, the decaf caramel latte he'd ordered steaming as he held it in both hands.

"Board games?" Nessa asked.

"Video games. I just signed a contract with a company out of LA to make a horror game based on a novel by Stewart Prince."

"Huh. Video games, then. Is that all you do?" Lici asked, definitely *not* holding back her distaste at his answer. I personally thought it was cool to have another artist of sorts around.

"Pretty much. I do some computer and tech work on the side when I can, but I usually only do that when business gets slow."

Lici raised her eyebrows. "Does business get slow often?"

Man, she was vicious today. I kicked her under the table and shot her my best "dude, knock it off" look. She rolled her eyes and brought her attention back to Seth. Before he answered, I interjected.

"That sounds really cool. I was thrilled when I figured out how to download a painting app to my phone." I bumped his elbow with mine and immediately felt like an idiot for sloshing his coffee around, sending it splashing out of his mug. "Oops. Sorry. I bet you figure that kind of stuff out like it's nothing."

He sucked in a breath at the hot liquid and reached for a napkin to wipe coffee from his hands.

Chuckling good-naturedly, he said, "I guess so."

I recalled the night I figured out I could do digital art on my phone, and how Adam had drawn a heart with his name in it with his finger. He was never great with tech, and we both liked the old-fashioned way of doing things—Adam with his pen and notebook, me with my sketchpad or canvas.

Nessa picked up the conversation from there. "So, does the gaming industry pay well?"

He thought about that for a moment. "Depends on the job, really. I'm definitely not rich, but the gig got me an upgrade from my mom's basement."

So the conversation went until each of us had finished eating our lemon bar pastries of the day and split the payment in four. Afterward, Lici and Nessa went their own ways, but I was having a fairly good day and didn't want to ruin it by going home to my deserted and depressing apartment, especially having gone out with someone new.

"Hey," I said to Seth after the girls had gone. "The park's just a couple blocks this way. Do you want to walk with me?"

He shrugged and took pace beside me.

The air was brisk, but we were both dressed appropriately for the weather.

"I've got to say, you handled those two like a champ," I said.

"Well, I had a fair warning, so I had time to prep the note cards."

I laughed a little, and he smiled. I instantly felt guilty for admiring a smile that wasn't Adam's, and I turned my gaze to the ground.

"I wasn't lying before, you know. When I yelled at you. I'm in... a really weird place right now, and I'm just barely starting to figure it out. I don't know if I'll ever be over it completely." I waited for him to respond. All the while I refused to make eye contact with him, but his response was incredibly understanding, and totally casual.

"Everyone has stuff. I get it." The leather of his jacket rustled as he shrugged again. I closed my eyes and swallowed past the boulder of anxiety that was slowly creeping up into my throat from my stomach. I took a deep, shuddering breath. *It's better if I just tell him everything now. That way it won't blind-side him if it comes up later.*

"My... my fiancé died. About six months ago." I gathered the courage necessary to peek up at him. He stopped walking, and I stopped as well. I was all too aware of how quiet it was in the absence of our footsteps. All the wusses of the world were inside, hiding from the early March cold. We were the only two living beings in sight.

"Oh, wow," Seth said, rubbing the stubble that grew on his cheek. "I'm sorry for calling that stuff." I shrugged, blinking the tears away, swallowing past the thickness in my throat.

"You didn't know. It was especially difficult because it happened right before our wedding, so I had a lot of things to cancel, a lot of hard conversations and pity glances. Anyway. I don't mean to dump this all on you, but I wanted to give you a fair warning since you're still here for some reason."

"Damn, are you okay?"

This question got me to look all the way up at him. Nobody had asked me that; not even when it happened. I guessed everyone probably figured that if you lose someone, you won't be okay. I started to really think about the word.

Okay doesn't mean you're doing well, or that you're happy; it simply means that you're alive despite the circumstances, and that you're doing your best to deal with them. I sighed.

"Yeah. For the first time in a while, I think I might be getting there," I said.

"Good. I can't imagine what that would be like. The only person I've ever gotten close to losing before was my stepmom, who choked on a chicken bone. And trust me, if she kicked it, I don't even think my dad would miss her," he said.

I watched a flash of guilt cross his eyes as, like most people who said things like that, he was probably worried he had offended me.

"Oh, god! That's bad!" I snorted, then I immediately covered my mouth. He smiled at me, but his smile quickly faded.

"So, your fiancé... how did he..." he started to ask.

"I don't think I'm ready to talk about that yet," I mumbled.

We started walking again, and he nodded.

He looked terribly upset. I felt terribly upset.

I only really talked about any of this with Dr. Will.

"Right. Sorry, no one I know has lost anyone, either. I guess you're not supposed to ask questions like that, huh? It's pretty inappropriate."

"Yeah, a little bit." I made a gesture with my thumb and pointer finger to punctuate.

"My bad."

I did my best to shrug it off.

"It's all right. So, you have a stepmom you don't care for. Are you close with anyone in your family?" I asked.

"My mom," he replied instantly. "My dad's kind of a loser. I think he knew my mom was too good for him, so he left to find an equal. My mom's great, though."

"Oh?" I raised my eyebrows. The park was still and totally silent as we rounded the corner and it came into view. At the moment, there was no wind, nothing to rustle the barren trees and bushes, nothing to stir the swings, and no laughter to stifle the silence. The only sound was that of our footsteps, which echoed off the sidewalk and buildings that surrounded the park.

"Yeah. After my dad left, my mom started adopting kids – or fostering them, I guess. Since I was sixteen, her house has been full of all kinds of kids. She's got a gift for it; I'll tell you what." Seth's entire face lit up as he recalled memories of the various children from his past. The whole time he talked, his hands swayed through the air, emphasizing every word.

"Your mom sounds great," I said after a time. I wondered what it would be like to have so many little kids running around. Then I remembered my mother talking about how she wanted me to start procreating. Adam *had* wanted kids. I'd always joked about how dogs were better. Man, I was an ass. And now I'd never know what our own family would have been like. Guilt sliced through my gut.

"Uh, hey, want to sit?" I asked, trying to distract myself, suddenly struggling to catch my breath. I put my hand on my stomach as we reached the edge of the park.

"The grass is probably wet now that the sun's out and the frost has melted," he started, looking around the park for benches.

I knew the city had removed all the metal park benches after one too many complaints about the material either freezing or burning its users. They'd promised to replace them with some kind of new and improved faux wooden ones, but that had been two years ago, and we'd heard nothing more on the subject.

I plopped down on the grass and patted the ground next to me.

"Oh, why not?" he asked himself and sat down.

"What about you? Any family *you* like?" Seth asked.

Bless you, I thought. *Thank you for moving the conversation in a new direction.*

"Actually, I'm pretty close to all of my family. Except my dad's parents. They moved to Germany when I was little. My grandma on my mom's side is great, though. I get my more practical grumpy side from her, I think."

"What about your parents? Are they still together? Any awful stepparents in the mix?" he asked.

His green eyes met mine as I finally looked at him.

"You could say that, yeah. Not the awful part, though. My stepmom is kind of a badass. Mom and Dad got divorced about ten years ago: Turns out Mom's... preferences... changed over the course of their relationship. Now she says she only met Dad because they were meant to be best friends and create my brother and me. She got a girlfriend pretty quickly after that, but Dad's always stuck around. They still live together, even after all this time, and the three of them get along great."

"Oh, shit. Is that weird for you?" he asked.

"It was. I thought I hated Nancy, my stepmom, for a while; but I can't imagine it any other way now. And then there's Jeremiah, my baby bro."

Seth laid back on the grass, putting his hands behind his head. "Sounds like your family's pretty great."

"Yeah, I guess they are. You'll probably meet Jeremiah soon if you keep hanging around Lici. They're a *thing* now." I made a face. He laughed.

We talked for well over an hour before I looked at the time and told Seth I had to go.

He offered to walk me to the bus stop, which I appreciated. A nervous feeling gnawed at me the whole walk back. When the bus pulled up the road toward my stop, I whipped around to face him.

"Hey, I'm glad I met you. I haven't talked like this in... a long time." Seth smiled and adjusted his weight and opened his mouth to reply, but I hurried to continue before he could say anything. "BUT. If you're looking for, well, pretty much anything, you're out of luck. I'm not ready to move on. Not yet. Maybe not ever."

He was silent for a few seconds, and then he threw his hands in the air. "Hey, I get that one hundred percent. How about friends? Everybody needs friends, right? I'm cool with just being pals. I just... feel like I met you for a reason."

The bus groaned to a stop behind me.

"Yeah, because you're a stalker, remember?" I said, narrowing my eyes at him. "*Just* friends?"

Now, one of his hands remained raised while the other found his heart. "Scouts honor, or whatever the hell they say. No ulterior motives here. Just a totally altruistic offer of friendship. Sound good?" The doors squealed open, and I started to board.

"Okay, then," I said. "I'll call you!"

Things got very busy with work after that. I had finished with my latest account project and was assigned two more, so it was a couple of weeks before I got around to calling him again. We spoke a few times on the phone, but we had a running conversation via text that kind of never ended.

I sat on my bed with my feet curled beneath me one night, scrolling through movies to stream online but not really focusing on the TV. I was immersed in a text conversation with Seth and intermittently adding crazy detail to yet another creepy drawing.

To be honest, I was kind of starting to enjoy them.

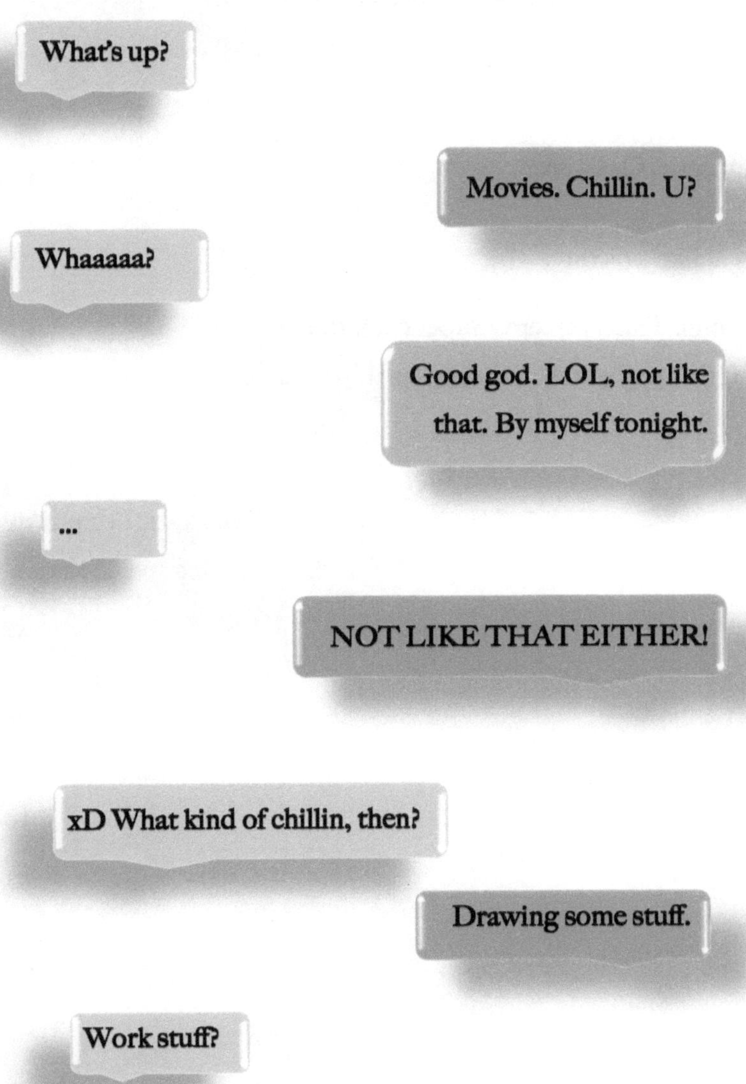

Some female comedian made a goat sound on the TV.

Nah. Could never show this to my clients. Theyd run screaming and I'd probably be out of a job.

Intrigue. Can I see?

I sent him a picture.

Damn. That is creepy. Super cool, though! I didn't peg you for a horror artist.

I wasnt until recently. I think I'm kinda starting to like it, tho.

Chapter 19: *A Second Date*

Approximately six and a half months after Adam's passing.

On Friday the next week, Seth called me.

"Hello?" I said when I picked up the phone.

"Wow, that's it? That's how you answer the phone?" Seth scoffed. This was the first time that he had called *me*, and apparently, he found my greeting to be lackluster.

"Um, yeah. That's how normal people answer the phone." It was late Friday night, and I'd just gotten out of the shower. I had pulled my hair into a tight bun, thrown on some sweats, and was about to attempt painting a watercolor landscape for the power bar account I'd just been assigned. Since I had finished my big project when I first came back to work, more and more people had been requesting me to work for them specifically. I had started taking my work home because I wanted to do an extra good job... and let's be honest, I was more than thankful for the distraction.

"Yeah, exactly. Normal people are so boring! Pathetic. Man, I'm so unimpressed," he said.

Even though he couldn't see me, I threw my hands to my hips, holding the phone between my jaw and my shoulder.

"Well excuuuuuuuse me! Not all of us can be as fancy as you are. Sometimes 'hello' is all we've got." I reached into a package of frosted chocolate cookies I brought into my studio a couple of days ago, pulled out a pretty stale cookie, and popped it into my mouth.

Stale or not, the cookies were delicious.

"Booooring," Seth said. "Hey, what are you doing tomorrow?"

I sighed and pretended to check my invisible planner. "Let's see… I've got 'wake up' at some point in the day, and I should probably schedule in 'brush teeth' and 'eat' in there somewhere. Not to mention my prestigious 'put deodorant on' event. That one will last a while. Man, I'm totally booked."

I stuffed a couple more cookies into my mouth and chewed so loudly I wouldn't have been surprised if Seth told me to knock it off.

"That's too bad," Seth remarked. "I've gathered a list some of my favorite more recent horror movies and was planning on having a marathon. Unfortunately, my companion would have to be free, as it's pretty much going to be an all-day event. I wasn't sure if you liked horror movies or not, so I also got a couple of what my mom calls rom-com classics, just in case."

"Man, you're just AMAZING at making plans in advance, aren't you? I've never been one for horror movies, but my imagination has been creating some very strange images lately. Sure, I'm in. Guess I can move 'brush teeth' to another day."

Seth sucked in a breath through the phone, causing way too much static for comfortable listening. "Oh, now... surely you can fit in both?"

The next morning, I got up and did some painting before Seth texted to let me know he was alive and to ask what I wanted in the junk food department. I told him whatever would be fine, so long as it was junk. He replied with his address.

Nerves gnawed at my stomach and had it flipping as I rushed to the bathroom to get ready. This was a friend date of sorts, and it was my first time going out of the house with anyone besides the girls in a long time. I wasn't sure how I felt about seeing Seth again in person, and I swear I saw Adam in every corner of the apartment as I got ready. But Seth and I had been talking a lot lately, and I wasn't sure I could avoid seeing him forever.

"What the hell does someone wear to a friend date?" I asked my frowning, perplexed reflection.

The only friend date I'd been on – aside from with the girls – was when I was eleven and this guy in my class asked me to see a matinee movie I forgot about almost as soon as it was over.

I decided to go with a pair of comfortable yet form-fitting blue jeans, a light sweater, and a rainbow striped jacket I kept for when I was feeling particularly adventurous. Going out in any form after

Adam, I needed a little courage to get me through. We were just friends. We'd made that very clear, but I couldn't help the flutter in my stomach at the idea of seeing him again. I pulled on the jacket and decided to do my makeup to tie the ensemble together.

I blended red, yellow, green, blue, and purple across my eyelids. By the time I was finished, I felt more like a fantasy book cover model than ever before.

"All right," I said to my reflection, who now looked much more confident. "You're ready, I guess."

I took the bus, but the stop was a few blocks away from the address he'd given me. When the bus pulled up, I climbed off. Seth stood there. In the mid-morning sun, the collar of his jacket was pulled up to shield his neck from the harsh March winds, and his hands were shoved deep into his pockets. His colorful comic book backpack was slung over one shoulder.

"Hey kiddo," he said, greeting me with a slow smile. His use of the word kiddo struck my heart like a bullet and stopped me in my tracks.

"Hey, could you call me something else? Kiddo doesn't really work for me," I said, doing my best to be polite.

He turned, and I forced myself to fall into pace beside him.

"Why? You don't have one of those weird inferiority complexes, do you? Like when someone calls you 'dear' and it makes you cringe because you're not that much younger than they are?" he asked, trying to keep the mood light.

"No. I just don't want you calling me that." I scowled.

I didn't mean for it to sound harsh, but it totally came out that way.

He just shrugged. "Okay. No more kiddo then."

We walked a block or two in silence. Seth lived in the more historical part of town, and the brick buildings loomed over us, tall and skinny, with intricate moldings and faded, hand painted signs. He attempted making conversation a few times, and I mumbled in perpendicular comments, mentally soaking in the view to paint later.

"I can't tell if you're admiring or judging," Seth said finally, totally aware of my obliviousness.

"Sorry. Definitely admiring. They don't make buildings like this anymore. God, you get to see this every day! You're so lucky."

He looked up at the buildings across the street, really trying to see them how I was. After a moment, though, he just waved his hand.

"Yeah, I guess. Hey, that's something I really need to focus on in my new project. The architecture makes a huge impact on a game's atmosphere. Thanks, Kalli."

"Sure," I said, still drinking in the scenery.

"Well, this is me," Seth said as he opened the door to his apartment. The building itself externally was as magnificent as the others. It was one of the buildings in the oldest part of the city, with detailed moldings of swirled waves of chipping material that cradled little cherubs and mermaids. The brick itself was old and multicolored due to bricks falling out and having to be replaced over the years. As dated as it was, the building was well maintained. The hallway inside had certain aspects that had been updated, but others that were still original and had just been restored. The railings were elegant wood-carved pieces that swirled gracefully up on the side of the stairwell from one floor to the next.

Seth held the door open for me.

"Why, thank you," I said as I crossed the threshold into his home. Inside was completely updated. I mean, totally modernized. The walls had been painted in light grays, blues and whites, and all electrical fixtures and appliances looked as though they had to be brand new.

As soon as I entered through the front door, I was in the living area, which had the thick, heated vinyl flooring that new constructions often had.

The majority of the floor was covered with a plush white shag rug, on which sat a white modern style couch absolutely covered in different nerdy video game plushies. In front of the couch was a metal framed glass coffee table with a bowl and a couple of miscellaneous video game controllers left out.

Across from that was the television: A seventy-five-inch 4K beauty that was mounted on the wall. Beneath that stood a short entertainment center with a much smaller TV. Large black bookshelves sat on either side of the double television setup, absolutely covered in strategically placed—and perfectly dusted—video game and popular movie action figures.

"Why do you have two TV's right in the same place?" I asked.

Seth busied himself hanging keys by the door.

"The big one's for movies – the little one's for gaming. And it's not a TV. It's actually a monitor. That entertainment center opens up to be a desk, and my computer's inside. I work in here. Sometimes. Anyway, that's a long and unnecessary description, but there you go."

I frowned.

"Wouldn't it be better to play games on the big one?" I asked.

"God, no. There are too many places to look and not enough time. Besides, many of the games look all funny on the big one. The graphics don't translate well to a screen that's bigger than what they were intended for, and if I'm playing on my computer, the game functions much better. Faster."

Although I really didn't understand, I appreciated his passion for his craft. I turned to scan the rest of the open area.

Just behind the living area was a wide open, well lit, and totally unused kitchen. Again, all stainless-steel appliances and updated fixtures. A few pots and pans hung unevenly from a metal shelf on the side of the island. Interesting, I thought as I turned my attention back to the hundreds of figurines that were placed just so in different categories: heroes, villains, horror type creatures, mentors.

"Is there anything you're not a fan of?" I asked, never taking my eyes off of the proud display.

"Not really. Comics, video games, movies of all kinds, yeah. I kind of have a thing for it all," he stated, the smile all too evident in his voice. I looked up to catch a glimpse of it before it faded. "Is that bad?" he added, as if my opinion would have changed anything. Actually, though, I thought it was cool. I, too, had my many nerdy moments – granted, they were never this extreme, but still. I was in no place to judge other people's interests, especially when they were cool enough to let me into their homes.

Still, I had to tease him at least a little...

"Man, I guessed you were a nerd, but still. This?" I gestured to the display on both sides of the television. He still stood near the doorway, holding his comic-book backpack, looking uncertain whether he should be honored or offended by my comment. "This has got to be a whole new level," I continued. "Comic books, anime, video games, I get. Typical nerd stuff. I can even understand the horror movie section..."

I slid my fingers delicately across the edge of the metal shelves. I knew better than to actually touch any of the figurines. Jeremiah had friends growing up that had collected things like these, and you definitely did not touch them.

"But what the hell is this?" I squeaked, pointing out one shelf that did not seem to have a particular genre or theme to it. On this shelf, and still just as strategically placed, it seemed, were all kinds of men, women, and couples that did not look to have any connection whatsoever with the world of the nerds.

Now, Seth stepped away from the door, airing more on the defensive side, but clearly eager to share with me the wonderful insight he was about to impart.

"That shelf is for the badass characters in other, more realistic shows, and a tribute to some of the greatest couples in our modern culture." He smiled again, and as he bent to retrieve one of the figurines, his curly brown hair fell from its gelled state onto his forehead. He looked it over with a dazed look on his face before placing it exactly back into the spot he had pulled it from.

"Yeah, okay," I said. "I guess they have just as much of a right to be idolized as any of these other characters, don't they?" I sighed, turning my attention to the couch. "I guess we should start those movies now, huh? If we're going to watch them all today, anyway."

He nodded, passionate rant forgotten.

"Sure, we can do that." He slung his backpack onto the couch and unzipped it. First, he pulled out a stack of probably seven different movies. He held them out for me to take. "Which one do you want to watch first?" he asked.

I took the movies from him and studied them. Most of them really were horror movies from the last few years, including top horror hits with a couple of rom-com classics, just as he'd promised, and good ones, too. I looked between the two more cheery titles, which had coincidentally been my top two favorite romantic comedies of all time. One was about a couple who were friends for years before they allowed themselves an opportunity to realize how they felt about each other, and another was about a young woman who closed herself off to having fun experiences because she moved around too often and ended up finding a reason to try and stay. I held those two up and fanned them out so he could see the titles.

"Have you seen either of these movies?" I asked, raising an eyebrow, trying to hide my smirk.

"My mom has forced me to watch that one like a zillion times. For whatever reason, that's our Christmas Eve classic. The other one I have yet to experience, but she says it's great."

"Huh," I mused aloud, letting my smile show. That was one we definitely had to watch. I rifled through the rest of the horror films and decided to go with a promising looking horror film adapted from a Hispanic wives' tale. Worst case scenario, I had another Hispanic culture reference to add to Lici's mental library. "Let's start with this one, shall we?"

Seth raised both of his eyebrows and continued rummaging through his bag as he spoke. "That one, huh? I was sure you'd have chosen one of the romantic ones." He pulled licorice, various soda pops (none of them diet, thank God—I just hated when guys assumed that I wanted diet anything—cheddar and movie-theater popcorn, chocolate-covered caramels, and of course, the absolutely necessary fruit snacks.

"Hey, I'm full of surprises," I said, taking off my shoes and curling my feet up beneath me on the couch, which was super comfortable despite its firm appearance. I wasn't sure if he had that rule or not, but my parents had raised me to be considerate and take my shoes off before putting my feet up on other people's furniture.

"There's a method to it, see," I started. "If we do it that way and watch the scary ones first, we can finish off with the happy ones without feeling like total wusses. And besides, that way, it won't be absolutely terrifying, because we still have plenty of daylight." I gestured to the two wide windows that overlooked the street below the kitchen.

"Ah, I see," he said, stepping away from the living room and into the kitchen. "So... I guess it might bother you then, if I did this?" He leaned forward and with a simple flick of his wrist, he released complete light blocking curtains. It was almost instantly pitch black.

"Shit," I said under my breath. "I guess I should have seen that coming..."

A moment later, the living room lights were flicked on and brightened the room again.

"Is that okay?" he asked, totally serious now. "I don't like the glare on the TV when I watch dark movies like these, but if you want them up, your wish is mine to command." He bowed to emphasize the remark and did a little twirling motion with his hand.

"Um..." I thought about that for a moment. I also hated when there was a glare on the TV, and both his windows and his television set were huge, so glaring was almost unavoidable. "Okay. We can keep them closed, but I don't have my girlfriends here, so if I need to go to the bathroom, you bet your ass I'm turning on every single light on the way there, got it?"

He grinned and snatched up two bags of popcorn off the table.

"Sounds good to me."

"And don't even think there's going to be any cuddling. Fair warning: When I get scared, I'm a kicker."

This comment made him laugh, but I was dead serious.

"Deal," he said. "Movie theater or cheddar?" He held both bags of popcorn up for me to inspect, and I pointed to the one in his right hand.

"Movie theater for me, please."

"Coming right up!" He juggled the bags of popcorn as he made his way back into the kitchen. In a matter of five or so minutes, all our goodies were laid out before us, and the movie day had officially begun.

Chapter 20: *The Date Continues*

Still about six and a half months after Adam's passing.

I WAS SURPRISED THAT SETH HADN'T KICKED ME OUT.

By the time the first movie was over, I asked so many questions it was getting ridiculous, and every time I got self-conscious about it, he made comments like, "See, that's what I need to implement more of!" and "Seriously, though. I can do better jump scares than that!"

When the second movie started, I was determined to be at least a little bit less obnoxious and resorted to pulling my sketchpad from my purse to write down the questions I had. I had to squint to see anything with the movie's dim lighting—he was right; these movies really were dark, not just in content but also visually—he spent the majority of the movie with my head bent over my sketchpad. When the second movie was over, I held out my extensive list of stupid questions, most of which he answered with, "Well if you had paid more attention, the movie would have answered this for you!"

About halfway through the third movie, we decided it was time for pizza. Seth and I spent a good ten minutes arguing about which toppings were going to be on the pizza, and who was going to let whom pay: We ended up going with a half and half pizza with my half being pepperoni, green peppers, black olives, and onions, and his half being a ham, black olive, and mushroom. We also ended up deciding to split the bill.

When the pizza arrived, we paused the movie. We both sat down and, without getting plates, started eating. Before long, the entire pizza was gone. Although we were both properly stuffed, the movie remained paused. We both sat back on the couch, stomachs ready to burst, and just looked at each other. I leaned with one arm propped up on the back of the couch, both feet tucked underneath me. Seth mirrored me, except both of his feet – with mismatching, brightly colored and hysterically designed socks hung over the edge of the sofa.

"Interesting," he mused, with no indication as to what he thought was so interesting.

"What?" I asked, suddenly self-conscious from the peculiar way in which he was looking at me. Interesting is not the best thing to hear when someone is staring right at you. I wiped my mouth with my sleeve, just in case.

He was silent for a few moments longer, and then he smiled.

The screen showed a long, darkened staircase that inclined to total darkness. The light from the TV was enough to eat by, and now, Seth's green eyes twinkled in the darkness.

"I've never seen you with makeup on," he said, leaning forward the tiniest bit. "You look really pretty."

I almost said something about how I'd worn at least some makeup when we met, and again on our "date" thingy, but I knew he meant that he hadn't seen me with makeup like this before.

"Thanks," I said, shifting beneath the weight of his gaze. "I like experimenting with different colors and things like that. Guess it's the artist in me. I used to do it all the time."

I shrugged.

Before I could even register what was happening, the space between the two of us closed. I had no idea how it happened, but all of a sudden, our faces were mere centimeters apart. Seth closed his eyes, leaning closer still.

I found my eyes closing as well, completely and totally without permission and despite the ball of anxiety that built instantly in my gut. That moment lasted an eternity before our lips met in a kiss that lasted two, maybe three seconds. It was sweet and soft, without tongue but far from some heatless, meaningless peck, and definitely not the kind of kiss that friends would share.

My stomach fluttered, and I felt my body relax just a bit as if somehow, it had found home again. This was safe. It was right. It was... Totally inappropriate.

When I opened my eyes and saw Seth, I freaked out. I knew I was kissing him, obviously, but the feeling I'd gotten was strikingly similar to kissing Adam. I threw myself backward, putting both hands over my mouth in case it got any weird ideas. I obviously wasn't in control of my own body anymore. My chest started to ache as, not for the first time, I thought *what if Adam was watching?*

"Everything okay?" Seth asked, green eyes hazy, still feeling the lingering effects of the kiss.

"Yeah, um..." I started. *Come on, Kalli, Think. Think.* "I have to pee. Where's your bathroom?"

He seemed to have bought my lame-ass excuse and pointed down the hallway. "Just down there. It'll be the first door on your right."

"Great. Thanks," I mumbled. Trying to get up off the couch without flying straight off of it was nearly impossible. I rushed as slowly and normally as possible without looking back until I found the bathroom door.

Once inside, I closed the door, locked it, and proceeded to lean with my back against the door and my hands over my face. When I finally let them down, I noticed that the bathroom was just as nice as the kitchen and living room had been. It was bright and very modern with white, brown, and gray speckled countertops and tile in the shower, which I fixated on in my attempt to calm myself down.

When I finally felt I could stand on my own without help from the door, and had to decide if I would faint, run home, or go back out there and continue what we started... I shuttered, half from the sensation of that kiss, and half from horror that I actually kissed him. What was I thinking? I made my way to the sink and stared at myself in the mirror.

Maybe I wasn't me. That would definitely explain my crazy behavior today. Maybe I'd accidentally switched bodies with somebody else, and *she* was the one manning the controls in my seriously unhinged brain. But when I looked in the mirror, I just saw me. Just blonde haired, blue eyed, light tan skinned... me.

"What the hell is wrong with you?" I whispered shamefully at my reflection. "What are you doing?" I gripped the edges of the sink and took some deep breaths, which did little to calm me further.

I knew that something had to be done about this, but what? *If I went back out there to talk to him, would I be able to say what I was feeling? Would we just go back to watching the movie again like nothing had happened? Oh, God. Would I kiss him again?*

"No," I said aloud. Then more quietly, I added, "I have to get out of here."

I took one last angry look at myself in the mirror and then opened the bathroom door, determined to get out of there as fast as humanly possible.

As I moved, I worked quickly to formulate an excuse about why I was leaving and where I was going.

When I got back into the living room, I picked up my purse without grabbing anything else, without checking to make sure I had all my belongings, and definitely without looking at him. I slipped my feet into my shoes without untying them, which made the backs fold in against my heels.

"Are you leaving?" Seth asked, standing up.

"Uh, I've got to go," I said. I was about to say something about how I forgot I had a work project that needed my immediate attention, but nothing came out.

I made a beeline for the door, trying to ignore the burning in my cheeks.

"Hey, I'm sorry about that kiss," he started. *Good god, did he just say kiss? Out loud?* "I don't know what came over me."

He got up to follow me to the door.

"Oh, no, that's okay." It was so not okay. What was I thinking? I grabbed the doorknob, twisted it, and I was out. He followed me into the hallway and called out for me once, but I was already out of the building, and I was not looking back. When I had walked a couple of blocks away and was sure he hadn't chased after me, I pulled out my cell phone. Silent tears streamed down my face and stung my cheeks as the cold wind whistled around me. I called Lici.

"Hey chika!" Lici sang. "What's up?"

I swallowed past the lump in my throat and uttered the only words I could think of. "We need to talk. Now."

I told Lici to meet me about four blocks from the bus stop. I didn't want to ride the bus, and I didn't want to keep walking, so I found a nice old building with wide front steps and waited for her to find me. As I waited, my mind involuntarily replayed that kiss, turning those two or three seconds into an eternity.

"No, no, no," I told myself sternly. "You are not going to think about it. You are going to ignore it until it's like it never happened."

An old woman sat on her porch a few doors down from me and put out a cigarette on the concrete.

She frowned at me as if I had lost my mind. Maybe I had.

Lici pulled up about half an hour after I called her—a good fifteen minutes after the old lady went back inside—and the moment she swung her passenger side door open from the inside, I got up, plopped into the seat, and slammed the door shut.

"What's going on?" she asked. I shook my head. Not here. I couldn't talk about it here... I needed distance. Maybe with the more space I put between myself and Seth, the clearer I would be able to think about this.

"Okay... Do you want to go home?" she asked, offering up the next best solution.

"Hell no!" I shouted.

I couldn't possibly go home to the place where Adam and I had been so happy together.

"Then where?" She raised her dark eyebrows at me. I silently thanked her for being so patient. I knew I wasn't making this easy.

What came out of my mouth wasn't a thank you at all. "Shit, Lici, I don't know. Just drive. Away, please."

I ran my fingers through my hair and tried to calm my breathing, slow my heartbeat, think of something, *anything,* else. When we were almost out of the historical part of town, Lici tried starting up the conversation again. She scrunched her nose distastefully at the old buildings.

"What were you doing clear out here, anyway?" she asked.

"I had a date, sort of..." I muttered, lost in thought.

"Oh! So you did decide to go through with it, then. I know you were on the fence about it last night."

"I kissed Seth," I said, my tone flat and disbelieving.

Her gaze shifted back and forth between the road and me.

"Oh shit, man! What happened? Was it nice?"

I leaned forward, putting my head on the dash.

"I'm a horrible person. I can't believe I did that to him."

"To Seth? Trust me, honey, I'm sure he loved it."

"Ew," I said, turning to face my friend as if she'd just said something completely uncalled for. "To Adam! I can't believe I did that to Adam!"

"Oh." Lici smacked her lips.

We were silent for almost twenty minutes, just driving around town with nowhere to go. Finally, we pulled into a little parking lot on the edge of town that was mostly used to hold empty cars from people carpooling. It was late in the afternoon, and most of the spaces were already empty for the day.

I stared blankly out into the forest that the lot overlooked. My mind was slow, my body numb. Still, I worked to figure out how I felt and what in the world I was supposed to do now.

"I guess I'll have to go into hiding for a while. Fake my death, move to a different city, somewhere far away from Seth."

After a while, Lici offered up her opinion. "Maybe you're falling for him, you know? Maybe it's time."

When she said this, I thought I would be sick, or angry, or something. But honestly, it felt like the thing I needed to hear. Despite how much I hated the idea, I thought she actually might be right.

"I can't do that, though. I can't just jump back into something, you know? Aren't I supposed to have some kind of a rebound phase? Like after a breakup? Seth can't be my rebound! I... I really like him."

Lici agreed that liking one's rebound was a recipe for disaster, but... maybe it was different when the person you're rebounding from left because they were dead and not because they were an asshole.

We pretty much left the discussion at that. After that, it was decided. Lici didn't necessarily give me the idea, but she definitely influenced it, and once the thought was in my head, there was no turning back.

I wasn't going to let Seth be my rebound. Maybe if I could find someone else, it would make all of this a little easier somehow.

That night, once I had calmed down enough to go home without feeling like my own weird kind of home wrecker, I went inside and curled up under the covers like I was a six-year-old afraid of the monsters in my closet.

I waited for Adam's ghost to come out of nowhere to haunt me. I imagined it going one of two ways: either he'd show up and ask me why I ruined the special bond the two of us had shared, or he would wrap me in his bodiless arms and tell me that it was okay, that he really did want me to be happy again.

I wished more than anything that he would appear and tell me everything would be all right. But of course, neither of those options was possible. Adam was gone, and even if he did somehow miraculously come back, conversation about Seth would probably not take any of the time we had together. I must have fallen asleep at some point, because I awoke to my cell phone ringing. Stupidly, I answered it without reading the name on the screen.

"Hey," an uncertain Seth said on the other end. "I wasn't sure if I should call... but you left your sketchbook here. Do you want me to bring it to you? It seems pretty important."

Yes! My heart screamed at me. *Any excuse to see him again. After all, it's not like I already have over a dozen other sketchbooks...*

No. My mind reasoned. I considered just telling him to toss it, but I couldn't remember if I had done anything I wouldn't want to lose in that one.

"No. Um... just hang onto it for me, will you? I'll come get it from you when I can," I replied after mulling it over for about thirty seconds too long. I rubbed my face, feeling like I hadn't slept in a lifetime. Man, this whole situation was exhausting.

"Okay..." he said. "Hey, I'm really sorry if I upset you today. I shouldn't have kissed you like that. You said you just wanted to be friends, and I shouldn't have..." He was silent for a moment. I ran my fingers in little circles against my temples. When had things gotten so complicated? Things had been going fine between the two of us, and now it was going to be all sorts of weird, uncomfortable, and more likely than not inappropriate. Not to mention that I was still so unsure of how to feel... about anything.

"Forget about it, okay?" I said as softly as I could. "I'll talk to you soon." I hung up the phone without waiting for a reply. Sure, it was probably rude, and the last thing I wanted was to offend him, but I needed some time to think things over, and talking to him was most definitely not going to help.

The next week went by pretty slowly. I'd wake up, get dressed, go to work, come home, paint a little—or do some more work, if I could find something to do—and go to bed. Rinse and repeat. I didn't want to see Lici or Nessa, who I was sure by then had gotten the memo. I knew they'd want to talk about everything that I was going through and what I was planning to do next, and I had absolutely no idea how to answer those kinds of questions.

I avoided taking the bus to work every day and instead took a taxi everywhere I went, which began to get entirely too expensive. But I kept at it that whole week, because I didn't want to chance running into... well, him. I feared that if I saw him again, I'd run straight into his embrace, and I just couldn't do that.

Seth called a few times throughout the week, but I was much more careful and made sure to let it go to voicemail each time. I didn't listen to the voicemails, because I was being honest with myself when I said I needed time to think; but for whatever reason, I couldn't bring myself to delete them, either.

Chapter 21: *Off the Deep End*

Almost seven months after Adam's passing.

By Friday, I was pretty much crawling out of my skin.

It suddenly felt weird isolating myself from everybody, even though that's exactly what I had been doing for months. On Friday afternoon, I went straight home after work, working quickly to put my plan into action before I could back out.

I put on the sexy dress that Lici let me borrow, which I still hadn't returned. I put on my black sheer tights and threw on a sparkly, midnight blue cardigan.

I did my makeup with blue, black and silver on my eyelids, and a little bit of gold for highlighting beneath my eyes, tossed on some light pink lip gloss, and pulled on the four-inch blue high heels. I made myself wait until it was eight o'clock, and then I left the apartment.

Rather than taking the bus and risking someone I knew seeing me looking like this, I took a taxi straight to the "club," the White Rabbit, which was really more of a bar with an over-hyped dance floor and less of an actual club.

When I got in the car, the driver eyed me from the front seat and smirked.

"Got a hot date?" she asked, raising her eyebrows.

"Something like that," I muttered, breathless, trying to get my heart to stop beating in my damn mouth. I slouched down as we pulled away from the apartment parking lot, hoping to God nobody saw me.

When we got to the White Rabbit, I tipped the driver, who I'd gotten to know fairly well in the twenty minutes or so it took me to get where I was going.

"Thanks for the ride, Shareece. I hope everything goes well with your Nanna's surgery," I said. I patted her shoulder from the back seat and climbed out, doing my very best not to show my panties as the dress crawled up my thighs when I stepped out of the car.

God knows how unattractive that looked, with me all hunched over, stretching my dress out so that it was at least a couple of inches closer to my knees.

"And best of luck to you on this crazy mission of yours. I hope you find the answers you're looking for," Shareece said. She shook her head like she knew I was out of my mind, and then she drove away.

I cleared my throat and stood tall, glad I'd picked these blue heels, because they matched perfectly with the cardigan I'd picked and gave me the tiniest boost of confidence.

Once inside, I made my way to the bar and ordered myself a margarita and leaned against the counter as I waited, scanning the floor. I did my best to ignore the raging anxiety that twisted my stomach into an intricate knot.

Was I actually expecting to hook up with somebody? No. Did I really want to? Hell no. I still didn't want to hurt or damage Adam's memory, but if I was going to do anything with anyone right after Adam's death, I worried that if it was with Seth—whom I had actually started to really care about—then I'd lose him, too.

I shook my head, feeling my hair bounce around my shoulders.

"Whatever happens tonight," I said softly to my drink. "It's my choice. I'm in control." I sounded crazy, and I knew I was acting even crazier, but all of this had been too much, and in the last six months, I felt like I'd lost myself. It was time I did something drastic, something that might help me figure out how I fit into this strange, new world.

Before Adam, whenever I went out to meet prospects, I always brought the girls. We would act like total idiots together, buy drinks together, dance together. We had done everything together. That was the problem this time around.

Yes, I was more terrified now than ever before, and I knew they would both be super supportive of my choice to put myself out there again—regardless of the results—but I didn't think I could handle it. No matter how well-meaning their intensions would be, their presence would be too much pressure. If they were there, I probably wouldn't have the courage to even stay.

I sighed and supported my chin with my free hand. Things really had gotten complicated. I ran my finger along the rim of my glass and admired the light yellow liquid inside.

This is stupid, I thought. *I should go home before I make a complete fool of myself.*

But I didn't leave. I took a deep breath, sat up straight, and eyed the crowd as more people started to show up.

The chairs and tables near the bar's small karaoke stage began to fill up, and people got in line to pick their songs. This place had done karaoke Fridays for long before the girls and I started going, but I had always been too chicken to try it out. I didn't have the best voice, and I didn't want to embarrass myself front of everyone.

Tonight, however, I did not give one single crap.

"What the hell," I muttered. My friends weren't there to see me screw this up, and I was still sober enough not to be completely tone deaf. I downed the rest of my drink and headed for the little sign-up area by the stage.

I studied the list. The cool thing about this particular club was that the owners were adamant about maintaining a fun atmosphere, and they encouraged singers to surprise each other with duets. The many times I had come here before I met Adam, I'd seen that situation turn out beautifully and horribly, but no matter the pair-up, it was always a good laugh.

The alcohol warmed my stomach and gave me just enough courage to sign up to co-sing one of my favorite songs. I didn't know the other singer, but that was the fun of it anyway. Mine was the seventh song down the list.

The first entertainer got up and sang a very interesting single person's version of a song he called, "I Got Myself, Babe." It was terrible but hilarious, and a great way to break the ice and kick off the night.

I watched as the next two acts covered songs that were vaguely familiar, but I didn't know the words. I sang along from the audience as they played and sang the songs I did know.

Finally, the manager got back onstage and tapped the mic, just to make sure that the last guy, who'd done a very violent dance with it during the last song, hadn't broken it.

"Please welcome Matt Tormina and Kalli Morgan to the stage as they join in a duet."

Three or four people clapped in the audience as I took to one side of the stage, and someone made a "whoop whoop" sound as my partner climbed the steps on the other side.

As the upbeat, staccato music began playing, I got the chance to take a quick gander at the guy I shared the stage with. Man, he was motorcycle model fine. If Lici had been with me, she'd have been all over him in a second.

Er, well, before she started seeing Jeremiah, that is. The idea gave me a weird, anxious feeling in my gut that quickly worsened when the guy smiled at me. He had almost shoulder-length blond hair that had been swiped back behind his ears. His rippling muscles stuck out just enough to be visible through his leather jacket and thick, semi-tight biker jeans. He had the squarest jaw I'd seen on anyone, and his smile took up basically the entire bottom half of his face.

Feeling particularly brave, when the words came up on the screen and it was time to begin singing, I jumped in before he had the chance, taking the main part. I wasn't sure if he'd be upset with me or not, but once I started, he threw me a bright, extra wide smile and jumped in on background vocals.

The song was a whirlwind of adrenaline, and the two of us got into it, dancing and spinning around on the stage as if we were the main characters in a musical.

When the song ended and the adrenaline dissipated, both of us stood on stage, slightly out of breath as the next singer approached.

The two of us climbed off the stage the same way we came, and I went to find a seat at a table, shocked and tired after the song, and a little unsure of what to do with myself now.

I definitely understood why people came back to do karaoke more than once, and I swore to myself that I would bring the girls as soon as things settled down.

"Hey," a gravelly, confident voice said from behind me. I turned around to see the guy I just sang with smiling at me.

"Hello," I said back. He used both of his massive hands to brush his hair behind his ears.

"You've got a great voice," he said.

I snorted. "I suck, but that was fun."

He laughed. "Can I get you a drink?"

"No, but you can come with me so I can get myself one." I narrowed my eyes playfully and, I hoped, flirtatiously. I knew Adam always loved when I looked at him like that, but he always made comments like, "You're such a dork" afterward.

I also knew he would definitely not approve of me going home with a stranger. Luckily, however, I'd already promised myself that I wasn't going to take this guy anywhere near my home, no matter how the evening panned out.

I bought myself a water and sat down near the edge of the room in a dark corner. It felt weird that I was planning all of this: *I* was planning on picking up a stranger. Did he know those were my intentions? What would he think if he found out? I shuddered but reminded myself that that was probably why he was here tonight, and probably why any guys showed up, unless they just really liked karaoke night, which I doubted.

We talked for a few minutes, making vague conversation about what he did for work, and when he asked me, I made some comment or another about being sort of in-between at the moment. The answer was vague enough that it wasn't an outright lie—I was currently switching back and forth between projects for two different accounts—but I didn't want this stranger to know anything about me if I could help it.

He spent another few minutes just talking to me about his bike, a topic that normally might have interested me, but between thoughts racing through my head about Adam's accident and the blaring, tone deaf karaoke performance on stage, I couldn't even make myself follow what he was saying.

After another minute or so of that, things grew quiet. Probably because neither of us really knew what to say. Then, out of nowhere, he piped up with, "You're sexy."

He leaned in closer to me as if he wanted to try and kiss me, and placed his large, calloused hand on my thigh.

My body actually had an instant physical reaction, and it wasn't a good one.

Is this what's supposed to happen? I thought. I felt sick, and so terribly out of place that my skin felt like it was crawling. *Screw finding a rebound. Who even needs a rebound, anyway?* I got the concept of not wanting to jump from one bad relationship right into the next, but what Adam and I had was the opposite of anything like that. What we'd had was good. It was right... and this was absolutely ridiculous.

"You know, Matt," I addressed him, pulling his hand from my leg and placing it on the table with a soft but awkward pat. "I've got to get going. Thank you for the conversation, and I hope you find someone to be with tonight, and I wish you luck."

With that, I stood and walked out of the bar, ignoring the man as he hollered after me. As I went, a warm feeling in my stomach told me I just made the right decision, and I felt confident with what I needed to do next. I walked to the nearest bus stop and pulled out my cell phone as I waited for the next available unit.

I dialed the number and put the phone to my ear.

It rang three times before he answered.

"Kalli, hey!" Seth said, and then more cautiously he added, "Is everything all right?"

I took the bus straight to his stop.

I knew it was late: It was already a quarter after ten, but this issue couldn't wait. When I got off the bus, Seth was already at the stop, waiting for me. He had both hands behind his back, and when I stepped onto the sidewalk, he held them out to reveal my sketch book. I took it and gave him a weak smile.

"I'm sorry if I freaked you out last week," he said.

"No, you didn't do anything," I said, shame heating my cheeks. "*I'm the one* who freaked me out. Can we go sit down somewhere?"

We walked the few blocks to his apartment together, chatting quietly about what had happened since we last saw each other, but the conversation stayed light until we got inside. I looked around.

I expected everything to look just as it had when I left last Saturday, with candy, popcorn and pizza boxes scattered everywhere, light-blocking curtains still hanging. The apartment looked pretty immaculate with only a couple of white sheets of printing paper littering the coffee table.

"What's this?" I asked as I took a seat on the couch. I took extra care to ensure I wasn't sitting where I sat the night we kissed, and I blinked away the memory.

I set down my sketchbook and lifted one of the papers. It didn't have any lines, and Seth had scribbled something down. Like most people, he struggled with keeping his words in a straight line on blank white paper; and the words made a gentle, illegible arc across the page, sloping down as it got closer to the right-hand side.

"My notes," he said simply as he put his backpack down on the counter in the kitchen before sitting beside me.

"Why blank paper?" I asked.

"Lined paper inhibits my creative abilities. If I write it down like this, whatever form it takes it takes for a reason, and the ideas always flow better."

"Interesting," I said, more to myself than to him. This little quirk of his made me smile. My smile quickly faded as I remembered what I wanted to say.

"Seth, this is going to sound awful, but I almost slept with someone tonight."

Seth's body stiffened as he waited for an explanation. I chewed my lip, struggling to find the best way to go on.

"What?" he asked. It was a quiet word, and it sounded more like "Whuuh?"

"Um... yeah," I said, realizing again how completely stupid the idea had been. "I had this plan that I was going to get all dressed up tonight, go out, get drunk, and sleep with somebody I don't know."

He looked slightly unsettled and more than a little confused. He shoved his hands into the front pockets of his jeans. "Why would you want to do that?" he asked. He didn't sound angry, just... genuinely dumbfounded.

I smacked my forehead with the palm of my hand.

"I got the idea in my head that I needed a rebound after Adam. You know? Like people do after a breakup?"

He moved off the couch and crouched down in front of me, pushing the coffee table aside.

"Right, but you two didn't just break up."

God, even Seth understood this.

"Yep. I feel really stupid about it. Anyway, I got there and had one drink. I sang this really fun karaoke song with this guy. It was going great, and we were all hyped after the song was over, and he wasn't bad looking. In another life I would totally have gone for him... and then..." I trailed off. I was babbling.

Why was it so easy to just word vomit all of this to him? I had never been this brutally honest with anyone but Adam.

"And then..." he nudged, as gently as his curiosity would let him.

"And then we sat down and started making conversation. I kept things light, casual, but then he called me sexy."

Now Seth looked totally lost. I'd never seen so many creases between his eyebrows before. He opened his mouth as if he wanted to say something, but whatever it was, he kept it to himself.

"At that point, I couldn't help thinking... You know what? Rebounds are stupid. For dating, sure, I guess it makes enough sense, but my situation is different. It's not like I had this crappy relationship and I'm trying to get over it before I try to find someone better. Adam was amazing. He treated me like a queen, and he *died*. And... I don't feel like I need a rebound, because... I like you, Seth. I really do."

Now his eyebrows raised way up, wrinkling his forehead beneath his dark brown curls.

"You do?" he asked, huge grin spreading across his face.

I nodded, and for whatever reason, I teared up.

"I do," I whispered.

My heart beat double time as Seth leaned in so close that I could feel his breath on my face.

His hands reached out to hold mine, and I searched his face for a better explanation for the way I'd been feeling.

I cleared my throat and blinked the tears away.

"Pretty much since I met you. There's something... familiar about you. You know how you said before that you felt like you were meant to know me?"

He nodded, and I watched his Adam's apple bob as he swallowed.

"Yeah... I feel that, too. Trust me, I don't want to. I'm not ready, and I can't tell you how guilty all of this makes me feel." I let his hands go, and they dropped limply in the space between our knees. "I'm supposed to be with Adam."

He was quiet for a moment as he considered my words. Then, he reached over to where I set my sketchbook on the table, and he flipped through the pages.

"Is this him?" he asked, stopping at a picture of a handsome, smiling man with dark hair, glimmering eyes, and just a tiny bit of stubble around his chin and jaw.

"It's supposed to be," I grumbled. "I haven't been able to get him right since it happened."

"Well, if he looked like this, I can see why you loved him," he said, letting out a sound that was half laugh and half sigh. We both looked a little longer at the inaccurate sketch in silence.

"Seth?" I said, drawing his green eyes from the sketchbook to me. "I don't feel... like Adam would be mad about this. It's thoroughly upsetting to me, but I don't think he would be, or maybe he would be and I'm just trying to find excuses to be with you."

He frowned. "What do you mean?"

I swallowed past the overwhelming urge to throw up.

"Well, before... before everything happened, Adam and I had a weird conversation." I picked at a hole in my tights just above my knee as I recalled the moment, and I wondered if this little rip had been there all night. "He said that if anything were to happen to him, he wanted me to find someone else. He said he wanted me to be happy."

I clenched my fists, tearing my tights even more. Even the memory of that conversation was infuriating, especially considering the mess I had made of things now.

"I see," Seth replied.

That was all either of us said for a moment. Seth really was strange. He didn't hardly react to anything I just said, even though it meant that the two of us may eventually be more than what we were.

This information was likely a lot for anyone to take in, so I took his silence as a sign that I should keep talking.

I had already told him what I felt and why I felt like it was somehow okay. Now I had to tell him what I wanted.

Okay or not, I was still going to need time.

"With… all of *that* said and out of the way, I do still feel like I need more time. I don't ever want to feel like we rushed into something we shouldn't have. I think it would kill me. Is that okay?"

"Of course," Seth said, warily brushing his hand against mine. "I think I would need time, too. But, if it's cool with you, I'd like to keep hanging out. I really do feel like I'm meant to be around you."

I let out a small laugh. "Sure. I like hanging with you, too."

Chapter 22: *A Conversation with Dad*

About seven months after Adam's passing.

APPARENTLY, IT REALLY WAS OKAY. SETH AND I BEGAN TO SPEND A LOT more time together. We called and texted and saw each other almost every day, but after that first time, we never kissed. There were a few times he held my hand when we walked places or we sort of cuddled during a movie, but we never shared another kiss.

My dad came by to visit in secret a few days after my discussion with Seth. Mom and I were still not speaking to one another, so my dad came alone to check in on me.

We'd never gone so long without seeing each other before, and while I was now feeling guilty and awkward about being so angry over a misunderstanding—and my mom had consistently been leaving messages over the last several months to apologize.

Truly, what it was is that every time I thought about that argument, I was reminded of just how deeply losing Adam had wounded me, and that wound reopened. Now I had let so much time pass that I wouldn't know how to go back to the way things were before.

I assured my dad that I was hanging in there, eating, breathing, bathing somewhat more regularly. He chuckled and sat down on the sofa, knocking throw pillows to the floor.

"Hey Dad?" I asked, feeling like a little kid again, curling up on the couch next to him. My feet were tucked up underneath me between the cushions, and my arms wrapped around my knees. I looked up at the man who raised me, the man who had always given everything to everyone around him. "Why did you stay? With Mom, I mean."

I expected him to sigh, to rub the grayed stubble on his chin and tell me that it was complicated like he had when I was younger. I expected him to say that he didn't know, but he had to have a reason. Getting an answer after so much time had passed meant more to me than it ever had before. If I could understand the complexity of his relationship with my mom, maybe I could get a grip on my own messy love life.

This time, though, he didn't say it was complicated.

For a minute, he didn't say anything at all. He just stared out into space as though he was trying to solve the problem of world hunger in his head. When he looked at me, the wrinkles on his face, his smile lines, his crow's feet, everything was accentuated by the shadows flickering from the muted movie playing on the TV across the room.

"I did it for a lot of reasons," he said. He turned his body so he could face me better, and then he also tucked his feet beneath his body. Man, we hadn't sat like this together in ages. "To start, I did it for you two. Yeah, I know kids survive divorce and separation all the time, but I couldn't see myself doing that to you. You were practically grown, and I knew I didn't have much time left with you living at home. I didn't want to take you from your mom, and I didn't want to lose a single moment with you. Biweekly visitation is bullshit."

He got that look on his face again, recalling what had happened all those years ago.

"Do you remember that weekend I went away, just after Mom said she wanted a divorce?"

I nodded. In all honesty, I didn't remember much. I was eighteen at the time, finishing up my senior year in high school, and while I was still living at home, a good portion of my time was spent participating in extracurricular activities or hanging out with Lici.

"Your mom was honest with me from the beginning. She told me about two months before that weekend that she'd met a woman and had started having feelings for her." At this point, my dad actually chuckled. "I was so worried, so afraid it was something I'd done, afraid it was just that she wasn't happy, and that she was acting out. I offered to go to marriage counseling for it. After a few weeks of that, the counselor looked at me like I was stupid. After your mom left one of our sessions, I went in to talk to him on my own.

"I told him that I didn't get it. We had always been so close, your mom and me. We hadn't even been fighting, and she up and sprung this absurd news on me out of nowhere."

"What did he say?" I asked. This was more than I'd ever heard before. I had no idea they had gone to marriage counseling.

Now, his face lit up with the smallest hint of a smile.

"He told me that she was feeling the real deal. He had seen cases of one spouse leaving the other for someone of the same gender for lots of reasons: abuse, cheating, mistrust, but there had been a few times in his career that a man or woman left because they discovered real feelings for someone else."

I frowned.

"Are you saying that you and Mom were never really in love?" I asked. No way. Even to this day my parents were some of the happiest people I knew, even with Nancy in the picture. They had to have at least been in love with each other at some point.

"Not at all. We were in love. Deeply. But more than that, we were friends. That friendship kept our relationship from turning rotten over time and allowed us to stay close even though things were changing."

Huh. Okay. I supposed that made some kind of sense.

"After that talk with the therapist," he said. "I still clung to the idea that she would change her mind, so it wasn't until she said she wanted a divorce that I knew just how much that wasn't ever going to happen. Then, I was pissed. I packed, gave the two of you some lame excuse I don't even remember, and went to stay with your uncle Paul.

"That weekend did a lot for me. It gave me the time I needed to think about what I wanted. Did I want to spite your mom for hurting me? For falling for someone else when I was still in love with her? Sure, you bet I did. But I wanted to be with you kids. I wanted to experience every minute I had with you and Jeremiah while you were still living at home. I thought I could stick through it until you left for college. But when that time came, I realized I still didn't want to leave, because I didn't want to be away from your mom. Even though she had hurt me, she was still my favorite person.

"I stayed in a hotel for a week or so while we sorted out the details, but after hearing my side of things, she agreed. My being at home was still the best idea." He laughed and readjusted to a more comfortable position. I took that moment to adjust as well. "Actually, I think her exact words were, 'I have no issue with you, hon. So long as we're clear about our relationship, I don't see why we can't still live together.'"

That sounded like Mom, all right. Colorful, caring, spunky ol' Mom. I still didn't understand the weird dynamics of my parents' relationship, but I did have a little more insight as to why he stuck around like he did, and how they were able to work things out.

"That sounds complicated," I said.

"Oh, one hundred percent," he replied, winking at me. "But life would be boring without the complex parts, wouldn't it? Mom just kept my life from getting boring."

Chapter 23: *Missing Mom*

Almost nine months after Adam's passing.

ABOUT A MONTH AND A HALF AFTER MY CONVERSATION WITH MY DAD, Lici, Nessa, Seth and I all went out to Mallorie's to celebrate Nessa's 29th birthday.

We wanted to celebrate it on her actual birthday, which this year landed on a Wednesday.

Lici brought Jeremiah, and it was the first time I'd really seen them together as a couple. To be honest, aside from Seth, I hadn't seen much of anyone in a while. I was still avoiding my mom, so I ended up avoiding pretty much my entire family.

Jeremiah and Lici, were great together. They were at that point in their relationship where they had begun finishing each other's sentences in that totally adorable, totally obnoxious way that happy couples do, and although I hated it, I was super happy for them. I had never seen Lici like this before in all the years I had known her.

Nessa's beau, Jules, was a five-foot four, very sweet banker with short, light blonde hair that she kept spiked up, and silvery blue eyes, just like Nessa had. I swear, if the two of them procreated, their babies would be super models from day one.

The idea of the two of them figuring out how to have babies in the future seemed like a real possibility at this point. They'd been together almost four months, and Jules still looked and acted completely smitten with Nessa.

I pushed the thought away, not wanting to think about my own weird, confusing love life, or the argument that ensued after my last conversation about reproducing.

Instead, I focused on how Nessa's new girlfriend was really cool.

I had one phone conversation with her a few weeks earlier, and now, she extended her arms for a hug as if we'd known each other forever and hadn't seen each other in a while. When she pulled out of our hug, she turned to give Seth the same greeting, and I looked around. I hadn't been back here in months.

Thankfully, Mallorie's had its crowd back. I was deeply grateful for this, because the quiet, crowd-less version we experienced last time had awkward enough memories associated with it that I hoped I never saw the place like that again.

It was at this birthday party, with everyone pretty happy, celebrating someone we all adored turning twenty-nine with her new lady, that I realized just how much I had missed my family. I had just gotten back from a quick bathroom break when I noticed Jeremiah mingling with the others at the table like he had always belonged right there with the group.

Suddenly, I was overcome with sadness. I realized now, looking in at this amazing group of people celebrating together, just how isolated I had been. I really had pushed everyone away, and I hadn't seen my family for months. It took everything I had not to cry as I pulled my cell phone from my back pocket.

I sent one text message:

> I miss u mamma. Can
> I come visit on Friday?

I chewed my lip as I waited for the message to send, then stared blankly at the screen and waited for her reply.

> We'll see you Friday. We have a birthday present
> for Ness. Will you bring it to her then?

I held my phone to my chest and thanked the universe that I might be able to finally put this tension behind me and allow myself to be a part of my own family again.

When I returned to my group, Jules and Lici were arguing about why it was important to pay off your credit cards before they were due. From Jules's standpoint, paying off your credit cards as soon as you spend the money is the best way to do it, because often credit card companies will end up having to pay you, and it reflects beautifully on your credit. Lici argued that doing so completely defeated the purpose of having a credit card in the first place.

Although Nessa had used her family's credit cards all her life, she was very responsible with her money. She was taught at a young age not to use the credit cards unless she could prove on paper that there were funds enough to cover those bills. That was one thing I'd always admired about her parents: They were filthy rich, but they still taught their daughter about financial responsibility. Nessa backed up Jules's argument with evidence of her own.

When I scooted back into our crowded booth, I found Seth's hand resting on his lap under the table. I took it and squeezed it. After that text from my mom, I decided I wanted Seth to meet my family.

When he shot me a surprised look, I smiled at him and mouthed the words, "Thank you." He responded with a confused frown.

"I'll tell you later," I whispered as the rest of the group joined in with their opinions on the proper way to use and pay for a credit card.

Seth smiled and piped in his own opinion from an entrepreneurial standpoint. I added in a comment or two of my own as the group bantered back and forth, but mostly, I sat back and watched all of these people interact over drinks and pizza.

After dinner, Lici and I told the server that it was her birthday, and that we had been the ones who called in a cake earlier in the day. The server gave us a huge, pearly white grin and turned to tell his co-workers. In another lifetime, Lici would be hitting on him relentlessly while the three of us girls would exchange remarks about what we liked about him. I guess things really had changed. Lici was totally serious about Jeremiah, and even now, while she waited and continued her earlier rant about why they needed more brilliant women in her department, she had her arm linked around his and her head against his shoulder.

Several of the serving staff members returned to our table carrying a huge German chocolate birthday cake.

Everyone—and I mean everyone—from the staff, to our group, to the drunk folks at the bar, to those outside of the drinking section, sang Nessa an obnoxious "Happy Birthday." She teared up as she did every year, but this year she couldn't hold it back, and she softly wept for a moment. We thanked the staff as they cleared away our dinner to make room for the cake.

It took a minute for us to calm her down enough to tell us why she was so emotional.

"It's nothing," she said, her giant blue eyes searching all of our faces before holding their gaze on Jules. "I'm just... so happy to have all of you. I've never felt so lucky in my life."

I guessed I wasn't the only one reflecting on things tonight.

After cake, we all shared our gifts with Nessa.

From Lici and Jeremiah, Nessa received a silver and turquoise tennis bracelet.

"Awe Lici, this will match those earrings you got me last year perfectly! Thank you!"

Jeremiah cleared his throat and faked being offended. "Hey, I helped her pick that out! It's from me too."

I rolled my eyes and let out a sarcastic, "Oh, come on."

At the same time, Nessa smiled brightly. "Thanks, Jer." In response, his offended façade faded quickly, and he beamed at her before sticking his tongue out at me.

I reached into my bag and pulled out a thin rectangular box.

"Seth helped me pick this one out, too," I said as I passed the box to her across the table. She smiled, untied the ribbon, and slid the top of the box off.

Inside was a silk knit scarf with blue, lavender, and silver threads. Nessa gasped and almost elbowed Jules in the face trying to put it on.

"So you don't have to borrow mine anymore," I said over the babble of the others. As Nessa smiled and thanked us, I added, "Unless you want to."

Now it was Jules's turn, and she reached into her pocket and pulled out a tiny box. With a box that size, I expected her to kneel, but instead she reached out and held both of Nessa's hands and looked her in the eye.

Nessa teared up again and fanned her face with her hands, but when she opened the box, it was not a ring. Her shoulders slumped for just a moment, but she perked up again quickly.

"Wow," she said, blinking away her tears. She turned the box so we could all see the diamond earrings Jules had gotten for her.

When it was time to hit the hay in order for any of us to get enough sleep to function the next day at work, I pulled Nessa aside.

"You okay?" I asked.

She smiled and sighed.

"Yeah. I don't know why I got myself so worked up over that little box. We've only been dating for a few months."

"Hey," I said, giving her a big hug. "Trust me, I don't think this one's going anywhere. She adores you, and she's stuck it out longer than the others. Give it time. Happy birthday, Ness."

She nodded and gave me a big smile as I turned to find Seth.

"Hey Seth," I said, pulling at his jacket sleeve as everyone said their goodbyes and headed for their cars.

"Yeah?" he asked.

"I want you to meet my family. Will you come with me on Friday?" Behind the look of complete shock, his eyes twinkled.

"No problem," he said, smiling.

Chapter 24: *Worlds Collide*

About nine months after Adam's passing.

Seth really did have a car, as it turned out.

A pearlescent, cream-colored 1964 convertible beauty. We had spoken on the phone twenty minutes earlier, and Seth just insisted that he drive us over there, since he'd finally gotten his car fixed. I waited in the parking lot for him to arrive, and I could not believe my eyes when he pulled up in that gorgeous car.

"What the hell?" I shouted, raising both my arms so high above my head that my purse spun around my shoulder. Seth parked the car and got out, walking around the back side to let me in. "God damn," I said, blinking my eyes rapidly. "When you said your car was under repair, I thought you meant, like, your typical four door sedan... not this!" I gestured to the entire car. "This is *not* a car; this is a work of art!"

"Yeah, well," Seth replied, shrugging as if his car wasn't the single most beautiful thing in the entire planet. He knew it, though. I could tell by the little smirk on his face that he tried to hide behind the collar of his jacket. "I thought this might be better than taking the bus. I want to make a good impression on your family."

"Well, you've got Jeremiah in your corner already," I said, shaking my head as if shaking a dream from my mind as I sat in the car. Seth closed the passenger side door and got back into the driver's side.

"I guess. Now we just have your Granma, dad, mom, and Nancy. And any other relatives you deem crucial, of course." I was silent for a moment, studying him as we pulled out of the parking lot. After a while, he noticed me staring at him. "What?" he asked, moving his gaze between the road and me.

"Why are you doing this?" I asked, my smile lingering on my face.

"Doing what?"

"Why are you coming with me today, and bringing this fancy car? Why are you trying to make an impression?" I adjusted in my seat to get a better look at him. I couldn't help the grin that spread across my face as he shifted up until we were going just over the speed limit, the powerful engine roaring all around us.

He shrugged with one hand on the steering wheel and the other hand hanging over it.

"Your family seems like something to be a part of... and besides, Kalli, I really like you. I know we're going slow, but I'm loving every second of it, and I'm not planning on going anywhere. Meeting the people that are important to you is a part of that. I know you and your mom have been fighting for a while, and I just... I want to make a good impression. That's all."

His words made my stomach flutter, and then I tensed. For the remainder of my ride to my parent's house one thought gnawed at me, twisting my gut and filling me with the old familiar guilty feeling.

Adam wasn't planning on going anywhere, either.

It felt like it had been a century since I saw anyone in my family besides Jeremiah and my dad. Usually when mom and I got into fights in the past, Dad or Granma would find me and try to convince me that Mom was right in her own way and beg me to forgive her. This time, however, I imagined they understood how complicated this subject was, and intentional or not, Mom had been out of line trying to talk to me about moving on so soon after Adam passed away.

You don't just tell a widow to move on only weeks after her husband's death. Well, we weren't technically married, but we were close enough that I thought the concept definitely still applied. Shriveling, aging ovaries or not, that's just not something you do.

Everyone had expected us to take the bus, so when we pulled up into the driveway in the breathtaking muscle car, I had the pleasure of watching everyone's jaws drop.

"Heyo!" I said, elated at the looks on their faces, and so happy to see them all again. I got myself out of the car, not giving Seth enough time to even open his door, let alone get around the car to open the door for me. Oops.

My family and I raced to each other. Mom wrapped her arms around my entire body, and her colorful shawl brushed against my chin. She smelled like... well, like my mom, like home, and I clung to the scent. Dad tackled my left side, and Nancy rushed my right.

Granma hugged me from behind, and we all stood there like complete idiots until Seth cleared his throat.

Our hug circle broke apart when Mom backed up. She eyed Seth, then looked at me as though I was absolutely insane. Clearly, Jeremiah hadn't told her anything.

I shot a glance in Jeremiah's direction, and he held his hands up as if to say, "It wasn't my place."

"Thank you," I mouthed at him.

Everyone's reaction to seeing Seth was priceless. The entire group stood there speechless. I could tell that Seth wasn't sure what to do with himself, and although he was making a huge effort to avoid being awkward, it was clear he didn't have much experience meeting people's families. I watched as he went in for a handshake and got pulled in for a hug by Granma, and I wondered if he'd ever met any of his previous girlfriend's parents.

Not that I *was* his girlfriend...

A cool breeze fluttered in around us, and I watched Seth as he noticed a plastic sandwich bag roll across the driveway from one of the houses down the street. Dad and Granma had started to fidget, Jeremiah held a hand to his mouth and tried to keep himself from smiling. Nancy had grabbed a hold of Mom's hand, and Mom just stared as though her eyes were no longer capable of closing.

I giggled.

"Mom, Dad, Granma, Nancy, this is Seth." I pointed with both hands to Seth, who stuffed his hands in his pockets and nodded.

"Nice to meet you," he said.

"Seth, these are my folks."

Finally, Mom seemed to snap out of her trance. She blinked about a zillion times, and her eyes started to water. She rubbed them with one hand as she extended the other to Seth, sniffling.

Seth took her hand and stated his own pleasantries, which I totally missed because I was so stuck in my own head wondering if my mother was actually crying about this. *Shit, should I have given her a heads up?* I wondered.

As everyone else took their turns shaking hands with the new guy, they talked over one another asking him a million questions there was no way he'd be able to answer.

Where did he come from?

What did he do for work?

Mom sneaked over to me, all hunch-backed and tip toed and everything.

"You didn't tell me you were bringing a guest," she said. Her eyebrows, dyed a bright green to match the top of her hair, raised on her forehead.

"Hey Mom," I said, smiling. "I'm bringing a guest over for dinner. Does that sound okay?"

She rolled her eyes.

"It's a little late for that, now."

Suddenly worry twisted in my gut and my brow began to furrow. "It is okay, isn't it? I'm sorry I didn't ask, I just thought—"

"Are you kidding?" she hollered before slapping her hand over her mouth. She looked around nervously. Everyone else was still absorbed in interrogating Seth, so Mom relaxed her shoulders and dropped her hand, revealing the crimson of her cheeks. "Of course, it's okay, Kalli," she added more quietly. "Here, let's go inside. I'll set another place at the table. Jeremiah! Run out back and grab one of the Thanksgiving chairs, will you?"

Dinner was going pretty well, so far. I had been relieved when Seth decided to sit across from me. Adam had always sat in the seat at my right, where Jeremiah now sat.

Mom had made roast beef with steamed carrots, broccoli, potatoes, celery, and everything else that went perfectly with my favorite meal. Typically, she had Nancy or dad or someone else go to the store to pick up rolls and pie, but since it had been so long since we had seen each other, she had pulled out all the stops.

That included her old recipe cards that she hadn't touched since I was little—not even for Christmas or Thanksgiving. Granma had tried getting her to use them for almost two decades now, but I guessed this was what it took.

We all sat around the dinner table. It hadn't been this crowded since the last Christmas I had with Adam.

"Wow, this food is incredible," Seth said, pulling me from my spiraling thoughts and speeding heartbeat. He scanned the group of people gathered around the table, and when his eyes found me, they stayed there.

"I've got to get a recipe like this to my mom," he said happily. "The kids would love this."

My body felt hot under his gaze with everyone else so close. I looked at my plate and stuffed a half-eaten roll into my mouth to hide the color that was forming in my cheeks. Thankfully, everyone was so focused on Seth that nobody even noticed.

"Oh," Mom said, eyebrows raised. "Do you have kids?"

The question was innocent enough. In this day and age just about everyone in town who was in their late twenties had kids. You didn't have to be married or with somebody to be a dad.

Besides, Seth was in his early thirties—that's plenty old enough to have children of his own.

Still, his eyes widened, and he almost choked on the drink of milk he had taken. After taking a very careful swallow, he replied.

"Um, no. I mean someday, I think I might like to experience that, but I haven't really found the right person to do that with."

I could have leapt over the table and kissed him right then and there for not bringing me into this conversation.

"Have you been single for long?" Nancy asked, just as ruthless as Mom. "Is that why you don't have kids yet?"

"Nance, not everyone needs to reproduce," I said, grinding my teeth together, the pain from my last dinner here resurfacing.

Seth waved off my comment and answered her honestly.

"Yeah, I guess it's been a while. I haven't had the best health, and it's only recently started to get better, so I suppose that's got some part to play in it, as well. It just hasn't been the right time. What I meant by 'the kids would love this' is the foster kids my mom takes in. She's a saint, but she can't cook anything besides macaroni and scrambled eggs to save her life."

Color flooded my cheeks as I sat across from Seth, listening to him go on about his mom.

Although it had been a pleasant enough evening for all of us so far, and Seth was handling his first dinner with my family with boatloads of grace, the occasional glance from the others told me I wasn't the only one who couldn't help thinking about my missing fiancé.

Still, however, the conversation continued, and it was genuine. My family seemed to be taking a liking to Seth as I had in the past few months, and as weird as it was for me, I was glad.

We all ate slowly, half wrapped up in our conversation and half hoping that the night would last. After we had stuffed ourselves with pie and cleared our plates, I studied my family.

"Hey, how would everyone feel about extending dinner into movie night?" I asked. I had missed my family terribly, and having them around kind of filled that void Adam left when he died.

"Sure, hon," Mom said, clearing the big serving dishes from the table. "How about you give Seth the grand tour while we get everything cleaned up?"

Dad raised his graying eyebrows.

"That sounds like a great idea!"

His hands clutched his full stomach, which over recent years had begun to stick out just a little bit over his belt.

Everyone else helped Mom clear the table and wash the dishes, and Seth and I were excused to wander the house I grew up in.

I put my hands in my back pockets and turned, gesturing with my elbow and shoulder to the area we just ate in.

"Well," I said. "You've seen the entryway. This is the dining room, and this..." I let the statement lag for a minute as I led him into the extremely crowded kitchen. "... is the kitchen, which is usually much less claustrophobic. Yeah... there are too many people in there. Let's go to the next room. If you want to see it later, I'll take you in. Deal?"

Seth nodded at the kitchen as a whole, drawing in the picture with his vivid green eyes. "Kitchen. Interesting. So that's what a real kitchen looks like... I've only ever read about them before."

"Come on, smart ass," I said, turning away as Mom shouted at me for swearing. Nancy—who was helping my mom with the dishes--chuckled.

Dad put the leftovers into various mismatched dishes and placed them in the fridge. Jeremiah wiped down the table, and Granma, as the elder, just kind of sat back and watched them all work.

"Sorry, Mom!" I shouted back toward the kitchen.

My childhood home had two flights of stairs across from each other leading up to two different parts of the house: The place that held my mom and Nancy's bedroom and the adult guest room, and the side which held my room, the "play room" which had been converted into an office when I moved out, Jeremiah's room, and the "little one's" guest bedroom. The guest bedroom on the kid side of the house was large enough to be a family room on its own and had been transformed into Dad's bedroom/man-cave when the two of them got divorced.

Seth followed me up the stairs on that side.

I quickly showed him the different bedrooms as we made our way down the hall.

When we reached my bedroom, I paused, unsure if I wanted him to see this part of my life. This is the room that I lived in from the time I was old enough to have a room until I moved out to go to college, and for some time between graduating college and moving in with Adam. It was the room in which I discovered much of myself.

I stared a moment at the door while I considered moving the tour onward. Little blue and green dragonflies made trails up the side of the white door. I reached up to the faded silver doorknob, drew a deep breath, and turned. *He's dealt with a good deal of crazy coming from me, and he's now met my family. Maybe it's right that he gets to bear witness to this, too.*

The door swung open, revealing the room that once contained my entire world.

The walls, which had been painted a different color for every phase of my life growing up, were just as I'd left them the year I'd turned eighteen and left home to live in the dorms on campus.

I was crazy about orange, my love for which had faded over the years, and green, which I still loved just as much as the day of my seventeenth birthday when I declared it my favorite color. Two walls, the one with the window and the one opposite it was painted a dark, orange, and the one with the window had quickly been covered up with drawings and small watercolor paintings.

The wall that held the doors to my tiny "walk-in" closet was painted a bright, not-quite-olive green, and the wall opposite it held a mural: a portrait of a woman's face with rainbow hair, which Mom and I had painted together the summer before my senior year of high school. The woman's mouth was slightly agape, full lips pouting, vibrant multicolored hair blowing fiercely around her, and a single tear slid down her cheek.

I saw many flaws in this painting that pretty much started my career, but the memories it revived were well worth each and every one of them.

My desk contained various makeup utensils, pens and half-sized colored pencils, papers and a couple of textbooks and library books I had neglected to return.

My bed was made with the same quilt I left on it, though I knew Mom well enough to know that she had washed it every three months whether or not I actually used it, just in case I ever needed a place to stay the night.

As I stood there, door partially opened, Seth still waiting in the hallway to be invited in, I wondered why I hadn't stayed here when Adam died. *Why had I gone to Lici's instead?*

Opening this door was like opening a portal to another lifetime, another dimension, another time when life revolved around passing geometry, getting a date to the next overhyped dance, and dramatic fights with Mom and Dad about everything.

When I stepped back to allow Seth to enter the bedroom, I thought back to the first time Adam had ever been in there. I recalled how he had looked around, touched various things, and then sat on my bed, where we proceeded to make out.

When Jeremiah, a sophomore in high school at the time, had come to get us for dinner, he complained about how we were gross and out of college and way too old to be doing that.

Right, I thought, sucking in a breath. *That's why I hadn't stayed here. Adam's memory lived here, too.*

"You okay?" Seth asked, turning around to face me with his eyebrows raised.

"Yeah, I'm fine. It's just... been a long time."

He nodded. He walked around the room in a clockwise motion that was almost identical to how Adam had all those years ago. Seth, however, was more reserved. He kept his hands in his pockets as he soaked up all the aspects of my teens that I'd left behind in that room.

After a while, I began to grow self-conscious. I stood in the corner and picked at my nails as he looked around. *What the hell was he doing being so quiet? Judging me? The dude has freaking "action figures" in his living room!*

I cleared my throat and shifted my weight.

"So anyway," I said, trying to muster an indifferent tone.

Finally, he looked back up at me, and there it was—that sweet, lopsided smile.

"What?" I asked, now smiling also. There was something about that smile that was just contagious.

"I can see you in here," he said, pointing around the room.

As usual, I pretended to take what he said at face value.

"Well, duh. I'm standing right here."

"Not what I meant," he started. "I mean, I haven't known you for that long, but this..." He gestured to the room as a whole. "Is definitely you. The bedding, the colors, the painting, the messy desk even. I just... see you."

"Oh," I said, shocked so much by this remark I could think of no witty retort. "Well, thanks. I guess this is sort of where I made myself."

"Well put," he said, shooting me a sweet look, and he exited the room without another word. Just like that. I took one more glance at the room trying to see it as he had before closing the door and following him down the hallway. Downstairs, we finished the tour quickly and join my family in the living room.

Chapter 25: *A Heated Moment*

Still about nine months after Adam's passing.

AFTER THE MOVIE, SETH AND I MEANDERED IN THE GENERAL DIRECTION of the car. It had been a fun family night, and a successful introduction. My family really seemed to get along well with Seth, which made me feel... kind of weird. It had taken them a while to warm up to Adam. Part of me felt guilty about this, but another part of me wondered if their quick fondness of Seth was because they, too, were just as shocked by Adam's sudden death that they wasted no time getting to know someone who might be a part of my life.

A part of my life... what was I thinking? Was the world spinning correctly? Everything felt so strange, and yet... it wasn't all bad.

My chest ached subtly, and I closed my eyes as Seth opened the door for me.

"Thanks," I said, my mind whirring.

He nodded and ran around the car to the driver's side. When he got in the car, he started it and let it idle in neutral for a minute.

At first, he didn't look at me.

He seemed as dazed as I had been since the movie ended and we walked out on the front porch and said our goodbyes to my family. I sat for a moment, suddenly feeling awkward, out of place, and unsure of what to say.

I took a deep breath, ready to start a conversation with an earth shatteringly brilliant, "Soooo..." Luckily, he opened his mouth before I did.

"I really like your family," he said. His green eyes twinkled, catching the dim light from my parents' front porch.

"I'm glad," I said. I wanted to tell him, "Of course you did, they're amazing people," but instead I just sat back and put my hands in my lap. "Why's that?"

"Oh, come on. You know why. They're so... real. Authentic. They're not nice because they have to be, and they really seem like the kind of people that are who they are no matter who they're around. Like... you."

My cheeks warmed, and I turned to look out the passenger side window into the darkness. I was still smiling, and now that I noticed it, the action felt weirdly mechanical.

"Oh, thanks," I managed to mumble.

He shrugged, and I could feel his eyes on me. *Please, please, please,* I thought. *Don't try to kiss me in my parents' driveway.* I was all too aware of the fact that my entire family was probably watching us through the living room curtains.

"We should go," I said, turning back to face him.

We spent the entire drive pleasantly discussing different parts of the movie we had watched with my family. When we got back to my apartment, I sat in the passenger seat, suddenly devoid of all motivation to ever get up again.

I didn't want to open the door.

I didn't want to even lift my purse or the licorice I'd snuck out of my parents' house off of my lap. I sighed.

Most of all, I didn't want this night to end. It had been forever since I spent an entire evening with my family, and I was grateful I was able to bring Seth along. He got to meet my family and experience for himself how cool they were.

For the first time in a long time, I actually felt happy. Really happy, not the kind of happy where you smile or laugh but it dissipates quickly. This time, the happiness spread throughout my body, showed on my face, and it lasted. It had lasted the entire night so far, and even though I missed Adam terribly, and I wished I were able to live the evening over with him, I really couldn't imagine it without Seth. I closed my eyes and silently counted to three.

Then, I decided to leap.

"Seth?" I said so quietly that I wasn't sure he heard me.

Sure enough, though, he looked over at me with eyes that were wide with curiosity. They looked almost completely black in the darkness of the lamp-less parking lot. I was silent for a moment, considering whether I really wanted to go through with this.

"Um..." I said. I sucked in a quick breath. My heart pounded in my chest. My muscles tensed as if I really was getting ready to jump. I leaned across the center console, reached a hand up in the darkness to find his face, and kissed him before I had any time to chicken out.

It wasn't a hard kiss by any means, but my eyes were closed so tightly I wasn't sure if I'd ever be able to open them again. Seth's body tensed, and after a couple of seconds, he kissed me back. The moment he did, both of us relaxed into each other.

Any awkwardness that had lingered between us throughout the night melted away in an instant. Suddenly, I wasn't Kalli the not-quite widow hermit who pushed everyone away and put up walls and constantly worried about disappointing her dead fiancé. Seth wasn't the undeniably attractive forbidden video game designer that would always come second after the legend that had come before him.

In that moment as our lips and tongues discovered each other, as the heat from our bodies pulsed around us inside the little front section of Seth's fantasy of a car, we were just people. Just two people, longing, kissing, living.

It was so nice to *live* for a change.

I ran my hands over his neck and chest, and his hands grasped my hips and played lightly beneath my shirt, the warmth of his fingers making my skin tingle. When we finally broke apart, the two of us were breathing heavily. Our faces were flushed, and shy smiles spread across our lips. Unsure what to do now, we just sat there, staring at each other. I leaned back into my seat once again and looked out into the empty parking lot.

Again, I felt him looking at me, but this time I didn't meet his gaze. Now that my heartbeat had begun to slow, I wasn't sure how to feel. Part of me ached, felt as though by kissing Seth I was betraying Adam's trust. Like I was cheating.

Another, larger, louder part of me felt incredible. That part of me worked to assure me that there was nothing wrong with what had just happened and wanted nothing more than to crawl back over the center console and experience more of that rush of life I just felt.

Shit. I had felt this way before.

I sat still in the passenger seat, frozen and drowning in my murky thoughts. Seth was the one that broke the silence.

"I've never seen your apartment before," he said softly, letting his sentence trail off as he leaned toward me.

Oh, no. If he asked to come in, would I be able to control myself? Would this guilty feeling be enough to stop me from doing what the rest of me wanted to do?

I pushed myself into the passenger door and felt the cold leather interior press against my back.

I didn't want him to think he did anything wrong, or that repulsion or displeasure was the reason for my distance, especially since I was the one who kissed *him.* I put my hand out, held it awkwardly in the air in front of him, and then settled on placing it on his forearm just above his wrist.

"Seth," I murmured. "You can't come in tonight."

Even in the dark I could see his subtle disappointment. His shoulders slumped and his body dropped ever so slightly.

"Not tonight," I repeated, watching as his eyes found my face. My thumb traced little circles on his skin, brushing against the soft brown hair on his arm. "I need time to think everything through. Make sure I'm okay with... this. I'm not saying I'm not. I just need to... you know."

"Make sure," he finished for me, nodding slowly. I squeezed his arm and leaned in to give him a soft peck on the cheek.

"Try me tomorrow," I whispered against his ear and retreated, letting myself out of the car and trying not to slam the heavy door behind me.

By the time I walked up the two small flights of creaky, carpeted stairs, I'd pretty much convinced myself that everything that had just happened, everything I felt, everything I wanted... was a dream.

It was all an elaborate hoax put on by my brain to trick me into thinking it was really happening. Surely, that was it.

Man, my brain was a dick.

I felt crazy.

When I reached my front door and jiggled the key around enough in the lock to let myself in, the other, more logical part of my brain told me that it actually had been real. I really had made out with a guy I'd only known a few months, and... I really had enjoyed it.

I pressed my fingers against my lips, where the memory of his kiss still lingered. My stomach flipped and fluttered, and I actually giggled.

As I placed my keys on the counter and walked back to the front door and to lock it, I replayed the moment over and over in my head, trying to wrap my mind around how I felt.

If I told Lici about what I'd just done and how I had left things off, she would tell me that I basically just told him to go screw himself, even though every inch of my body, which had been so used to mourning and being neglected that it barely remembered what touch was, wanted to.

I shuffled into the kitchen without turning on the lights, pulled a cereal bowl out of the cupboard and grabbed a spoon from the drawer below it. The dishes made little clinking sounds as I placed them on the countertop and abandoned them in search of some chocolate marshmallow cereal.

Maybe filling my body full of pointless sugar would satisfy the urge I felt. Maybe it wasn't lust I was feeling; maybe it was just plain old hunger. I poured myself an excessive helping of cereal that was so old I couldn't even remember buying it, and drowned it in milk.

Shoveling the treat into my mouth, I pulled out my phone.

In that moment, my head was swimming furiously, and I felt as though I drank half a bottle of wine in the time it had taken me to get inside.

I thought having my girls around would help me figure out what to do, and more importantly, how to feel about it. I clicked through my messages, tapped on Lici's name, and pressed the dial button. She answered her phone in four rings. In that time, I had already begun to doubt my decision to call her.

"Hey chika," she said sleepily when she answered the phone. "What's up?"

"You know what?" I said, making up my mind. "I made a discovery and I thought it was super urgent, but now that I think about it, I can wait to share. Sorry for bugging you so late!"

"Psh! You're totally fine. You know my sleeping schedule better than I do. If I was anywhere near dropping into a beauty sleep, you would have waited."

"I guess you're right. Have a good night!"

"Buenos nochas, señorita. Call me tomorrow about this discovery of yours."

I hung up the phone and rubbed my forehead.

Yes, I did need my friends. And yes, in the past, they had helped me make all of my major decisions regarding the guys in my life. They had even helped me figure out when it was the right time to be intimate with Adam for the first time, and how to go about sending the right message. This time, however, I felt I needed to make that decision for myself.

As much as it scared and confused me, I knew this was something I was going to think over without any excited, giggling voices putting in their two cents.

I suddenly felt extremely tired, and more than a little bit dazed. I decided to sleep on it.

Chapter 26: *Change is at the Door*

Still about nine months after Adam's passing.

By morning, I had made my decision.

I went about the apartment doing my regular early Saturday morning cleaning. Since I started going out and doing things, I realized every time I got home that, although I have always been a little bit on the messy side, I was turning into a full-fledged slob.

After that, I decided that I was going to make a routine, which included basic cleaning once a week. I'd dust, do the dishes and clean the bathroom.

All of my chores took me a total of about thirty-five minutes if I did them slowly. Once I finished my housework, I decided it was still probably too early to get ahold of Seth with the result of my thorough thinking the night before.

I took to my studio and painted some colorful Peruvian lilies and stared at my work for a while.

The more I looked at the painting, the more I liked it.

This was the first time in forever that I had created something beautiful that wasn't for work.

Finally, Seth sent me a good morning text.

Hey there.

Ive been thinking a lot about last night...

I chewed the inside of my lip for a minute. I spent the majority of last night thinking through how I would tell him what I had decided, but now that he was actually asking, I wasn't quite sure how to do it. I decided to go with,

Call me.

Within seconds, my phone was ringing.

"Hey," I said when I picked up. Anticipation stretched through the miles between us. Without waiting for him to ask again or even greet me back, I got straight to the point. "I thought about this a lot last night, and I'm going to give you the results of that thinking. I... want you to come over. I feel like it's a crucial part of you getting to know me to see how I live, and it's only fair because I got to see your place forever ago. I also really like you, and I want you to feel welcome here. But. I don't want to do anything here. Not... not yet at least. I don't know if I could handle that. Does that sound okay?"

"That sounds fair enough," he said.

Within the hour, Seth had called me again.

"Hello," I said, then I smiled because I recalled the conversation we had when I first answered his call with that response.

"Seriously with the 'hello' still? Ugh. We need to work on that. Anyway, I'm here, but I don't know which one is yours."

"Oh! Hold on just a sec. I'm coming. I didn't know you were going to show up today!" I hung up the phone and tried not to run to the door, though excitement had me rushing. I twisted the knob and swung the door open to reveal Seth, standing with his back to me, holding horror movies in one hand and a bouquet of my favorite lilies in the other. I assumed both were supposed to be a surprise because he held them behind his back.

I giggled, and he turned around, eyes wide and mouth open.

"Oh," he said. A light pink graced his cheeks. "I guess it's that one, then. I, uh, got these for you." He held out the flowers, and I took them and stuck them beneath my nose to take a deep, whiff.

"Why didn't you go with roses?" I asked as I led him inside. "Most guys do."

This question seemed to take him by surprise, and he stumbled over his words as he struggled with an explanation. When I looked back at him, he smacked his hand against his forehead.

"Shit, I knew you'd like the roses better. I just saw those ones, and they looked like something you might like, so I felt like I had to get them. I should've just gone with the roses. Sorry, I'll remember that for next time."

His embarrassment awoke a bubble of laughter that had been resting deep in my stomach. It rose, and with it came a loud bout of laughter that echoed through my kitchen. It was almost visible as it bounced off the sink, the counter tops, and the cupboards, and I realized... I couldn't remember the last time I had laughed in this apartment.

I shook off my bewildered feeling and brought the flowers to the sink, letting Seth ruminate on his "mistake" for a few seconds longer.

I snuck a peek at him as I bent to get a vase from beneath the sink. One of his hands rubbed the back of his neck nervously as the other still clutched the stack of horror movies.

"Actually," I said, sifting through the pile of miscellaneous objects under the kitchen sink that I had never cared to organize.

Blindly, I pulled a vase out and looked at it. It was a crystal vase that Adam had gotten me with a huge bouquet of flowers when I got the job position that I was in now. Before, I was working mainly in secretarial with a couple of trial projects thrown at me every once in a while. It had been a big deal when I got my own office space.

Adam had the vase engraved with beautiful, sparkling cursive letters that spelled out, "You're incredible." I realized as I put the vase back that I'd been quiet for quite a while, and I cleared my throat.

"I'm glad you didn't go with roses."

I stuck my head under the sink, terrified of pulling another vase like that from under there. I found a tall, thin glass one that I couldn't remember getting and decided that would do.

This bouquet of flowers needed to have their own memory, not be attached to an old one.

"You are?" Seth asked as I turned on the water and began cutting the stems. He tried to hide it, but relief was spelled out across his face like a neon sign. I smiled.

"Sure. Roses are lame ass flowers that men get women because they want to do something nice but don't care enough to get to know what kind of flowers they prefer. These ones," I said as I held up the now full vase of flowers. "Just so happen to be my favorite."

"Really?" he asked, raising his eyebrows in disbelief. I set the flowers on the island.

"Yep. Come and see." I led him through the hallway to my studio and showed him the flowers I had finished painting earlier that morning. They were slightly different in color, but I was amazed at how closely they matched the flowers he brought over. I gestured to the painting.

"See? I painted these this morning. It's crazy you brought flowers that look so similar."

He took a moment to close his mouth.

"Damn," he muttered. Then, as if he'd just picked up on what I said at the sink, added, "Hey, what about the girls whose favorite flowers are roses? Are the guys who get those girls roses still insensitive?"

I pondered the question for a second, tapping my finger against my chin. "Probably."

He scoffed, dropping his hands to his sides. "What?"

"It depends on whether they knew that roses were her favorite, if he ever paid enough attention or cared enough to ask, or if he just lucked out because he got her roses regardless of her favorite flower, because roses are a catch-all."

"Damn," he said again, and I fought against the urge to laugh at him. I settled instead for a quiet smile. "Getting flowers for a girl is a lot more complicated than I thought. You make all guys sound like complete dickheads."

"Oh, no, not *all* guys are like that. Take you, for example. You looked at other flowers and for whatever reason thought I would like these ones better. Which I did. See?"

"But... I went in there to get you roses."

"Hmm. True. But at least you didn't. So... you're only half a dickhead, I guess." Now my smile broke into a full grin. The wide eyed, shocked look on his face was absolutely priceless.

"Hey!"

I threw my hands up, palms out. A sign that hopefully said, "I have no qualms."

"It's fine, it's fine," I said. "All guys *can* be dickheads. Even Adam was at first. I had to tell him after the first few months of us being together that I do *not* like roses."

After that comment, the conversation lagged. *Idiot,* I thought. *Way to kill the conversation. Just bring up your dead fiancé, why don't you? He's trying so hard to be cool, and you're totally ruining it.* I tried to think of something that would get the conversation back on track.

I cleared my throat for the second time since Seth had arrived.

"Anyway, you've seen the kitchen and the hallway, but would you like the official grand tour?" I asked. This brought back his smile. "Beware, it'll take quite a while. Like, at least three minutes."

"Lead the way."

"Great! Let's start back at the front door, shall we?" I asked, already shooing him out of the studio.

He shrugged, literally trying to wipe the smile off his face.

So, I led him back to the front door and pushed him outside. I told him to wait three seconds, then knock. He did, which made me think he was that much cooler.

I opened the door and put on my most professional face and tried on my best French accent, which was absolutely horrendous. Aside from giving me a confused look, he didn't seem to mind.

"Why, hello monsieur. I have been awaiting your arrival. Please, come right in." I made a grand, exaggerated bowing gesture, and he entered my apartment for the second time in ten minutes.

"To your left we have the chef's kitchen." I put a hand on the side of my mouth and whispered, "Except the chef doesn't really cook anything besides frozen pizza." Seth nodded and pretended to be blown away by my exceptional cooking skills.

"To the right, you have the dining area living room combo. This is where all the party guests lounge... if there were any parties, or guests, for that matter."

Now I led him back through the hallway, which I only just noticed was full of pictures of Adam and me, which had been too painful to take down. There were a few pictures of my family, and some of me and the girls, but for the most part it was Adam and me, smiling, kissing. Oh, God. I hoped he didn't notice them, but he would have to be pretty blind not to.

I wasn't ashamed necessarily, or embarrassed, I just felt really weird having him see that part of my life, for the same reason I felt strange bringing up Adam around Seth. It felt like a whole other lifetime, and I wondered if he felt as strange about it as I did.

I didn't want to ask. Instead, I just went along as I had been, making my silly accent even more unbearable to hear in hopes it would distract him from the photographs.

"In here we have ze bathroom. In it lies ze finest toilet paper in all the land. Here is ze washroom, where... as you can see... not a lot of washing gets done." I waved a hand at the pile of dirty clothes I'd forgotten to wash and was grateful I always washed my underwear with the light clothing, which had been washed the day before. "And of course, the studio, which is also a weight room, but I rarely use the weights anymore. I've mostly been hibernating."

"So, this is where the magic happens," Seth said, eyeballing all the paintings and drawings that were scattered about the room. "I love it."

"Why, thank you, good sir. Okay, I'm dropping the accent now."

"Yeah, that's probably a good idea. Your accent kind of sucks."

"Hey, now! I'd like to see you do a better one!" I stuck my tongue out at him, and he totally one-upped me with a glorious accent as I led him through the rest of the hallway to the bedroom.

"Holy shit! If I knew you could do accents, I never would have challenged you. Sheesh! This room here is the bedroom," I said.

Having him there, looking around at the place I slept... the place I had spent much of my time with Adam made me feel uncomfortable. I shifted my weight, reaching forward. This was too intimate.

"Anyway," I said, grabbing hold of the knob and closing the door a little too quickly.

"On with the last and best part of the tour. This way, please."

We retraced our steps through the living room and out to the balcony. I pulled back the curtains and opened the sliding glass door.

"This is the coolest balcony I've ever seen," Seth said, noticing the way it wrapped around the entire side of the building, going all the way from the living room to my bedroom.

"Yeah, it's amazing out here. And the thing I love about it is that the roof doesn't overlap this side of the building. When they made it semi-residential, they added a sloping roof, but it's angled so the slopes go off the front and back, so the balconies always have a clear view of the sky. At night, it's breathtaking."

"Sounds like it," he said.

"Anyway, why'd you bring those movies?" I asked.

"Well, I figured we could finish what we started a while ago. You still have quite a stack of movies to experience, and since you said you didn't want to do anything romantic here, I thought it would be the perfect time."

I raised my eyebrows at him.

He shrugged. "Nothing kills a romantic mood like fear."

We spent the rest of the day together sitting close and watching movie after movie, and he was so right. I was so focused on every intense or chilling part of the movies we watched that I practically forgot the lust I felt for him the night before.

There was a moment, though, after it got dark out that we paused our movie so I could show him the view from the balcony at night. I brought out a couple of the many throw pillows from the couch so we could have a more comfortable place to sit.

When we got out there and looked out at the city and the night sky above, Seth actually sighed.

"You weren't kidding," he remarked reverently. "If I had a view like this, I'd never sleep inside again."

"Until you froze to death in the winter," I muttered, but I totally understood what he meant. We spent the rest of the night out on the balcony, talking about anything that came to mind. As the night drew later, we migrated closer and closer together until we fell asleep practically spooning on the hard wooden surface. It wasn't until six in the morning that we woke up and realized we had fallen asleep.

"Shit, I've got to get going," Seth said, his voice sleepy. We both got up, and I stood there rubbing my eyes.

"Yeah, no problem," I said, hearing the disappointment in my voice. Seth reached forward and caressed my cheek.

His hand was like ice on my skin.

"I've got a ton of work to get done today, but… Kalli, this was amazing. Thank you for having me over."

Stifling a yawn, I nodded. "Thanks for coming," I said.

"I hope you get some more sleep," he told me, kissing me softly on the forehead. "Text me when you get up for the day?"

Lici and Nessa came over later that morning and got to hear all about the awesome night I'd had with Seth. I honestly had an incredible time.

I couldn't stop thinking about how we had talked until we had fallen asleep, or the way his body felt against mine when I woke up.

"Oh my God, that sounds amazing. I could just die," Nessa said, fanning herself. "I can't believe you've found someone you *like*."

Lici had already given me her two cents worth when she found out Seth and I had kissed for the first time, but this time she remained silent. Surprising, as she used to jump at the chance to tell me to sleep with somebody... but I think she already knew how I felt about the whole Adam-Seth situation.

Still, the way I felt after having Seth over... after how alive he made me feel when he brought me home from my parents' house... I felt like *maybe* it was time for me to let myself relax and let whatever was going to happen... happen.

Chapter 27: *Kalli's 30ᵗʰ Birthday*

Ten months after Adam's passing.

SETH WAS A SWEETHEART.

He must have asked Lici or Nessa when my birthday was, because I was pretty sure I had never told him. Yet here he was, standing at my bus stop when I got off work that day with the best caramel filled chocolates in the world in his hands. These were my absolute favorite, so I was certain he had to have asked somebody.

"Hey, you," I said, smiling.

It had been a good day at work—cupcakes, balloons, the works—and it didn't have anything do to with the fact that people pitied me. My boss went all out for all of our birthdays, so this attention was a breath of fresh air. Seth's surprising me at the bus stop was the cherry on top of a lovely day. Now if only I could rid myself of the gnawing reminder that this was my first birthday without Adam in six years... it would be perfect. I greeted Seth with a small, sweet kiss.

"Man, if I'd chosen any other stop to get off on today, you would be feeling pretty silly, I bet," I told him.

He grinned and pulled me into a tight hug.

"You smell like an office full of painting supplies," he replied, his embrace lingering for a moment before he let me go. "And yeah, I would probably feel like an idiot, so thanks for choosing this one."

I nodded and pulled away from him.

"So, what's up? We going to watch a movie or something?" I asked, hopeful. Since I turned thirteen, my birthday tradition had been to get ice cream and watch birthday-themed movies. It was silly, now that I was an adult, but that was part of the charm.

"Nope." He smiled, kind of crushing my hopes. Okay, I supposed other plans would work out, too. Lici could always come over and watch movies with me after work tomorrow.

"Huh, okay, then what?"

Now his grin outstretched the limits of his face.

"We're going on a scavenger hunt." Before I could reply, he added with a wink, "Blindfolded."

"But I haven't even been home yet. I'll need to get changed..." I trailed off, wondering what in the world I should even wear to a scavenger hunt.

Seth shook his head, and the navy-blue baseball cap that held his hair back wiggled out of place. He adjusted it as he spoke. "Nope. You're sexy as hell just like that. We're on a mission, and time is of the essence."

So... we went on a scavenger hunt.

It was amazing. Seth had gone through town earlier in the day and set everything up.

For our scavenger hunt, he would read me these little clues that said things like, "Where did we first meet?" and then I would have to think of the answer. When we got to each location, he would remove my blindfold, and I would search for the next clue. On and on this went until we had been on the bus, at the coffee shop, outside his apartment, and to every other significant place we'd been together since we met. It was a wonderful time. By the time we had gotten through every clue, we had ended up at the park.

He led me carefully through the park and removed my blindfold when we reached a small pavilion. My parents, my friends, my brother, Granma... everyone was there.

"Surprise!!!" they all shouted. I eyed the decorations Seth had put up. Orange and green ribbons were tied to every surface, balloons floated all over the place, and a big orange and green cake sat on the table with big, sloppy letters that said, "Happy Birthday Kallifornia" on it. It was the cheesiest, sweetest attempt at a birthday party I had ever seen.

We spent the rest of the afternoon together, laughing, eating, and enjoying each other's company.

Toward the end, Lici and Nessa cornered me and congratulated me on how cute my birthday celebration had been.

Mom, Nancy, and Granma told me once again that they really liked Seth. As the hours passed, the sun crept lower and lower in the sky, painting the clouds in vivid pinks and yellows until there was nothing but a few magenta clouds on the horizon. Slowly, our little crowd began to disperse, until it was just Seth and me, cleaning up the paper plates and pulling down the decorations.

"These decorations were... so unprofessionally set up," I joked, pulling one of the tables toward the edge of the pavilion to reach the last of the hanging ribbon a little bit better. "I love the colors, though."

Seth whipped around, acting as if my words had physically wounded him.

"Oh yeah?" he asked. Within seconds, he was wrapping his arms around my waist and pulling me down from the table I'd just climbed up on. He held me tightly, clasping his arms together under my backside, and spinning me around in quick circles. "Unprofessional, huh?"

"Stop!" I shouted. "Stop! I just ate, like, an entire cake! I'm going to puke!"

I couldn't help the bubbles of crazy laughter that burst from my lungs as he turned us around and around. When he finally set me down, I slid against his chest, placing my hand on the corded muscle over his heart. Without backing away, I smiled up at him.

"This has been the best birthday. Thank you."

He leaned in and kissed me so softly.

"Well, there is one last thing..." he said, smiling down at me. His green eyes searched mine, as his scent held me in place.

"Oh?" I asked, my question barely audible.

He nodded, and the two of us stood together in silence.

Then out of nowhere, his energy was back.

"Hurry!" he exclaimed. "Get the decorations in this bag and let's get out of here."

We rushed around the pavilion, stuffing everything that was left out into a large garbage bag. As soon as we were in the car, Seth basically peeled out of the parking lot and raced to his apartment.

When we pulled up, he ran around the car to open the door for me. Then he led me up the stairs, through the front door, and I walked into his apartment to a bottle of wine, a huge carton of movie theater popcorn, and a rom-com ready and waiting to be played on his huge flat screen. I doubted the night could get any better.

"Wow," I breathed. "You really did think of everything."

He smiled that sweet, crooked smile at me, and I sat down on the couch, doing my best to ignore the fact that the effort Seth had made to make my day so spectacular made my knees feel funny. He popped the cork on the bottle of white Moscato and poured each of us a glass.

"Wine?" he asked, bowing like an absolute dork. His brown hair fell out of his baseball cap, curling against his forehead.

"Sure," I said. "But only one glass. I do have to work tomorrow, you know."

"What the lady wishes, she shall get. It's your birthday, after all."

He clicked a button on his remote as I got situated on the sofa, and the movie began.

About thirty minutes into the movie—and about halfway through my second glass of wine—I couldn't stop glancing over at Seth, who really seemed to be enjoying the film. He caught me staring before long, however, and he smiled, gesturing for me to cuddle closer to him. I scooted in, putting the popcorn on the floor at our feet. I tried to cuddle with him, but my mind was whirring, and I found myself struggling to sit still.

The entire day had been absolutely magical. Seth was warm, and sweet, and he smelled delicious. I leaned my head back to look up at him, getting his attention.

"You're missing the movie," he said, pointing his free arm at the screen. I reached up, angling his chin down toward me, and pressed my lips to his.

"I've seen it before," I whispered against them.

The kiss started out gentle and sweet, but it quickly deepened. I adjusted my body, putting my knees up against his thigh as I wrapped my arms around his neck. My fingers played with the hair that curled against the back of his neck.

Seth's hands explored everywhere, caressing my arms, my back, the sides of my torso. His lips tasted like popcorn and mint chocolate ice cream.

For a moment, he pulled away and just looked at me, smiling, hair tousled, out of breath. He looked like he wanted to say something, but before he could, he was kissing me again. First on my lips, then my cheek, my jaw, down to my neck. I let out a soft moan and leaned back, adjusting us both again so that we were horizontal.

"Mm," he said, pulling away again. He placed a crown of small kisses on my forehead and sat back up semi-awkwardly. My heart pounded so loudly I was sure he could hear it. Hell, I wouldn't have been surprised if his neighbors heard it.

"What is it?" I asked, exasperated, struggling to steady my breath.

I ran my hands longingly across the width of his chest. How could I not have noticed the muscle that stood so firm beneath his t-shirt?

I scrambled to get up after him, taking my turn to kiss the base of his neck, which was slightly sweaty.

"Not here," he groaned, lifting me off the couch, wrapping my legs around his waist. He carried me from the living room—leaving the movie playing in the background—to his bedroom. He set me down on his bed, which embraced my body like a warm hug.

His hands grasped my hips, then found their way to the skin beneath my shirt. I lifted my arms, giving him permission to slide it off. He did, keeping eyes closed the whole time. I took the moment of privacy to slide off my work pants, temporarily self-conscious of the fact that I was wearing my pink laundry day panties and a mis-matched bra. At least it was black. I sat back against the bed, and when he opened his eyes, he moaned.

"Oh, god," he said, his voice husky. I couldn't tell if it was from pleasure or frustration or something else, but he followed it up with, "You're so fucking beautiful." I felt my face begin to burn. I pulled him back in, yanking his shirt and pants from his body, and I noticed briefly his uneven chest hair. We pressed together, hearts thundering in our chests.

Before long we were melded together, a pulsing, living thing that had both of us gasping at our newfound closeness.

Afterward, Seth and I laid together in his bed. My head rested on his sweat-slicked chest, and I marveled at the familiar feeling I got as

I listened to the sound of his quick and steady heartbeat. Seth brushed his fingers over my hair rhythmically, both of us lost in thought.

I was surprised that, in this moment at least, I wasn't overcome with guilt. Instead, all I felt was this strong sense of familiarity and the happiness that felt as if it would burst through my ribcage.

All the times I'd heard Lici rave about the sex she was having, all the times I'd been with Adam, all my other firsts... This was different. Whatever this thing blooming between us was, it was something else entirely: It was a spark that would light my world on fire.

Chapter 28: *Wise Words and Stomach Aches*

Eleven months after Adam's passing.

Vanessa didn't show up for work.

I had been a little bit worried when Nessa didn't show up for work in the morning, but I brushed it off. Every once in a while, her family would fly into town and expect her to drop everything so she could go vacation with them for a couple of days.

It was pretty much to be expected every six months or so, and Nessa was due for another spontaneous visit. Whenever this happened, Nessa would always call in sick with some excuse for not getting a doctor's note and take off work for a couple of days while she "got better." Mr. Walker always knew it was total bullshit, but he let her have the days off anyway.

Usually, though, Nessa would text Lici and me and let us know what was going on, but sometimes she just got wrapped up in all the fun and forgot to reach out.

It was only after work that I really started to get worried. I pulled out my cellphone to give her a call as I walked to the bus stop on my way home. As soon as I lit up the screen, Lici called. I answered in a hurry, almost dropping my purse.

"Hey, have you heard from Ness today?" I asked. "I've been waiting for her to reach out and say her parents came into town, but I haven't heard anything from her. She usually texts us by now."

"Actually, I was thinking the same thing, so I called her," Lici replied. "I just got off the phone with her. I don't know what's up, but when I called, she was hysterical. I couldn't even understand what she was saying, but she definitely said no when I asked if she wanted me to call 911."

"Shit," I mumbled. Most likely, Ness was having relationship troubles, but Lici and I kept our phones ready to dial the police as we both headed to her house. Damn, she and Jules had seemed so happy.

Rather than taking the bus, I decided to jog. Nessa's house was only six or seven blocks from UpAndComing, so I would get there much faster on foot.

There was a small gas station at the corner about a block from her house. I ran inside, grabbed a big box of tissues and a couple little containers of orange breath mints. Nessa absolutely loved those things, and I hoped they might help her feel better.

I juggled with my change and thanked the cashier as I hurried the rest of the way to Nessa's. I stepped into her driveway just as Lici was pulling up at the house. Out of her little black car she pulled a white orchid and a little purple teddy bear.

"Nice touch," I said, meeting her on the sidewalk.

"I swear, I'm going to kick this chick's white ass to China," Lici mumbled as we stormed up the walkway.

"Hey, I've got a baseball bat at home. I'll help."

Without knocking, Lici and I used my spare key to let ourselves inside. The house was immaculate, and Lici and I shared a look of complete horror: Usually by the time she started crying after a breakup, Nessa pulled out everything that reminded her of the person she had fallen for and either broken it, set it on fire, or given it a good throw around the living room.

"Nessa?" I shouted, hoping to hear some kind of response.

I hadn't seen Jules's car in the driveway, so I was fairly sure that Nessa was alone. Shame. I would have liked to bust her face in for hurting my friend. I listened carefully, but Nessa didn't answer. Lici and I silently agreed to split up. She took the main floor, and I took the upstairs. I checked the bathroom, the guest bedroom, and every single closet along the way, but I found nothing. Finally, I burst open the door to the master bathroom and heard crying from within the huge, connected walk-in closet.

"Ness, what is it?" I asked. This time, I gave a gentle knock before sliding open the large, full-length mirror-covered door. I crouched down to get a better look at my friend. Her face was red, swollen, blotchy, and covered in layers of mascara. The layered streaks on her face told me that she'd been crying off and on throughout the day.

"Why didn't you call us?" I asked.

"I..." she started, her sentence trailing off as she worked to gain her composure, only to end up sniffling so badly she snorted, which made her start sobbing all over again. Then she shouted, "I screwed up!"

I leaned back on my heels and called over my shoulder.

"Lici, I found her! Get your ass in here, please!"

I was definitely going to need reinforcements for this one. Lici came running, her high, black ponytail waving furiously back and forth behind her as she entered the closet.

"Crap," she murmured as she joined me on the plush carpeted floor. She carefully set the bear and orchid down beside her. I had been too busy searching to realize I still had things in my hands, and I dumped my gas station goodies onto the floor as well.

Noticing the box of tissues I had dropped, Nessa snatched it up, tearing open the box and pulling out an entire fistful to bury her face in. She sobbed something into the hoard of tissues, and I looked desperately at Lici.

Neither of us could understand what it was she was trying to say. I placed my hand gently on her shoulder.

"Honey, can you try that again?" I asked as calmly as I could.

"She asked me to move in with her!" she screamed, loudly enough that I was certain her neighbors heard. She thrust her head into her hands and sobbed uncontrollably while Lici and I sat there, totally dumbfounded.

A quick glance at Lici told me she was just as confused as I was. After a minute or so of this awkward silence where neither of us knew what to say or do to help, I cleared my throat.

"Ness, um... sorry... but I don't get it. Why is that a problem?"

She stopped crying for a moment and with great effort, she lifted her head.

"Because I asked her to leave. *She* asked *me* to move in with her, finally someone in this god-forsaken planet wants to commit to me, and I asked her to leave. I was so shocked, and I still haven't told my parents that I'm with a woman, not that I think they would mind, but it's just scary, and I... I didn't know what to do. I told her to go home."

"Why the hell would you do that?" Lici asked. I could tell by the strain on her face that she was trying to be gentle, but she definitely wasn't coming across that way.

Nessa blinked those big blue doe eyes at Lici without saying anything. Then she looked at me, and I raised my hands.

"Sorry girl, but I'm with Lici on this one. I thought you guys were going great, and clearly, she seemed to think so, too. So why did you say no? Do you not want to be with her?"

"No!" she raised her voice again.

"Well," Lici sighed. "Guess that's settled, then. I'm glad it was you who ended it, this time. Good going, girlfriend."

"*No,*" Nessa said, letting out her breath in an exasperated huff. "Not no I don't. I *want* to be with her. More than I've ever wanted to be with anyone. I was so happy when she asked that I just didn't know what to do. I didn't feel like... like I deserved her. Like I deserved to be as happy as I am. Maybe it's too soon for all of this. Maybe it's not real. Maybe we need to wait—"

I reached forward and gripped Nessa's shoulders, which caused her to flinch away from me.

"Vanessa. Listen to me right now. If you feel this way about Jules, don't you waste a single second thinking about it. Life is too short as it is. Don't you dare make your time shorter by putting things off. If that's how you feel about her, there's no need to worry about anything else. Don't worry about me, or Lici, or your parents, or Jules's family, or anything else. Just do it. Nothing else matters but the time you have together. Do you understand me?"

I didn't realize until after I stopped talking, but my face was burning. My entire body felt hot with a rage I hadn't known I had. Lici and Nessa both looking at me like I was absolutely crazy, but when I met Lici's gaze, her face softened. She turned back to Nessa.

"Agreed. Move in with the lady already. You wanted her to propose at your birthday party, didn't you? Just take the leap."

Nessa sniffled and wiped her entire face on the handful of tissues she still held in her hands. "Really?"

Lici and I nodded.

"Really. Call her."

So, she did.

As she gushed over the phone about how she felt to Jules, I found myself deep in thought about what I had said to her. I couldn't believe it had taken me so long to understand that I didn't want to waste any more time. I had wasted too much of it with Adam. I had spent too much time already denying what I felt for Seth, and I had learned that one can never truly know how much time they'll have someone for.

Three weeks later, Nessa and Jules were completely moved in together, and the two of them invited us out for a housewarming party. It was just the few of us: Nessa and Jules, Jeremiah and Lici, and Seth and me. Seth and I had picked out a large potted plant to bring as a housewarming gift, and the two got so excited. Jules, I later learned, was a bit of a plant nerd, and she was psyched to have a new green friend to care for.

At the party, despite the fact that I was over the moon excited that Nessa had finally found someone who loved her exactly the way she was, I couldn't help obsessing over the pit in my stomach. I had been feeling anxious lately, and the last couple of days had been especially tough.

Tonight, I spent most of my time off by myself, picking the nail polish off my fingers until it was completely gone.

When the others started telling stories about the weirdest places they had ever had sex, I couldn't help myself as memories of my last night with Adam flooded back to me with full force.

I made my way to Seth and tugged gently at his elbow to get his attention.

"Hey, I'm getting pretty tired. Can we get going?" I asked as the dread in my gut grew ever larger.

Seth looked at his watch, then he shot me a concerned look.

"It's seven thirty," he replied, tilting his freshly opened beer toward his watch for emphasis.

I put my hands in my pockets and raised my shoulders.

"I know, I just... I want to go."

Seth clicked his tongue. "Sure, we'll go. Let's just say goodbye and we'll get our jackets and catch a bus."

The cacophony of laughter and clinking glasses echoed in my ears, and my vision blurred. My chest felt tight, and I decided I didn't need my jacket. What I needed was air. I mumbled something about coming back another time for it, when I backed into the large floor plant, knocking it to the ground with a crash and sending potting soil flying everywhere.

Everyone in our group looked up at me with worried expressions, but I couldn't even catch my breath well enough to apologize. Instead I jumped up and spun on my heels, nearly crashing into the door in my haste to exit. I turned the knob and rushed out of Nessa and Jules's new townhome and onto the street.

Outside, the cool evening breeze brushed against my face, but it did little to calm me.

I put my hands on my knees and worked to catch my breath.

In, out. In, out. I stared at the horizon, but the vivid colors of the setting sun only brought back more memories of Adam, which caused my chest to constrict even more.

Then Seth was beside me with one hand on my shoulder and the other carrying both of our jackets.

"Hey, is everything okay?" he asked.

Concern was spelled plainly across his face. I shook my head.

"No. I don't... I don't feel good," I said.

"Do you want me to take you to the hospital?" he asked, immediately patting down his pockets in search of his keys. "We can go right now."

"No, no hospital. I just want to get home."

"Okay, no problem. I'll drive you." He started ushering me toward his car, which was parked on the street right a few houses down. He had barely opened his first beer when I asked if we could leave, and now, he offered to drive me home.

I remembered the first night I rode in his car, and how badly I had wanted him to come upstairs with me, and although we had been having sex fairly regularly for a month now, the guilt I felt that first heated night when I wanted him so badly came rushing back to me.

"No, I'm going to take the bus."

Seth looked at his car, then at me. He lifted a shoulder. "Okay, no problem. We'll ride the bus, then."

As he approached, I put my hand on his chest, halting him in his tracks. "No, Seth. I'm going alone."

"Kalli, if you're not feeling well, I really don't think you should be riding the bus across town by yourself."

God, he sounded just like Adam.

"You don't need to take care of me!" I shouted at him. My heart beat a million times a minute, and I just needed to get away, get some space to myself so I could catch my breath. "Just leave me alone!"

Seth's green eyes widened like saucers.

"What the hell, Kalli? Did I do something? You're acting crazy."

I scoffed. "Right, crazy. Just..." I waved off his comment with a shaky hand. "Just leave me alone, okay? I'll call you later."

At that, I left him standing on the sidewalk with both our jackets still in his grasp and made my way to the bus stop.

Chapter 29: *Dark Days*

A year after Adam's passing.

I WOKE UP LATE ONE MORNING A FEW LONG DAYS LATER FEELING LIKE absolute garbage.

Seriously. I couldn't remember what I had dreamt about, go figure, but whatever it was had left me to wake up feeling so depressed that my entire body ached. I had been inexplicably short tempered the last few days, but this was getting a little ridiculous. I let out a grunt and rolled over to check my phone. I tapped the screen, let my eyes adjust to the brightness, and then my heart stopped beating. The pain in my chest throbbed, and each new wave was more unbearable than the last. It was September 7th.

September 7th. How could I have forgotten?

Two images flashed across my memory. One of Adam, alive, vibrant, hair and suit just so, smiling at me the way he always had, and the other also of Adam, stone cold and unmoving on that hospital bed.

I sat up too quickly and threw the blankets off of me. This, of course, only made me cold and dizzy. I pushed through it, rolling off of the bed. I stood up. I had to do something, but I had no idea what to do with myself. Leaving my bedroom door wide open, I wandered through every room in the apartment. I put my jacket and shoes on over my baggy t-shirt and calf-length pajama pants, ready to leave.

Then I took them off again. I resorted to sitting on the couch, then laying down, then staring blankly into space as I stacked every pillow I had on top of my body. *What am I doing?*

Memories of Adam flooded my mind, and along with those memories came a reminder that I hadn't truly felt in a while.

Adam was gone.

My phone pinged to alert me that I had two new voicemails.

The first message was from Dr. Will's office.

"Hello, Kalli, this is Will Jacobi. I'm just calling to see how things have been going, and to let you know that my office is still open to you if you ever feel you need to talk. Whatever you're feeling right now is perfectly acceptable. Call me if you need anything."

The second voicemail was from Seth.

"Hey Kalli, I... uh, sorry. I'm just calling again because I wanted to say I'm sorry for our argument the other night..." I had forgotten all about how I had told him to leave me alone.

I had been feeling guilty about being with him again...

I blinked, bringing my attention back to Seth's words. "... shouldn't have called you crazy. That was rude. Look, please call me when you can, okay? Thanks. Uh, bye."

I wondered if this day looming over me was the real reason I had been so out of the blue awful. Had I subconsciously known that the anniversary of Adam's death was right around the corner? Even worse, how could I have let myself forget?

That thought made me sick to my stomach. *I should get back in touch with Dr. Will...* I thought. *It's been a while, and he always knows what to say.* I sat up again, knocking the majority of my throw pillows onto the floor. I called in sick to work. There was only one place I felt like being today. It wasn't at the office, and it wasn't with my shrink.

I made the effort to get dressed into something slightly more presentable, throwing on Adam's old workout hoodie and pulling on an actual pair of jeans, and I headed to the bus stop.

On the bus, I tried sketching to make myself seem busy and repel people from wanting to talk to me. I typically didn't mind the friendly chit chat I'd get when riding the bus, but today I wasn't in the mood. By the time I reached my destination, I had covered three full sketchbook pages with stupid, meaningless scribbles and frightening, twisted creatures. I snapped my sketchbook closed and put it in my satchel as I made my way down the aisle and off the bus.

The dark brick house hadn't changed since the last time I had visited, almost a full year ago.

Jerry answered the door when I knocked.

At first, he looked totally surprised, but then he pulled me into a huge bear hug. When Alice came to see who was at the door, she quickly joined in. Before long, the three of us were huddled close together, sobbing, and no one had even said a word. Adam's parents understood my pain, because they had been experiencing it, too.

When we all calmed down enough to speak, Adam's parents invited me inside. They sat me down in the living-room with a cup of peppermint tea and a plate of oatmeal raisin cookies--Adam's favorite.

I expected them to ask me what I was doing there, or why I hadn't called since the funeral, but they didn't. Instead, wiping away her free rolling tears, Alice said, "It's wonderful to see you again."

"I've been meaning to call," I started, setting my cookie on the napkin they had given me. "For so long. I just..."

Jerry put his hand up to stop me from talking.

"We understand. It's... We've been meaning to call you, too."

The tension in my stomach eased a little, and I let out a heavy sigh. I asked how things had been, and Jerry told me about his work. Alice told me about how they had made themselves busy renovating the basement. When they asked about me, the guilty feeling in my gut returned stronger than ever.

"I... Um... I've been better," I mumbled. I did everything I could to hold back my building sob, but it just turned into a weird squeaking sound somewhere deep in my throat.

Totally alarmed, Alice leaned forward from where she was sitting on the couch opposite me and placed a warm, soft hand on my knee.

"What is it, honey?" she asked.

"I'm going to hell!" I shouted through quaking sobs. "I started seeing someone. About six months ago. Ugh, I'm awful. How could I do this to Adam? I didn't even wait a year before I hopped along to someone else."

I really hadn't meant to dump all of that information on Adam's parents like that, but once I started talking, I couldn't stop. When I finally did, I threw my hands up to hide my face. My shoulders shook with the powerful emotions I couldn't contain.

"Oh, wow," Adam's mom said. "Okay, this... isn't easy for me..."

She stood up, and the thought that she was walking away from me, the thought that I had disappointed her made me cry even harder. But then she sat down beside me, and I felt her warm hand rub my back between my shoulder blades.

"Kalli, let me tell you something," she said softly. "Waiting six months after someone you love has died does not qualify as 'hopping' to someone else. Besides, I know you pretty well by now, I think. Did you even go looking for someone else?"

This question got me to look up at her.

"No!" I said in pure horror at the idea.

"That's what I thought." She nodded, then placed her hands gracefully in her lap. She looked as exhausted and conflicted as I felt. "We human beings have very little control over the people that enter our hearts. You're doing only what comes naturally to you."

I sniffled unattractively.

Jerry passed me a tissue box.

Hearing all of this from my dead fiancé's parents was extremely disorienting, but it did help to calm me a little bit.

We spent the rest of the morning going through old pictures, sharing memories of our favorite moments with him. We talked and reminisced and allowed ourselves to grieve over Adam's death as if it were only yesterday that he left us behind.

For the next two days I kept my head down, going straight to my office and straight home, ignoring all calls and texts, avoiding as many people as I possibly could.

I woke up that Saturday afternoon feeling like absolute trash fire. I couldn't believe I had slept so long, but I honestly didn't care. Even after talking with Adam's parents, I felt like the world was coming to an end, and there was nothing I could do but lay in bed and hide under the covers. Which I did, until I got a call from my therapist's office.

"Hello?" I croaked.

"Dr. Will says he wants you up this morning," his receptionist said.

Rolling over, I threw the blankets off my head, but I didn't get up.

"Since when is he the boss of me?" I asked. Was it immature? Yes. Did I care? Nope.

Dr. Will's receptionist sighed, and I wondered how many times she had to deal with phone calls like this one. "Since you started paying him to tell you what's good for you," she said.

During our last therapy session, Dr. Will had told me to buy a calendar and look at it every day. Apparently, I had been letting time slip by out of my control, and I was definitely feeling the effects of that issue over the last week. More reluctantly than I'd ever done anything in my life, I pulled myself out of bed and checked my calendar. *Ugh*, I thought. My heart dropped. My muscles froze—which was a good thing, or else I would have collapsed on the floor.

Today marked the one-year anniversary of Adam's funeral.

When my muscles finally started working again, I paced back and forth around the room. Part of me felt like crawling back in bed. Part of me wanted to walk into the middle of traffic and see what happened.

I had to do something, anything, and everywhere I looked I was reminded of just how much time I had allowed myself to ignore in the last few months. I wondered why I seemed to be having a harder time today than I was even on the anniversary of his death.

Seth called me a couple of times, his calls spaced out far enough that it felt like he was trying to respect my boundaries but then got concerned. I texted him in all caps after the third call:

NOT IN THE MOOD.
PLEASE LEAVE ME ALONE.

I decided to take a shower—a huge sign of personal growth on my part, considering how smelly I had gotten after the first few months after Adam passed away.

I let the hot water run over me until I felt I would fall asleep.

Then I turned the temperature to cold and forced myself stand under the icy water, which helped.

When I got out of the shower, I got into the closet to find something to wear, and my wedding dress—still hanging on the inside of my closet door—taunted me.

I reached up and pulled the dress from the hook it had hung on for the past year. I unzipped it, stunned once again by its gorgeous design and filled with a terrible sadness that I had never gotten my chance to wear it.

I ran my fingers over the soft, silky material. I decided I was going to wear this dress. Adam's death had taken from me the only opportunity I had to wear this beautiful gown in public, but I could still wear it in my own home.

I pulled it off the hanger and put it on, struggling to zip myself into it, because it no longer fit me the way it had when I bought it. The material shuffled as I made my way back to the bathroom. I threw the towel that hung on the full-body mirror to the ground and looked myself over. My hair was wet, but I had brushed it, at least, and my blue eyes stared back at me, wide and bloodshot.

My mind raced a million miles an hour, but one thought repeated clearly over and over. *What about Seth?*

I made a call to my therapist and asked if he had any time available that I could come in today. His receptionist was in a much better mood now and said that he had left a 3:15 timeslot available for me if I needed it.

Jeesh, that dude was scary. I got dressed and headed for the bus.

By the time I got to my appointment, I realized how tired I was. Today had been emotionally draining and absolutely exhausting. Dr.

Will sat down and looked at me from across the room, but he didn't say anything, for, like, three straight minutes. I supposed this was a good thing, because when I finally opened my mouth to say something, I had a vague idea of what it was that had actually been bothering me.

"I moved on too fast. I got a calendar like you asked, so I didn't really lose days anymore, but I lost track of time in a different way. I've been spending so much time with Seth and everyone that I didn't even think about how much time had passed. Or how little time it had been before I just moved on... I guess."

I put my face in my hands. I probably confused him as much as I was puzzled myself, but he just sat there, looking at me.

Finally, he spoke.

"What did you do this week, Kalli?"

"What?" I asked, lifting my head only enough to take a look at him.

"It's likely been a very difficult week for you, and you haven't made an appointment until today. What else have you done this week?"

I sighed, suddenly feeling guilty and weird about my actions earlier in the week.

"I worked... and I... visited Adam's parents."

Dr. Will raised his eyebrows at me.

"Interesting," he said. "How did that go?"

I considered his question for a moment before responding.

"It was okay, I think. I told them about Seth. We cried a lot. They were wonderful about everything. Should I not have gone?"

He scratched his gray peppered beard, which was short and neatly trimmed. He pondered my question for a moment, then he stood up only to move to a chair that was closer to me.

"Did meeting with them help you feel any better?"

"Well, yeah, actually. I guess it did."

I sat up a little straighter in my chair.

"I think doing things like this... as long as they're healthy and help you to heal... can be a good thing. I think both parties could stand to gain some closure from an interaction like that, so long as it's positive."

I frowned and looked down and my hands. I had bitten my fingernails on the bus ride over here, and they were now short and serrated.

"Then why do I still feel this way? Why did I feel like death this morning? I felt so awful, doc, like he died yesterday. That doesn't sound like healing to me—that sounds like reverting. Only now, I've got another guy hanging around."

He shook his head slowly.

"Today was the anniversary of a day you experienced great trauma. Losing someone you love, especially in such a violent and unexpected way, is extremely traumatic. Those things you felt today are bound to recur. Just like many people experience good feelings year after year on their birthdays, if you experience something terrible, those feelings are likely to resurface time and again, especially on its anniversary.

"But Kalli, what's important now is what you do with those feelings when they do resurface. Adam's death is marked. His funeral—the day you realized that he really was gone for good—is marked. You'll have an anniversary of these painful events every year. Doing something that brings you a little bit of peace, that heals you and the others that lost him instead of falling into the darkness you were in before... well, I think that says a lot."

My eyes had filled with silent tears as I listened to what this man had to say. His words filled my broken heart with hope. I had been a mess, but I had also lost someone I was getting ready to spend the rest of my life with. Change would come; that was just life, but if I could keep making progress somehow... I just might be able to get through this. I wiped a few stray tears from my cheeks and nodded as he continued.

"You're allowed to feel sad, angry, lost. What happened to you a year ago was life changing, and I am proud of you for doing something good this week. I recommend you continue to let yourself do things that will help you heal."

Chapter 30: *A New Day*

A year and one day after Adam's funeral.

EVEN THOUGH I FELT LIKE DYING AFTER MY MEETING WITH JERRY AND Alice on that dark day, and I felt even worse when I woke up on the anniversary of Adam's funeral, when I awoke the next morning, I was filled with a strange feeling that I couldn't pin down. I had dreamt of something—I didn't remember what—but I was inspired.

I went to my studio and got painting. As I worked away at my canvas, I allowed my thoughts to wander, and my mind kept returning to trying to figure out whatever I had dreamt about.

After a while, I took a good look at how my painting was turning out. Without paying much attention, I had created a fairly detailed painting of a ladybug—not red as they usually are, but a bright, vibrant orange.

The little creature hung on the tip of a drooping blade of grass, two legs extended forward to another blade that was just out of reach.

I was satisfied with how it had turned out, and grateful that I had painted something so colorful for myself.

The image was strangely familiar, and I wondered if that was what I dreamt about the night before.

Then, like a bag of bricks, it hit me.

The air left my lungs in a painful gasp and my chest ached as if I'd been pummeled by a wrecking ball.

It was the ladybug from the hospital.

My eyes widened.

"Holy shit," I whispered. "I'm healing."

Seth came by a couple days later to drop off another handful of movies that he insisted I had to watch. Honestly, I thought he was getting tired of my minimal responses to his messages and wanted to check up on me.

He said he couldn't stay long because one of his foster siblings had an orchestra concert at her school. He set the movies down in the living room as I convinced him to stay long enough for a cup of coffee. When we walked into the kitchen, Seth eyed the ladybug painting that hung on the bottom half of the kitchen island.

"Um, that's new," he said, gesturing to it without taking his hands out of his pockets.

"Oh, yeah. I finished it a couple of days ago," I said.

I reached into the cupboard to pull out two cups and got a pot of coffee brewing.

"Nice location. Not enough wall space?" he asked, looking around the apartment.

"Nah, that's not it," I said. "That painting deserved a special spot."

"Gotcha. Well, the kitchen island is a very underrated place to hang art," he said, and I smiled, proud of myself for the connection I had made.

We stood there in silence for a moment as we stared at this new painting, and I let every emotion wash over me. The pain of losing Adam. The darkness I fell into. The support and love and friendship I had experienced, and the bond I had forged with Seth.

"Hey, I'm sorry for losing my shit with you this last week," I said, rubbing the back of my neck. "I didn't mean it when I said I wanted you to leave me alone. I just I needed some space to process things. There's... there's been a lot on my mind, and everything this year has been so much to navigate through..."

Seth reached out and took my hand.

"Hey, it's all good. I'm super sorry I called you crazy. You're not crazy, you're just different. And I happen to love that about you."

On Thursday that week, Seth called me just as I was getting ready for bed. Even from his greeting, I could tell that he was struggling to contain his excitement. I didn't think I had ever heard him so energetic before.

"Hey," he said before I could even properly greet him. "Listen. This is super important. We need to go on a date tomorrow. I have something that I've been wanting to do for a while, and I want you to be there with me. I was thinking that afterward we could celebrate by taking you to go meet my mom, and whatever new siblings I have at the moment. We could stay at her place for a few days. What do you think?"

He and I had spent several nights together by now, so it wasn't a new idea for me. Still, hearing his request for me to stay with him was a little surprising.

"Well, sure, I guess," I replied. "That sounds like fun."

Seth refused to share with me what he planned to do, adamant that he wanted it to be a total surprise, so I wasn't sure what to wear. I ended up going with some cute stretchy jeans, a peach-colored tank top and my soft, light gray hoodie.

I stayed up late to complete all the work I had planned to do the next day, and I reached out to my boss to let him know I would not be coming in to the office.

It had been about a week since my last dark day, and the heat from the summer has started to fade. On Friday morning, a bubble of excitement fluttered through my chest as Seth pulled up in that gorgeous classic car of his.

I let myself into the car, and like always, he frowned at me.

"Why do you insist that I can't be a gentleman?"

"I can open the door for myself, thank you very much," I said, grinning at him. "I've been doing it my entire life. Now, are you going to tell me where you're taking me, or are you still keeping it a secret? It's not nice to keep secrets, you know."

"Fair point. I'm taking you to the hospital," he said, and his entire face lit up with joy.

"Um... okay, are you serious? Listen... I know we've been seeing each other for a while, but if you wanted to get rid of me, all you had to do was make a phone call. A surprise visit to the hospital really isn't necessary." When Seth didn't respond to my joke, worry twisted in my gut. "Wait, is everything okay? Is your mom okay?"

Seth smiled and shook his head.

"Everything and everyone is fine," he said and left it at that.

I leaned back in my seat, relieved to hear that at least everyone was okay. I stared at the blurs of green and brown that passed us by as we drove the back roads to the hospital, all the while trying to guess why Seth would want to visit the hospital of all places for a date. It was a little bit of a longer route to get there from the back roads, but it actually ended up being much faster after bypassing all the late morning traffic.

When we pulled into the parking lot, Seth's smile stretched across his face and his eyes beamed.

"Okay, you're, like, freakishly happy right now," I said, stifling a confused giggle. "What are we doing here?"

"Remember when I said I recently went through a major surgery?"

He reached over and wrapped his hand in mine as I recalled him briefly mentioning it in a text message a while back. A cool breeze fluttered through the open windows, filling the space between us. I was definitely glad I had decided to wear something warm and comfy. This was bound to be the most unromantic date I'd ever been on.

"Yes..." I said.

"Well, apparently you have to wait an entire year before you can donate blood or any bodily fluid. It's been about a year for me, and I'm finally allowed to contribute. Help save someone else for a change."

"Did you donate blood often?" I asked. He seemed so enthusiastic about this that I was certain it had to be something he enjoyed doing, though I had no idea why. "Before the surgery, I mean."

"No, not before," he said. "But I'll tell you what, Kalli. That experience changed my life. I want to contribute. I want to be better."

"Well, then, can't argue with that. Let's go get your blood drawn."

We walked through the winding, brightly lit, over sterilized hospital hallways to find the correct information desk. When we did, Seth leaned over the counter and talked to the woman behind it.

Meanwhile, I decided to sit down in the nearest waiting room chair. I tapped the chair's skinny armrests with my fingers, but it wasn't long before I grew restless.

"You know what?" I said, jumping out of my seat, approaching the woman behind the desk. "I'm going to donate. Sign me up too, please."

The look that Seth gave me in that moment, the way his eyes watered and his smile reached up into the rest of his facial features, my stomach warmed, and I knew I made the right choice speaking up.

"You afraid of needles, Kalli?" he asked, a glimmer of humor playing in his eyes, crooked smile lingering on his face.

I tiptoed, leaning into the countertop for balance as I placed a quick kiss on his cheek.

"Hell, no."

"Let's do this then."

And we did. The whole experience was kind of surreal. I had donated blood before, but never on a date with someone. Truly, the only other person I had donated blood with was Lici for a blood drive in high school.

Seth's words echoed in my mind and I couldn't help but smile at his excitement. This was important to him, and I was grateful to be invited to join him.

When we were finished, the lady wrapped our needle-pricks with yellow medical tape, and we picked up a cookie from the front desk on our way out.

Chapter 31: *Close to Home*

A year and two weeks after Adam's passing.

FOR THE ENTIRE DRIVE TO SETH'S MOM'S HOUSE, I TRIED TO IMAGINE what it looked like.

He had told me that they came from humble beginnings, but I kept imagining something bigger and nicer than what I'd grown up in. However, it turned out to be a pretty average house after all. The house was yellow painted brick, and as we pulled into the driveway behind a silver minivan, I couldn't help but stare.

We fished our suitcases out of the car as a super short woman with red-brown hair, freckles across her entire face, and smile lines for days came running out.

"Sethy!" she called, small arms waving through the air. She wore a little yellow apron over a faded maroon blouse. Her hair was pulled back into a messy bun, she had baking flour on her pants. She looked like, well, a mom.

"Hey, ma," Seth said warmly, and with one arm, he picked the small woman up into a hug and spun her around before setting her back down. I couldn't help grinning at the scene before me.

This is where Seth came from. It was warm and beautiful. My family was great, and we were all super close, but looking at this woman here, knowing that for a while, it was just the two of them, I knew there was something special there. I felt so lucky to be able to finally witness it.

When Seth's mom found her balance again, she turned to me. She looked me over.

"So, this is the infamous Kalli Morgan." She frowned for a moment, and then her face broke into a grin so similar to Seth's it was spooky.

"Hello Sonjia. It's nice to finally meet you," I said, reaching out a hand for her to shake.

With the way she greeted Seth, I'd expected her to come in for a hug, but she didn't. She did, however, take my hand and pull me in close enough to whisper in my ear.

"You're stunning," she said. "Your photos do not do you justice."

Shocked, I stumbled backward.

"Wow, uh, thank you." My face grew hot, and I tried to hide it by brushing my bangs back. "I've heard such incredible things about you."

"Seth, honey, the kids are in the back. Can you go make sure they're actually taking down the pool and not just swimming in it? I've been telling them all day and they just won't listen to me."

"Sure thing," he said. He kissed my cheek and jogged off behind the house. Sonjia rolled her eyes.

"You let them have a kitty pool for one month in the summer and they're so sad to see it go they just won't put it away. "

I laughed.

"Well, you know those experiences are super hard to come by. I never had a pool growing up," I said.

She raised her thin eyebrows at me. "No?"

"Nope. My mom was too worried that my brother and I would drown in it."

"Smart woman," she said.

Sonjia led me into the house, where she put on a kettle for tea. She walked me though the house, giving me the tour and showing off the three extensions she had added to the house in the years after her husband left. I had laughed when Seth originally told me his dad left to find someone more on his level, but now I could see that he was absolutely serious.

I was struggling to find anyone at this incredible woman's level, and I just met her.

"After the last group of kids left, I decided to turn this back portion here into a sunroom. I've always wanted a sunroom!"

I could tell that this had been a bedroom with large windows before. This was the westernmost part of the house and the newest addition, and its large windows that overlooked the backyard made the space perfect for a sunroom.

Outside, Seth wrestled with two little kids, a boy with dark skin and dark hair, and a little tan girl with huge brown eyes and long brown hair. They splashed water all over the place defending their pool from him, and finally, he scooped both of them up, set them on the lawn just outside the pool, and flipped it over, throwing his hands in the air and shouting his triumph.

I hadn't noticed, but I'd been grinning the whole time I watched him with those kids. I only realized it when I looked over and saw that Sonjia hadn't been watching Seth as I had: she'd been watching me. I covered my mouth and realized for the second time since arriving here that my face was red.

Seth had the kids come inside and he introduced us before the three of them went to find a change of clothes.

For dinner, Seth and I helped Sonjia make "stuffed pasta," which required us to stuff the giant shell noodles with several miscellaneous vegetables and cheeses. By the time we had all the ingredients arranged in the pan ready to be baked, I was a little leery.

As dinner baked, we followed Sonjia to the living room, where she told me she had made a habit of reading or telling stories while dinner cooked when Seth was little. This, she said, kept the kids distracted long enough for dinner to cook without asking her endlessly when it would be ready.

"Wow," I marveled. "That's kind of genius."

She winked.

"Works every time, even now." She spared a look at Seth, who was already sitting on the floor with a fluffy rainbow pillow in his lap. He patted the floor next to him and looked up at me expectantly. I wanted so badly to capture the memory that I actually pulled out my cell phone and snapped a picture of Seth and his two little siblings, who leaned on each other to get into the shot.

The warm light that flooded in through the windows on the west side of the house filled the living room with a homey sensation. I stuffed my phone back into my pocket and got down on the floor with them, listening as Sonjia spun one of her tales.

Soon after dinner was ready, we all gathered around the table, which was made of well-worn wood and had several different shades in different areas and had about eight mismatched chairs tucked in around it.

The pasta concoction turned out to be delicious. I had three large stuffed noodles placed on my plate with a big helping of canned pears on the side.

We talked about all kinds of things, starting with baseball—which apparently Sonjia was a huge fan of—but Seth quickly changed the subject. We caught Sonjia up on the progress of Seth's most recent project, and I told her how cool I thought it was that the game he was making would be compatible across all consoles. Although I was never much of a video game player, I was catching on quickly.

"You know, I've seen bits and pieces of what he's designed so far, and it looks really good," I said, beaming with pride. "I've seen other games that have really low-quality graphics where it looks like the characters are just stop motion animated barbies doing menial tasks. His is so realistic, and it has a super lifelike movement. From an artistic standpoint, it's pretty incredible. I was certainly impressed," I said before stuffing another big bite of pasta into my mouth.

Seth turned to me, smiling that smile. My insides fluttered, and I looked quickly back to my food.

"Woah, now, is that a compliment? From a real artist?" he asked.

I swallowed and nodded at him. "It most certainly is."

Seth pretended to dab a tear from his eye and the kids laughed. Now, he turned to them.

"Did you hear that, guys? If Kalli's approved it, that means it really might be worth playing! Maybe Mom will let you guys play it."

The kids, who I had quickly learned were named Zach and Isabel, lit up as they begged their mom to let them play when it comes out.

"Oh, see what you've done? Fine, you can play it. When you're eighteen. You two don't need any more horror in your lives until you're grown up and I can no longer control your environments."

When their little shoulders slumped, Seth piped back up. "Don't worry, you two. You won't be missing much. You deserve the best quality games, anyway."

Sonjia rolled her eyes and pointed her fork at him from across the table. "Oh, you stop that. You know your game is going to get tons of attention when it's finished. I'd be surprised if they don't line up around the block to drop awards in your lap." We all laughed.

"Thanks, Mom," he said softly.

She nodded, satisfied, and went back to eating. Between bites, she addressed me.

"So, tell me more about what you do. Seth told me that you work in a marketing department. What do you do there, and how did you wind up with a job like that? I've got to tell you, with what he told me about your work, I thought you'd be much different."

"Oh?" I said, taking a sip from my water. "What did you expect?"

She shrugged. I could see where Seth got his loose shoulders.

"To put it bluntly, I thought you'd have a stick up your ass. Pardon my language, kids. You should never say 'ass.' You've been very cool and down to Earth, and I'm happy you could join us today."

The water I tried to swallow almost came back up through my nose at her use of the word 'ass'.

"Thanks, Sonjia. I'm grateful to be invited. Well, I went to school for art. I guess I discovered my love for it in high school, when my mom and I painted a giant mural on my bedroom wall. After that, I couldn't leave it be.

"When I graduated college, I submitted my portfolio to pretty much everybody: magazines, small businesses, publishing companies, and one small company that had just started up. They advertised that they helped all kinds of businesses gain traction in their marketing.

"They got back to me within a week and asked if I had any receptionist skills. They already had a few artists on call for their marketing, but they said they had a position available for someone to manage the phones. After a couple of months, they started giving me little marketing jobs here and there. I think they were sizing me up. Soon enough, I had my own office. It's a great job, but I work there because my boss is amazing, and I get to do art all day. I don't manage numbers, I don't trade off companies, I just get paid to do art."

"Cool!" said Zach.

"I want to be an artist!" Isabel cried out.

Sonjia smiled, clearly having changed her mind about the whole stick up the butt thing.

"Right?" Seth said. "Being a marketing artist sounds pretty great, doesn't it?"

Sonjia nodded and opened her mouth as if she was going to say something, but she was interrupted by Isabel and Zach, who took turns asking me if I could draw things for them. My ego was a rocket headed straight for the moon.

When the kids settled down, Sonjia cleared away their plates. I picked up mine to take it to the kitchen, but Seth intercepted, stealing it from me before I could scoot my chair back. Before leaving the dining room, Sonjia smiled at me, and I couldn't help being thinking about how similar she was to my own mom.

"I heard you recently had a birthday," she said.

"Yes, ma'am. About a month ago."

"Good. Birthdays are a big deal around here. I'll be right back." She passed Seth the pile of plates, and they headed into the kitchen. While they were gone, I had a funny face contest with Zach and Isabel, who was particularly good at crossing her eyes.

Soon, Seth and his mom returned to the dining room with a beautiful homemade German chocolate cake with extra coconut sprinkled on top.

"Oh my god," I said, covering my mouth with both hands. "You did not have to do this! My birthday was forever ago!"

"As far as I'm concerned," Sonjia said, placing the cake down carefully on the table. "Your birthday is now."

They sang me happy birthday, and as we started eating it, Seth caught his mom looking at him with such adoration I thought he would melt.

"What?" he asked, licking some icing from the side of his hand.

"I'm so happy you're here," she said, her eyes filling with tears. He smiled at her before turning his attention back to me.

"Birthdays are a big deal in this family," he said.

"You don't say," I joked.

Sonjia perked up. "We never miss one, even if we're a little late. You never know when a birthday will be your last." She looked at Seth, who suddenly focused intently on getting himself a second helping of dessert. "I don't know if he told you or not, but it's kind of a birthday for Seth, too."

I frowned. "It is? Seth, I thought you told me your birthday was in February.

"It is," he said, passing a plate with a second piece of cake to Zach.

"Seth used to have serious heart problems," Sonjia said. "We almost lost him. No matter what we tried, he kept getting sicker and weaker. He was on wait list for a transplant for years."

Sonjia sniffled and wiped her sleeve across her face. Again, the look of pure love pierced the space between mother and son.

"I'm so glad you had that transplant last year, honey. It saved you, and it saved me, too." She turned her attention back to me again. "If he hadn't, I don't think he would have met you. He's had girlfriends in the past, but none have ever made him as happy as you have."

Her words were so kind and sweet, but I barely heard them.

"Wait... A transplant?" I asked. "A year ago?"

I couldn't quite explain why, but my stomach twisted into a knot that dropped like solid matter to the bottom of my torso. My heart stopped beating and I paused, mid-chew, to stare blankly at the family in front of me.

"Yeah," Sonjia said, matter-of-factly. "A year and... two weeks ago, wasn't it honey?" She looked at Seth.

"Yep." He smiled too. Grateful to be alive, probably. God damn. I gripped the bottom of my hoodie beneath the table to steady the shaking in my hands, suddenly feeling too warm.

A year and two weeks ago.

No. Fucking. Way.

Even if this all of this was a coincidence, it sure dredged up a lot of complicated emotions for me.

I backed out of my chair, scooting it too loudly against the blue and white linoleum floor. The chair almost tipped over, but I caught it at the last second. I wiped my mouth with my napkin before setting the cloth on the table. My head was spinning like I'd just downed half a bottle of wine.

"Um... I have to go," I said.

I pulled at my hoodie, trying to get some air.

I couldn't look at Seth. I spared a quick half glance at Sonjia as I backed away from the table. I made a half-hearted effort to scoot my chair back in before retreating toward the door.

"Sonjia, thank you for having me. It was... really great. Um... yeah. I love your house. Seth... I'll call you."

I could hear Sonjia say something, totally shocked by my crazy actions, and I couldn't blame her.

My mind thrummed. Sweat beaded on my forehead.

The edges of my vision blurred, and I thought I might faint, but instead I began to cry. Hot, salty tears trailed down my cheeks, one after the other, dripping off of my chin, splattering like tiny bombs on my chest and the ground as I made my way to the front door. I heard someone get up from the table, heard Seth's voice say something to his mother, and then heard heavy footsteps tracing the path behind me.

I closed the door behind me without looking back, not caring that I probably slammed it right in his face, not caring that I had probably offended everyone in there, and I may never be allowed back in Sonjia's home again. All I cared about was relieving this tightness in my chest.

This anxiety felt as if it would suffocate me. This feeling nagged at me and told me that the donor of Seth's transplant had been Adam.

Had Adam died so Seth could live?

I had to know. I stopped at the curb, looking up and down the decrepit street hopelessly. I knew I needed to get away from that house, go to the hospital, access Adam's medical records, but first I had one major problem to solve. I came here with Seth. I was in the middle of nowhere, with not a single bus stop in sight. How was I supposed to leave?

Just then, Seth's footsteps jogged up behind me. He walked around me so fast that I didn't have time to turn away from him without seeing that he held a dishtowel covered in blood to his nose. I supposed I really had hit him with the door, after all.

"What the fuck?" Seth demanded, totally exasperated and out of breath with the towel against his face. "I don't mean to be rude, but seriously. What the fuck?"

Anger bubbled up inside me like mints in a soda bottle. For a reason I couldn't explain, I balled up a fist and hit him in the stomach. He bent over, but I hadn't hit him hard enough to do any damage.

"Ow! Have you lost your damn mind?" he shouted.

Probably.

"Why didn't you tell me about this?" I asked.

"About what?" He looked plain silly now, with one hand holding the dishtowel to his face and the other holding his stomach where I hit him. My hand wasn't even hurting yet. I flexed my fingers and realized that my hand actually hurt like hell. Oops.

I scoffed and shook out my hand.

"About the transplant!"

Seth raised his eyebrows. Confused, he lowered his voice. "I told you I had a major surgery. I told you that more than once!"

"Yeah, a major surgery. That could be fixing a broken bone. Could be a tumor removal. Could be an appendectomy. It could have been any number of things other than a God damned *organ transplant!*" I was vaguely aware that we were shouting at each other at the top of our voices in the middle of the street, and I lowered my voice. "You never told me it was a transplant."

I couldn't tell for sure, but from behind the towel, he looked genuinely concerned. "Why are you so worked up about this?" he asked much more gently.

I fell quiet for a moment. I found myself rubbing my arms despite the pain that now throbbed in my hand. Now that I was outside, my body had cooled off. I definitely couldn't tell him about my suspicions until I found out if they were correct or not. "I... I need to be alone for a while. I just need to be alone."

"This again, huh?" Seth nodded and turned away. I knew he was probably so tired of me, and I couldn't blame him. I'd been a damn mess this year. I turned toward the street, and then remembered once more the predicament I was in.

"Wait, Seth?" I asked, loathing myself, feeling like I'd hit an all new low. Seth turned back around again, as I asked, "Uh... could you give me a ride?"

Chapter 32: *Matters of the Heart*

A year and two weeks after Adam's passing.

But Seth didn't take me home.

Home wasn't really where I wanted to go.

While Seth was inside apologizing and smoothing things over with his mom and siblings, I called the hospital to ask if there was any way I could get access to the files that stated which of Adam's organs went to whom.

All the people I spoke to were adamant that those files were kept highly classified under normal circumstances, and since Adam and I were not technically family, those files were off limits to me.

I knew I was probably overreacting. I knew the chances of me falling for someone who had received Adam's heart were slim to none, but the knot in my gut told me there was something more to this, and I couldn't rest until I knew for sure. I could tell the woman on the phone was doing her best to be friendly with me, but she sounded perturbed, like she answered this same exact question a thousand times a day.

They could not grant me access to any of that information, even if I begged. Those files were kept classified for the safety of the donor's family and for the safety of the recipients, that even if I *was* married to Adam when he passed away, the information they would have been able to share would still be limited.

I knew I couldn't just give it up. I had to find out one way or another. So, instead of taking me home like I had originally asked him to, Seth drove me to see Adam's parents. They were both home; both cars were parked in the driveway.

Although I had only spoken to them once in the year since the funeral, they had made it clear I was always welcome, even after I had told them I was seeing Seth.

I sincerely hoped they still felt that way now.

When I turned to thank Seth for the ride, he frowned at me: an expression that was equal parts confusion and concern.

"Kalli, please. Tell me what's going on. You're freaking me out. Look, I'm sorry I wasn't more specific when I told you about my surgery..."

I put a hand up to stop him from finishing his apology. As shaken as I felt, I needed to at least let him know it wasn't his fault I was acting crazy... again.

"Stop. Seth, I promise I will explain everything to you when I can. I just... can't right now. Okay? Not until I have more information." He looked at me like I was an apple being offered up by an evil queen. I raised my eyebrows at him. "I mean it."

"All right," he relented with a heavy sigh. He rubbed the stubble on his chin with one hand while the other clutched the steering wheel. "Okay. Do what you have to, I guess. Call me when you can."

I threw a hand up in a quick wave as he drove away down the street. When I could no longer see his car anymore, I drew in a deep breath and tried to get myself to calm down. Whatever happened after I knocked on those doors, after I entered that home, would be okay. It had to be.

No matter what, Adam wasn't coming back, though I feared deep down that digging up the evidence I needed would resurrect him. If that happened, I would be stuck with absolutely no idea what to feel or how to explain myself. Shit. This was going to be a disaster.

I straightened my back and tried not to hang my head as I approached the door. I focused on the little welcoming wreath, with its small wooden sticks, fake leaves, and little bluebirds beneath a hand-painted sign that said, "Welcome to Our Nest." I raised a closed fist and knocked, instantly regretting the action because pain shot through my knuckles and up my arm. I winced and tried knocking with the other hand.

Before long I heard talking, and then Alice's voice said, "No honey, I've got it."

Then the knob turned as she opened the door. When she saw it was me, she smiled her usual sweet, warm smile.

Her smile quickly faded to a look of concern as she saw my somber expression and the way I babied my hand. Without saying anything she backed away, motioning for me to come in.

"Jerry," she called. "It's Kalli. We'll be in the kitchen!"

She led me through the house that I had visited frequently with Adam over the years we were together, the home that I had always loved. We went through the living room with its big, plush brown couches. We walked through the hallway with picture after picture of Adam with his family and childhood friends. Finally, we entered into the kitchen with its grey granite countertops, red cupboards, and bright yellow walls with birdhouse wallpaper trimming the walls near the ceiling.

My heart squeezed as I thought back to the first night Adam and I had gone ice skating together, how we decided to go to a place just a few blocks from his parents' house. I remembered how we had slipped, and my skate had cut his shins. I recalled how I had driven his car over to his parents' house—poorly, because I never drove anywhere—and how Adam had used his spare key to let us in so I could patch him up. That was the first time I had visited his parents' home, and I had loved it just as much then as I did looking at it now.

My eyelids fluttered, holding back tears at the unexpected memory, and I squared my shoulders, determined to get the information I came for.

"Alice, I'm sorry for barging in without calling again, but I was wondering if you might have any information on the recipients of

Adam's organ donations. Files? Anything?" I took a seat at the table, never moving my gaze from her face.

She looked a little shocked, and she frowned.

"Well, they gave us very little information, and anything we did get was vague and came through the hospital, just in case someone from our family disagreed with Adam's decisions to donate and wanted to take action. I do have a few letters from the families of some of the recipients, though. Let's see... where did I put those letters?"

Absently, Alice paced the kitchen trying to remember the location of those letters. She reached into the fridge and pulled out some mango pineapple juice and poured me a glass. The cup gave off a soft clink as she placed it on the table in front of me. Just then, Adam's dad came walking in with his reading glasses in one hand and a novel in another. He looked up and smiled at me. Then, when his eyes met his wife's, he grew concerned also.

"Something wrong?" he asked.

"Honey, do you remember where we put those letters from the people who got Adam's donations? I can't seem to recall where we put them." She chewed the inside of her cheek, and he continued to frown.

"I'm sorry to be a bother," I told him. "But it's important. I wouldn't have come by without calling ahead if it wasn't. I already did that recently..." I silently prayed I wasn't putting them out by being here again so soon.

"Nonsense," he said as he stuffed the paperback novel in his armpit and snapped his fingers. "You know what? I think we put them in the chest in his bedroom."

Alice's face lit up as she remembered as well.

"That's right. Kalli, you stay here and drink your juice," she said, as though I was her kid.

"Sure thing," I replied. The thought of going back into Adam's bedroom filled me with sorrow. I'd rather not be so surrounded by him right now.

Alice left and Jerry followed to see if his memory had served him correctly. I sat there at the table, listening to the clock ticking quietly on the wall above the sink. I stared blankly at the kitchen.

I always loved it, and I even told Adam that when we bought our own house, this is what I wanted our kitchen to look like.

It was strange, being there in his childhood kitchen, knowing that he would never again walk into this room, never again step foot into this house. I wondered how many times a day his parents had to brush away thoughts like that and wondered why they still stayed there after everything that had happened. I didn't know if I could handle living in the same house I raised a child in if that child was no longer living. I shuddered. I couldn't imagine what it would have been like to go through what they had.

Within minutes the couple returned to the room. Jerry was still holding his book, but his reading glasses now rested atop of his balding head. Alice carried a thin stack of letters. *This is it*, I thought. My heart skipped a beat.

"Here you are," she said, passing the stack to me.

My blue eyes stared unblinking at the pile of envelopes before me.

One by one, I sorted through the letters. One by one, I began piecing together where these little parts of Adam had been sent off to. I flipped through most of the letters, only scanning them for pertinent information. Every one of them was so sincere, thanking Adam's family for his gift to them.

As I looked through these letters, I was filled with an urge to find out who else had gotten a part of Adam, but right now, those people had to wait. Right now, I was on a mission, and tension built up inside of me with every passing second. Tears flowed silently down my cheeks, but I was so focused on learning the truth I didn't even bother brushing them away. I let them fall down my face and into my lap.

Liver, kidneys, pancreas, lungs, so on and so forth. Finally, as if by cosmic design, at the very bottom of the stack, I found a letter from the recipient of Adam's heart.

My eyes scanned the page, and there in bold, black, slightly sloppy handwriting, was my answer.

Dear family,

I am so sorry for the loss of your child. I can't even begin to imagine the suffering you must be going through, and I think about you every day.

I wanted to thank you so much for the wonderous gift your child has given mine. My Sethy is thirty-one years old, and your child saved his life. He has struggled with his heart condition for his entire life, and thanks to your son's donation, he's healthy again for the first time in a long time.

Thank you. A million times, thank you.

Sonjia

Sethy? Holy crap.

Was this for real? I rubbed my eyes, looked again. Sethy. Thirty-one years old, heart condition. Signed Sonjia. It was him—it had to be. My hands fell to my lap, still clutching the paper. I noticed the worried looks on Adam's parents' faces, but for a moment, I couldn't bring myself to tell them what I'd just discovered. No way. No. Fucking. Way. My hunch had been right...

"Kalli, what is it?" Alice asked me finally, when the silence had become too much for her to bear. I held out the paper with a shaky hand. They searched the page, then both sets of eyes trained on me again, this time full of confusion.

"That... Seth..." I tried to tell them, but my breath kept catching in my lungs and I feared it would soon turn to heaving sobs. I cleared my throat, blinked away the tears that clouded my vision, and tried again. "Seth has Adam's heart."

They were silent for a full minute. I heard each and every second tick by on the clock on the wall.

"Wait a minute. Your Seth? The gentleman you're dating now?" Adam's dad asked with a softness in his voice that made me want to curl into myself and jump up to hug him at the same time. The interests conflicted with one another, so I sat still with my hands in my lap. Adam's mom rubbed her face with both hands. She rubbed her eyes, her cheeks, her neck. I nodded.

"That's him. Sethy is what his mom calls him. That's his mom's name on the bottom of the page. How does this even happen?"

Again, the room fell silent as we processed the information.

It seemed like there was nothing any of us could say, and although I was struggling to make sense of any of my thoughts, I told Adam's parents that I needed to go home and think about things.

Adam's dad offered to give me a ride home and I accepted, though the ride took an eternity with each of us lost in our own thoughts.

When I got home, I thanked Jerry for the ride and walked numbly up the stairs to my front door. I went straight to my room and crawled into bed, pulling the covers over my face. I folded my arms and was jolted by surprise at the pain in the crook of my right elbow. I forgot it was the same day that Seth and I had gotten our blood drawn.

I ran through every detail of the day over and over again until I finally drifted off to sleep.

Chapter 33: *A Sign*

Still a year and two weeks after Adam's passing.

I WOKE UP IN THE SAME CLOTHES I WORE YESTERDAY.

I was beyond groggy. My mind felt like mud, my eyelids felt like sandpaper, and the pounding in my head was an obnoxious reminder that I had fallen asleep crying. A moment later, I was reminded of the reason I'd been crying, and a newfound sense of dread filled me.

What was I supposed to do now? What *could* I do?

It wasn't fair for me to treat Seth any differently now, and we had only just gotten to the point where I felt semi-comfortable in my feelings for him. Now there was this obstacle in our way, which felt insurmountable. But was it really even an obstacle? I had loved Adam first. I suddenly felt sick to my stomach, and I swallowed back a wave of nausea.

A thousand thoughts flooded my mind. I picked up my phone, first to call the girls, which I quickly decided against. Then I thought I'd call my mom, then Seth, and finally, I wanted to call Adam's mom.

But with each person, my fingers froze and wouldn't dial. I stared at my phone, contacts list up, screen starting to dim from not being used.

Finally, I decided I was actually going to call my mom. Of all the people I knew, she had experienced the most complicated love affairs. I found her name in my list and called.

"Hey cutie poo! What are you up to?" she chirped cheerfully when she answered.

"Um, Mom? I have something I want to talk to you about. Can you... Is there somewhere we can go to talk without anyone else overhearing?"

"Of course, honey," she said, voice now anxious. "What's wrong?"

"I don't want to say on the phone. I need to talk to you in person."

Mom pulled up to my apartment half an hour later in her deadly minivan. At this point I had chewed all of my nails short, and I now picked at the stubs that were left. I had been waiting on the curb in front of the building since we hung up the phone, and as she drove up, I pulled my hoodie closer around my body and raced against the wind toward the van. Mom leaned over without unbuckling her seatbelt and opened the passenger side door for me.

"Hey Kalli," she said, her mouth a tight line. Her hair was starting to grow out again, and it was died blue on the bottom, green over that, and hot pink just outside the roots. It was cut into a lopsided bob with one side two or three inches longer in the front than the other and the back spiked out.

"Hey mom," I said nervously. "I like your new hairstyle."

She pretended to fluff out the back. "Oh, this? Thanks baby. Where to?"

I looked straight ahead out the windshield, doing my best to ignore the knot in my stomach. Tears welled up in my eyes.

"Remember that place with the waterfalls that we used to go when I was a kid? The one Dad proposed to you at?"

I wasn't sure if she was remembering the proposal or the times we went there when I was little, but whatever she was thinking about brought a smile to her face and made her eyes twinkle.

"Of course, I remember."

"Can we go there?" I asked, raising my eyebrows.

I knew in this time of year that there probably wouldn't be many hikers, so it would be the perfect place to get all this confusion I felt out in private. I also knew that the leaves would just be starting to change up there, and that the scent of the woods that surrounded the little clearing would be calming for me. I got excited at the thought of being up there again.

"Right away, ma'am," she said, making a little gesture by her forehead as though she was tipping an invisible chauffer cap. At that, she flipped a U-ey right in the middle of the parking lot and headed toward the woods.

She tried to keep the conversation going, making small talk and trying to bring up what it was I wanted to talk to her about without outright asking. I looked out the window and answered her little questions with mumbles and head nods.

Before long, we were outside the city limits, and fields passed by the van in green and golden blurs.

We ascended up the winding mountain roads, and finally, mom turned off into a small parking area. We'd been driving for nearly an hour, and it felt good to get out of the deathtrap that my mom refused to get rid of.

The moment Mom shut off the engine, the sounds of the woods came to life: birds chirped and twittered, a soft breeze shuffled the leaves on the trees, which were just starting to turn. Even louder than these sounds, though, was that of the river rushing by, and the waterfall splashing against the rocks below. Mom got out of the car and slammed the door on the driver's side so it would stay shut.

We hiked up a small dirt path until we reached the clearing right beside the waterfall. It was every bit as beautiful as I remembered. Moss covered a large, flat rock that I claimed as my throne when I was little. Beneath that rock sat long, yellowing grass that waved with even the lightest of breezes. The waterfall was now almost deafening, but it was a comforting sound that I hadn't heard in far too long.

I made my way to my rock and sat on the part closest to the water. Just like old times, I ran my fingers along the never-quite-dry moss, still loving its squishy, bumpy texture beneath my hands. Mom sat down next to me, expectant but patient.

I sighed.

"I'm not quite sure how to even *start* telling you about this..." I said, dropping my hands in my lap.

Mom shrugged.

"Best way to get uncomfortable information out is to just spill it. No sense in beating around the bush trying to find the right words. But that's just my opinion," she said, taking my hand so I would look at her. She gave me an encouraging smile.

Well, I thought. *Here goes nothing.*

Without giving myself another second to rationalize myself out of asking for my mom's advice, I spat out the issue I'd been thinking about for the last fifteen hours or so.

"Seth has Adam's heart."

I swallowed past the lump in my throat. *Holy hell. Will that ever be easier to say?* She frowned as if she wasn't sure if she heard me correctly. I nodded.

"Do you mean, like, metaphorically, or..."

"Definitely one hundred percent literally."

"Oh, wow. Wow. But wait, I thought Adam wasn't a donor. Isn't that something that the two of you fought about?"

"He wasn't, until about a month before he died. Then he up and changed it right before we started planning our wedding. Said he finally came to terms with the fact that I was right: refusing to donate was stingy and a waste of perfectly good body parts." I chuckled softly at the memory. Tears stung my eyes, but they didn't fall. "Apparently... his heart... went to Seth when he died."

"My God. What are the chances?" she asked in the way people do when they really aren't asking because they know how slim the chances are. She squeezed my hand.

"I know. I found out yesterday and I still can't believe it."

I stood up, full of so much energy all of a sudden that I couldn't sit still anymore. Mom's hand dropped into her lap as I began to pace. With the pacing came the ranting.

"I didn't even *want* to move on after Adam, damn it. You know that. And then I met Seth and I opened myself up again, and I *really* care about him. Mom, I think I love him. Is that shitty? I mean, I definitely didn't *mean* to fall for him, and now I just feel so weird knowing that it's the same goddamn heart I fell for in the first place. What do I even do?"

Mom was silent for a long time while she processed the impossible information. She chewed her lip as she thought, and finally, after what felt like a thousand years, she finally smiled.

"I think it's poetic."

"I'm sorry, what?"

Mom stood up and approached me, placing her warm hands on my elbows, turning me to face her.

"Think about it, Kalli. You know Adam wanted you to be happy. Who better to move on and be happy with than the man who literally received his heart? It's perfect. I don't mean to get all hippie on you, hon, but I think it's a sign."

I just stood there staring at her for a long time.

We spent much of the remaining daylight hours up by the waterfall, talking everything through as I processed and reprocessed everything. I was so grateful I called her. I really needed my mamma for this.

Chapter 34: *Life Saver*

Still a year and two weeks after Adam's passing.

MY MOM THOUGHT MY BOYFRIEND HAVING MY DEAD FIANCÉ'S HEART was a sign. Now, I had to figure out what that sign was.

I thought about the argument my mom and I had when she first suggested I try to move on after Adam's death. I thought back even further about the fight I got into with Adam when he brought up my finding happiness with someone else if he passed away before me. I recalled how angry I had been, how I had told myself there was no way I could ever fall for another heart but his.

As it turned out, I had fallen for his heart all over again.

By the time I got home after spending the rest of the day with my mom, I did feel some small sense of clarity. I felt good enough about the conversation she and I had that, even though I still had absolutely no clue what any of this meant, I was able to muster up the bravery needed to text Seth and ask him to meet with me. Seth responded quickly, and he agreed to meet with me, but his text showed how frustrated he felt with me. I really couldn't blame him. I had been all over the place since we met.

Not wanting to be picked up again, I decided to take the bus and meet him at the park we walked through on our first date. Because taking the bus is much slower thank driving, Seth arrived at the park quite a bit earlier than I did, and I found him sitting on the grass by the playground writing on a clipboard stacked with plain white paper.

"Hey," I said, standing above him, both hands stuffed deep into my jacket pockets.

"Hey," he replied, putting his clipboard and pen into the colorful comic backpack that caught my eye an eternity ago. "So, are you ready to tell me what's been going on with you lately?" he asked. He raised his eyebrows at me and patted the ground. I sat down beside him, letting my breath out in a huff.

"Sorry about that," I muttered.

"Seriously. I mean, no offense, Kalli, I know you've had a rough year, but damn. I've never seen you like that before."

"I know... how's your nose?" I asked, remembering how I slammed the door in his face yesterday. When he gestured to a dark bruise beneath his eyes, I put my head down. I took a deep breath and held it, only letting it go when I figured out how I wanted to answer him. "I'm sorry for freaking you out, and... I'm sorry for slamming the door on you. And for my general erratic behavior over the last few weeks. I just... found out some really unsettling news."

Seth adjusted so his entire body faced me. He crossed his legs and pulled the grass with his fingers.

"Unsettling how?" he asked.

I kept my mom's wise words at the forefront of my mind, clinging to them and trying to be brave as she would be. The best way to get uncomfortable information out is to just spill it. *No sense in beating around the bush trying to find the right words.* Sitting there now, with Seth, I knew she was right. If I took the time to search for the right words, I would lose my nerve, and we would sit here forever.

"Seth, the donor you got your new heart from… did you ever find out who it was?" I asked. I knew his mom had found out, because I read her letter to Adam's parents; but I wasn't sure if Seth had known or not. I prayed that he never knew. If he did, our entire time spent together would have felt like a massive lie.

"No," he said, frowning, clearly not understanding where I was going with this just yet. "I felt guilty too guilty. I didn't want to know who it was, because that person was dead…" he trailed off, and his eyes widened to the point I thought they just might pop out. "Wait a second… did Adam…"

I nodded slowly, making a weird clicking noise with my mouth. We were quiet for a moment as the thought sunk in.

"Oh." We just sat there for a minute. I searched his face, which was twisted with some emotion I couldn't quite read. Seth plucked a few fistfuls of dying grass and discarded them into two neat piles between us. "Kalli," he said, meeting my gaze after what felt like forever. "I had no idea. I knew Adam passed around the time I had my surgery, but I never thought... the chances of that are so low I never even *imagined* it would be his."

I swallowed past a lump in my throat and nodded.

When Seth spoke again, his voice was thick with emotion.

"He saved my life, Kalli." The words were so softly spoken that I wasn't even sure if he had actually said them. When I looked at him, his eyes were glossy; and they searched mine, pleading for me to understand. When he spoke again, his voice rose barely above a whisper. "God, this is crazy. I didn't... I feel like I took him from you."

I shrugged half-heartedly.

"It's not like you killed him." I was so shocked by the conclusion he'd somehow come to in the last couple of minutes. I wrapped my arms tightly around my torso, silently begging my chest to stop aching.

He shook his head.

"I guess so, but Kalli?" He stopped pulling grass, and now he ran his fingers through the piles, lifting up the broken blades and letting them fall back to the ground. Over and over he did this, until I thought he might have forgotten what he was going to say.

"Hmm?"

Mesmerized by the action his hands were performing, I was taken totally by surprise by the words he spoke next. I honestly didn't know if I would have been able to see it coming if I had been looking directly at his face.

"I don't know what you're thinking right now, and I know this information may complicate things, but Kalli, I love you."

Suddenly my eyes couldn't blink fast enough.

I had been feeling the same thing for a while now. Hell, I even said it out loud to my mom, but hearing those words from him... I just wasn't prepared for it, especially in the middle of the conversation we were currently having.

"God, Seth. I.... I love you too."

Seth's entire body relaxed, and he let out a huge sigh of relief. Suddenly the big doubt rushed back to my mind, and I had to say something. I had come to terms with my feelings for him for the most part, and after learning about this whole heart situation, I wasn't super worried about things on my end. When he saw the frown on my face, his smile faded.

"What's the problem?"

"I just... uh, would you?"

"Would I what?" he asked.

"Would you still feel that way if it wasn't for Adam's heart? Would you feel anything for me at all?" I asked, wiping some stray tears from my face.

Seth's frown deepened. The look on his face was a mix of what looked like disgust and defense.

"Does it matter?" he asked me. "If that's how it worked out, why does it matter what would have happened if things had gone differently? I probably wouldn't have even met you if things hadn't turned out this way."

Bristled, I straightened my back.

I didn't want to admit it, but I knew he was right. We likely wouldn't have met if he wasn't the one to receive Adam's heart. I worked to figure out why it was I was so upset.

In my mind, it was simple: If Seth hadn't gotten that surgery, we never would have met, so the possibility of him asking me out, becoming involved in my life, falling for me... all about zero. I knew that. For some reason, that really pissed me off, and my face flushed with an unwarranted sense of anger.

"That's what I thought," I said, standing back up.

He scrambled up after me, leaving his backpack laying discarded on the grass.

"Okay, look. I get it. That's not the answer you wanted. Do you want me to say that no matter what I would have found you? That I would have loved you? I could, but you and I both know that would be a lie."

I glared at him. Everything he was saying made sense to me. I understood it, and still I was furious. Why did he have to ruin this good thing with his honesty. If he had just told me what I wanted to hear, we could be going home happy together right now.

"I just wish... I wish it was meant to be," I mumbled, hating how naïve I sounded. My shoulders slumped. After Adam died, I was hopeless, lost, disconnected from the human race as a whole. Seth brought me back to life, and I guess he kind of brought Adam back, too. He gave me hope and reminded me what it was like to live. "This has to mean something, doesn't it?" I asked, gesturing loosely to the both of us. If not, was I even allowed to feel this way about him? I heard the pleading in my voice, and I tried to ignore it, hoping it didn't sound as completely desperate to him as it sounded to me. I blinked the tears from my eyes.

I expected him to shrug; I'd gotten used to that response from him. Instead, he stood perfectly still, unfazed by the wind that began to blow furiously around us. He just... looked at me, and as he did, I almost wondered if this had all just been a bad dream that I would soon wake from.

Suddenly, a look so absolutely passionate—a mix of anger, joy, sadness, and desperation all rolled into one—crossed his face. With a level voice that so did not match his expression, he spoke.

"Can you honestly say it doesn't? Kalli, everything that's happened has brought us here, together. If Adam hadn't... If I hadn't gotten his heart, I would have died. I was so close this time. And even if I hadn't, if someone else had miraculously come along and given me their heart... even if all of it played out that way, and my car had still broken down, and we still ended up meeting on that bus, you would have been married to Adam, and you wouldn't have spared me a second glance."

He was right. Again.

When I noticed him in the lobby getting coffee that one time, I barely looked twice at him, and the main thing that captured my attention was that colorful backpack of his.

Even after our first interaction, I'd been irritated and annoyed more than anything, and by the time I got to my office, the incident had completely left my memory.

"Yeah," I said, watching the bottom of his unbuttoned flannel shirt flap in the breeze. "I know."

He stepped forward again, closing the distance between us until we were almost chest to chest. My stomach fluttered, and warmth spread throughout my body, but I couldn't bring myself to look at him. I was confused and ashamed of how weird I was making things.

"The fact that it wouldn't have happened any other way proves to me that this thing between us was *meant* to be. There were too many other factors that could have changed this in the blink of an eye that would have made it so we were never even on that bus together. I know it was hard for you, and that you went through a lot to get here, but I'm so glad it worked out this way. Kalli, every single thing that has happened brought me to you."

Seth's words were the key that unlocked my broken, battered heart. I looked up at him then, and as I did, Seth leaned forward, closed the remaining space between us, and kissed me with a passion that told me he meant every word he just said.

For a moment, we allowed ourselves to get caught up in one another. The rest of the world—including my fear—faded away, and we were just two people who had met and fallen in love against all odds.

When we parted—breathless and flushed—Seth took me home, and I invited him inside. I struggled against the butterflies that stirred wildly in my stomach. After learning about everything and getting Seth's viewpoint on it all, I felt better. Weird as it was, everything was starting to make sense, puzzle pieces beginning to click into place.

The strange coincidences.

His familiarity, and the pull we had felt between us since our meeting on the bus.

His ridiculously accurate guesses.

Seth and I wandered the apartment with our lips colliding, exploring our connection with all our newfound knowledge. We made it to the bedroom, and for the first time in my apartment, with everything we had learned and discussed, Seth and I made love.

Soon after Seth and I had discussed the newest change in our strange relationship, Lici, Nessa and I met at Mallorie's for the first time in what felt like centuries.

"Hey Niña," Lici said when I walked in. She waved me over frantically. "Okay, so we all have news," she paused, sharing an excited glance with Nessa. "But your mom talked with Jermiah, who might have let your big news slip just a little bit, so you're first."

I rolled my eyes.

"Great, yet another thing I have to get used to with your new relationship," I muttered. "Now my brother will get to tell you everything before I do."

She smiled innocently and threw her hands up.

"Well, what can you do? So? Spill it. It has taken every last drop of my self-restraint to keep the news from this one, who—"

"I'm dying to know!" Nessa interjected. She clasped her hands together, her nails sparkling under the overhead lamp. "Please!"

So, I took about ten minutes telling them the story about my recent discovery and facing yet another of the same reaction.

"Oh my god!" Nessa said for about the fiftieth time.

"Yeah, yeah, yeah. I know, it's absolutely nuts and way unlikely. But we've talked about it, and we're good."

Lici and Nessa raised their eyebrows at me.

"I promise," I told them. "He... he thinks we're meant to be. Right now, we're better than good." I blushed, recalling our moment together at the park.

"Well you better be," Lici said, reaching her hand into the pocket of her jeans. "Because now it's time for my news.... It would be really bad if you were sad and sullen and didn't have a date to my engagement party." When she withdrew her hand, it was embellished with a stunning princess cut diamond engagement ring.

"What the fuck?" I said, scooping my jaw off the table. "Excuse my language, but seriously. Has the world started spinning in reverse? *You* are getting married? I'm so happy for you!"

Nessa and I swarmed Lici with hugs and giggles. When the three of us settled down and tried to ignore the many awkward glances coming our way, two things crossed my mind.

One: I was seriously pissed at Jeremiah. Not only did he give away my big news before I could, but he'd been keeping this *huge* secret from me. Two: When I broke the news of mine and Adam's engagement, Nessa went to a dark place. I sent her a worried glance.

"How are you feeling about this?" I asked.

She waved her hand at me. "I'm really good, actually. Jules is absolutely a godsend, and she treats me like a queen. We've been together for a while, and living together seems to be going well. I'm really good. No rush, over here."

I looked at my two best friends. I was in love with a man who was not Adam but had Adam's heart. Not only was Lici committing to a relationship, but she was getting married... to my brother. And Nessa was with a woman for the first time in her life, and she had finally found her perfect match.

Man, things really had changed.

Chapter 35: *Another Big Reveal*

About a year and one month after Adam's passing.

I'D FELT SICK FOR THE LAST TWO WEEKS.

And I mean, really sick. Either I ate something really bad, or my body was reacting poorly to the information about Seth that I still found myself trying to digest even after our conversation.

Either way, I had called in sick to work the last three days, and I really couldn't afford any more time off after all the days I had taken this year. I called in once more and told Mr. Walker that I was going to see a doctor today and I would bring in a note for the last few days. My boss had been super cool about all the time I had taken, of course, but I insisted on the doctor's note. I had been all over the place for over a year now; the least I could do was get a note to excuse my absence the last few days.

When I went into the doctor's office, I had to do that stupid thing where I told the people at the desk what was wrong, then the nurse, and then for whatever reason I still had to tell the doctor, too. This was always frustrating to me, but it was worse this time because my nausea made me feel like I was going to puke every time I opened my mouth. They had me pee in a cup, they drew some blood, and then they had me wait forever and a half before the doctor came back in.

The doctor sat down on her spinning stool and checked her computer screen for a moment before she looked me in the eye.

"Miss Morgan, your results are in. The reason you've been so nauseous lately is because you're pregnant."

"I'm sorry," I said, blinking about thirty times per second. "What did you say?"

"You're pregnant." The doctor started going over the various options I had and droned on and on about the benefits and downsides to each option. Although she was speaking slowly and clearly, I didn't hear much of what she said through the ringing in my ears.

I found myself returning to my sex-ed lectures from high school. "To put it simply, sex equals babies," my teacher had said. I *just* started to wrap my head around my feelings for Seth, and the insane truth of where Seth's heart transplant had come from, and now this? The universe was throwing me some pretty serious curveballs lately.

When I was with Adam, we had talked about having kids, but I had always brushed the topic off, unsure if I even wanted kids. Now was definitely not the time in my life where I felt like I should be spawning offspring, but...

Something about it also really excited me.

Knowing that there was something living inside me—something that Seth and I had created together—felt right. I was definitely going to keep it; there was no question about that. I knew my parents and my brother would love having a baby around, and they would be there for whatever support I was going to need.

For the first time in my life, I could picture myself with a little kiddo running around.

Now, I just had to figure out how in the world I was going to break the news to Seth. I knew I wanted him to be the first person to know, but I was honestly pretty terrified.

What if he didn't want it?

Seth and I were just barely starting to adjust to our relationship after everything we had learned. *What if finding out that I'm pregnant is too much for him to bear? What if it's too much for me?* Doubts and worries and excited little thoughts swirled around my head for the next several days as I tried to come to terms with this new set of life-changing news.

I spent a lot of time reflecting on the arguments that Adam and I had when he was alive. I thought deeply about how badly he wanted to have kids, and how against the idea I always was. A large part of me felt as if I was betraying him, getting pregnant with another man's child, but I wasn't ready before.

I honestly didn't know if I was ready now, but I knew I was going to do everything I could for the little creature growing inside me. I spent two days on the internet searching what foods I should or shouldn't be eating, what exercise I should be getting, and so on. I was going nuts sitting on this information without telling anyone. There were several times in those few days that I considered just texting the news to Seth, but I wanted to tell him in person. I wanted to give him just a little bit more time before I sprang any new craziness on him.

I wasn't sure if I loved the little thing yet. In my mind, as soon as I received the news, it felt real to me, and although I learned—through endless online search spirals—that I wouldn't be able to feel the baby move for weeks, I swear I could feel it in there. I could feel it growing and living, and that feeling connected me to the little creature more than I had ever been connected to anything.

Over the next two weeks, I kept my head down as much as possible. I still spoke with my family and saw my wonderful friends, but I was quiet as the anticipation nearly ate me alive.

I wanted desperately to share this huge thing that was happening with me, but I had to find the right time, and with each day that passed, I wanted more than ever for Seth to be the first to know. After everything we had been through this year, after everything that I had put him through, he deserved to know before anyone else.

But I had to find the right time.

Over those next two weeks, Seth and I were both pretty swamped with work.

Seth was working to finish up his big project, and I spent a lot of time slowly making up for the days I had missed from being sick, so it was nice that most of our communication during these weeks was through brief phone calls and short text messages.

I wanted to do this right, and I was grateful to have something so wonderful to focus on. I had experienced some of the very darkest moments of my life in the last year.

I had lost my fiancé, the love of my life, I had fought with myself over feeling happy and finding love again, I had distanced myself from my friends and family. After all of that, here was this new little spark of hope. I was with a man that I adored, someone who accepted all of my craziness and loved me for it. I was finding my stride with my family again and finally, I had a new reason to mark the days off my calendar.

Chapter 36: *Saying Goodbye*

Three weeks after the doctor's appointment.

THE SUN HAD NEVER SHONE BRIGHTER.

The day of Lici and Jeremiah's engagement party started out to be a gorgeous day. The sunrise was bright, painting streaks of gold and pink across the sky like a sunset would. Guests arrived sporadically as Seth and I helped the rest of my family get everything ready, and I was bubbling with excitement—and nerves—waiting for the right time to tell Seth that we had created life together.

We had just gotten all of the food outside when the first wave of rain hit us out of nowhere. I'm not talking little sprinkles, either. I'm talking inches of water on every surface within seconds.

We scrambled for a plan B, which we didn't have because the weather app had reported clear skies all day. Plan B involved sixty-five people—some close friends and family members, some people from work, and then some more random people that we'd gathered along the way, like Mel from the Happy Place and Lici's shoe guy—all cramming into my parents' house. Despite the downpour that had us all packed in the small space like a bunch of sardines, we had a phenomenal time.

The cherry on top of the whole thing had been when Jeremiah got out his guitar and played an absolutely adorable song that he had written just for Lici. And even better, the whole song was written and sung in Spanish.

My baby brother had never taken a Spanish class that I was aware of, and Lici barely understood a word of it, but the whole thing was perfect.

Lici turned totally red and waved her hands like a maniac, as if that would dry the tears in her eyes. Needless to say, she loved the song. When it was over, before Jeremiah could even put his guitar down, Lici jumped him and wrapped both arms in a chokehold around his neck.

"Nothing like true love, huh?" Seth murmured beside me, startling me. Instinctively, I put my hand to my lower abdomen, which warmed at my touch.

"Hey, where've you been?" I asked, giving him a light peck on the cheek, his stubble tickling my lips.

Seth put both hands in his front pockets.

"I was helping your mom clean some things up," he replied simply.

"Thanks, you didn't have to do that," I said, smiling at him.

"Hey, I'm on her good side for now. I've got to do what I can to stay that way!" I nodded as if that made perfect sense, but really, I was lost in thought again.

A year and a half ago, if someone had told me that this was how my life was going to be, I would have laughed in their face.

My stomach fluttered and I chewed my lip, remembering the news I'd been meaning to tell Seth for the last couple of weeks.

I squinted at him and made a small gesture to the sliding glass doors behind us that led into the backyard. By now, the rain had almost completely stopped falling, and little rays of sunlight filtered down through holes in the clouds above.

"Wanna take a walk with me?" I asked.

"Sure," he said, holding the crook of his elbow out for me to take.

It was surprisingly easy to sneak out of the party, especially since everyone's attention was on the bride and groom-to-be. Once we were outside, I pulled him around the side of the house and down the block before anyone could spot us and call us back inside the house.

Seth laughed, and when I stopped yanking his arm out of its socket, he grinned at me.

"Okay, if anyone were to catch us now, they'd have to have some damn good X-ray vision," he said. "What's up?"

We took up a more reasonable pace, and for another half a block, I fought the urge to bite my nails trying to find the right words. Finally, I whirled around, deciding to just spit it out, my mom's wise words from before echoing in my brain.

"Seth, I'm pregnant."

His eyes widened, and his jaw dropped.

Slowly, I watched him put the pieces together. He pointed a thumb at his chest and mouthed, "Wait, mine?"

I rolled my eyes, fighting the urge to say, "No shit, Sherlock." Instead of saying those words and offending the poor guy, I decided to go with, "There's definitely no way it could be anyone else's."

At my response, a slow smile crept across his face, then that small smile erupted into a huge grin.

"No way. No fucking way. I'm going to be a dad?"

I'd imagined this conversation about fifty billion times since I found out two and a half weeks ago, and this is definitely not how I expected things would go.

"You're... you're happy about this?" I asked cautiously.

"Are you kidding?" He laughed and rubbed his palms together. "I'm stoked! Who else knows about this? Your mom? The girls?" I shook my head, and my rain-dampened ponytail brushed over my shoulder and hung in front of me. Grateful for something to do with my hands, I played with it.

"Just me. And now you." I gestured to him with both of my hands "And the doctor lady at the clinic, of course. Maybe some people at the lab who ran my tests, but I doubt my pregnancy is on their minds."

"Pregnancy, wow. What a weird word! Why haven't you told anyone? This is huge news! This is amazing!"

I turned my gaze to my shoes.

"It's Jeremiah and Lici's big moment right now. I was going to wait until after the wedding or something. I don't know. I didn't want to steal her thunder. And you don't know my mom that well, but she's been hounding me to have a kid since I was basically fresh out of college. There's no way the spotlight would still be on them, which it should be. More than that, though... I really wanted you to be the first one to know."

"I guess..." he said, letting his sentence off for a second, and then his face grew much more serious. Gently, he placed his hands on my elbows, rubbing tiny circles on my arms with his thumbs. "What... uh... What about Adam? How are you feeling about all this?"

I blinked back my surprise. I choked up at the reminder that, in an alternate reality, this would have been Adam's baby. I wanted to hug him for asking.

"Actually," I said, reaching up and locking my fingers behind his neck. "I've been thinking a lot about that, and I got an idea that I think will put all three of us at ease. How do you feel about having a little date after this?"

That question got him smiling again.

"Love to. Man, I can't believe I'm going to have a kid. That's nuts! What do you think? Should we get married?" His green eyes were wide, equal parts thrilled and terrified.

I knew exactly how he felt.

"God, no," I said. Hurt flashed across his face, and I waved my hands in front of him as if somehow that would take back those words. "Let me back up a second. Seth, I'm not going anywhere, and if you want it, there's no way I'd want to have this kid without you. But A: I don't think we should rush to get married just because we've got a baby on the way, and B: the last time I planned to get married didn't turn out so well, and I really don't feel like going through that mess again."

"Oh. Right, sorry. Understood." His eyes went to my belly, which was showing about as much as it shows when I eat too much fast food. He put his hands out hesitantly.

"Can I?" he asked, unable to contain his smile. I took his hands and let him feel my stomach, though there wasn't much to feel yet. I thought it would be weird, but having his hands on the space where our child would grow for the next several months was actually very sweet, and very comforting.

I decided right then and there, though, that no one else would be allowed to place their hands on my stomach. No way.

We snuck back to the engagement party without so much as a suspicious glance, which I was grateful for. With the weight of this news finally off my chest, the rest of the party was so much better than it had been when it started, and by the time the guests began leaving, everyone was feeling a kind of sentimental euphoria.

These two people were in love. They were going to be together. Seth was by my side, and totally on board. At last, everything seemed like it really was going to be okay.

Throughout the rest of the party, every time I looked over at Seth, he sent me a big smile and a double thumbs up.

When the party was over, Nancy, Mom, Dad and Granma retreated to clean the house and make any excuse possible to ogle at Jeremiah and Lici, who were dancing to no music whatsoever on the back deck. It was surreal, watching Lici curl up in someone's arms, eyes closed, swaying to the rhythm he created, smiling like a fool.

I guess I wasn't the only one experiencing life's crazy curveballs this year. I knew for a fact she never expected her life to turn out this way, either.

Seth, eager to see what I had planned for our evening, bounded up beside me, disrupting my happy introspections.

"Everything's good to go, here. Do I need to bring anything?"

"Just your car," I whispered back. I had everything else we would need with me.

I gave Seth very vague directions, and eventually, we reached our destination.

"A cemetery?" he asked, frowning at the Springworth Cemetery welcome sign.

"Oh, come on, you're not scared, are you?" I asked playfully, bumping his arm with my shoulder across the center console.

He scoffed.

"No! I just don't see what we could possibly be doing in the cemetery so close to sunset. Are you sure you don't want to wait until tomorrow?"

I rolled my eyes. The man was in the middle of creating a horror video game, for crying out loud.

"Nope," I said. "It has to be tonight." *If not tonight, I might lose my nerve.* "Besides, it's not even dark yet, silly." I didn't wait for him to come around and get my door. Instead, I wrapped my jacket around myself, pushed open the door, and climbed out of the car. Seth scrambled out of the car after me, slamming the driver's side door in his attempt to keep up with me. I kept up a steady pace, and I only slowed when I found the headstone I was looking for.

"This is where he was buried," I said, a reverent tone hushing my voice. I hadn't been here since we buried him. It was too painful. But now, the love I felt overshadowed the pain and fear.

"Wow," he replied in the same soft tone.

I reached into my pocket and pulled out two pieces of blank sketchbook paper. I knew what I wanted to write, but I wasn't sure if I would require the second paper or not.

I unfolded them and placed the second one on the ground beneath my knee. Then, I reached into my purse and pulled out my best calligraphy pen.

Placing the piece of paper on his headstone, I began writing.

Seth cleared his throat.

"Hey, um... could I do that, too?" *What the hell?* I thought. I passed him the second piece of paper and dug around in my purse for another pen.

For several minutes, the two of us sat in silence. Each of us bent over Adam's headstone, drafting our own letters to him.

When we were both finished, we sat back on the grass. Seth handed me his letter.

"Want to read it?" he asked.

"I'd love to," I said.

Dear Adam,

I'm sorry I stole your girl. Really. And your heart, I guess. But you made all of this possible, and I can't tell you how happy I am. Kalli is the best thing that's ever happened to me, and whatever happens next, I promise to take good care of her if she'll let me. Thanks again, and best of luck out there.

Seth.

"Awe," I said, smiling at him. The sun was now low in the sky, and the majority of the atmosphere overhead was already beginning to turn a deep, dark purple.

The rainclouds from earlier reflected the last bit of the sun's bright rays. The leaves in the cemetery reflected those last rays in tones of bronze and gold. A beautiful picture.

I pulled out my phone, snapped a picture, and moved it to my folder to paint later. I titled it, "New Beginning."

"That's really sweet," I said to him at last. "Morbid as hell, too."

"Can I read yours now?" he asked, raising his eyebrows.

"No way, my friend. This one is just between us."

He gasped, but then quickly relented. "Fair enough." The hair that wasn't tucked under his baseball cap curled around his face.

I read through my letter one last time.

Dear Adam,

Well, here we are. Apparently, you <u>can</u> fall in love twice in a lifetime, and it's messy as hell. To make it even messier, I had to go fall for your heart all over again. But Seth isn't you. He never will be, but as weird as it is to admit, he isn't any less than you, either.

I'm sorry we didn't get the happily ever after we pictured for so long, and I'm sorry I fought you about having kids. Turns out, I do want them. It just took losing you to realize it. Seth and I have one. A kid, I mean. She's not due yet, but she's on the way. Or he. Not sure which it'll be yet.

Wherever you are, I hope you're doing well, and I hope I get to see you again. I've always believed I will, though it's going to be a hell of a lot more complicated than I imagined before. Just take it easy on me, okay?

When you told me before that you wanted me to find someone to make me happy if I were to ever lose you, I was pissed. I never thought I'd need to, and then you were gone so quickly. I hope when we do finally see each other again, we can figure it out. I hope it's not a total nightmare. I love you, Adam, but you were right. I do need to take care of me while I'm here, and Seth...

well, he makes me happy. Although he won't ever replace you, he has helped me to heal the hole in my heart from when you left.

A part of me will always be yours, and weirdly enough, a part of Seth will be, too.

Love,

Kalli

I reached into my pocket and ran my thumb back and forth across the smooth surface of my lighter. Then, I took both of our messages and set them aflame.

It took a while for them to catch, but eventually they did, and I set them down on Adam's headstone.

So what if things were confusing, and messy, and so damn complicated that even we couldn't understand them? We were together. This was how it had worked out, and I was going to work like crazy to hold onto it like I should have done with Adam.

Taking Seth's hand in mine, I watched as the late fall breeze lifted up the glowing embers of the words we had written to Adam and carried them off into the ever-darkening sky.

Acknowledgements

As I mentioned in my author note at the beginning of this story, This story took me ages to finally get to a point where I felt like I could share it with anyone. There have been many people along the way who have supported me in this process.

Brandon, thank you for all the long walks and chats and brainstorming sessions, and answering all my questions that typically started with, "Do you think this would really happen?" Thank you for your endless support, and for showing me how deeply I can love. It helps a ton with my writing.

Mom, thank you for bugging me five times a year about wanting to read this book. I told you it was on my list… it just took longer than I originally expected.

Elivia, thank you for all of your support. Even from across the country you still make me feel celebrated. You make me feel like I'm famous every time we talk about my books!

Imogen, thank you for taking a chance on this book long before it was actually ready for anyone to look at it. Thank you for your patience and your thoughtful notes. They helped more than you'll ever know.

Hannah and Gilbert, thank you for beta reading this book and for hyping it up. Your phone calls and text messages are morale boosters for sure, and I hope I never lose my amazing cheerleaders.

Kerry W., thank you for teaching me that there is no "right" way to grieve. Thank you for teaching me that grief is a messy, complicated and fluid process.

Baylan, Grandpa, and little creature, thank you for the joy you brought me in the time I had with you. Thank you for teaching me that loss doesn't mean you'll never heal, that healing means your life and perspectives might just look a little bit different, and that moving forward doesn't mean forgetting. I love you all.

About the Author

BREYANNA I.L. EVANS IS A MULTI-GENRE AUTHOR OF SEVERAL PUBLISHED books including children's stories, poetry, a novella, romance, fiction and fantasy, with more books always in the works.

After graduating with a bachelor's degree in creative writing from Utah Valley University, Breyanna taught middle school and high school English. She now works as a reading intervention specialist through the University of Utah Reading Clinic, always hoping to assist educators and struggling readers enhance their skills.

In her free time, Breyanna enjoys watching movies, painting, drawing, writing, reading, playing Dark Souls, and spending as much time as possible with her family. For release and book signing event updates, you can join Breyanna's email list at breyannaevansauthor.com

@breyannailevans

breyannaevansauthor@gmail.com

breyannaevansauthor.com